THE RUSSIAN'S GREED

ALSO BY CAP DANIELS

The Chase Fulton Novels

Book One: *The Opening Chase*

Book Two: *The Broken Chase*

Book Three: *The Stronger Chase*

Book Four: *The Unending Chase*

Book Five: *The Distant Chase*

Book Six: *The Entangled Chase*

Book Seven: *The Devil's Chase*

Book Eight: *The Angel's Chase*

Book Nine: *The Forgotten Chase*

Book Ten: *The Emerald Chase*

Book Eleven: *The Polar Chase*

Book Twelve: *The Burning Chase*

Book Thirteen: *The Poison Chase*

Book Fourteen: *The Bitter Chase*

The Avenging Angel – Seven Deadly Sins Series

Book One: *The Russian's Pride*

Book Two: *The Russian's Greed*

Book Three: *The Russian's Gluttony* (Autumn 2021)

Stand-Alone Novels

We Were Brave

Novellas

I Am Gypsy

The Chase Is On

THE RUSSIAN'S GREED

AVENGING ANGEL

SEVEN DEADLY SINS SERIES

BOOK #2

CAP DANIELS

ANCHOR WATCH
PUBLISHING
** USA **

The Russian's Greed
Avenging Angel
Seven Deadly Sins Book #2
Cap Daniels

This is a work of fiction. Names, characters, places, historical events, and incidents are the product of the author's imagination or have been used fictitiously. Although many locations such as marinas, airports, hotels, restaurants, etc. used in this work actually exist, they are used fictitiously and may have been relocated, exaggerated, or otherwise modified by creative license for the purpose of this work. Although many characters are based on personalities, physical attributes, skills, or intellect of actual individuals, all of the characters in this work are products of the author's imagination except those used for historical significance.

Published by:
ANCHOR WATCH
PUBLISHING
** USA **

13 Digit ISBN: 978-1-951021-22-1
Library of Congress Control Number: 2021907293

Cover Design: German Creative

Printed in the United States of America

"Earth provides enough to satisfy every man's needs, but not every man's greed."

——*Mahatma Gandhi*

THE RUSSIAN'S GREED

Zhadnost' Russkikh

CAP DANIELS

1

ZAPAKH DYMA (SMELL THE SMOKE)

March 2004

Anastasia "Anya" Burinkova gripped the brushed nickel handle of the heavy wooden door, raising the handle and silently moving the door through its arc. Providing the precisely measured amount of lifting force on the door, she kept the tell-tale creaks of the hinges from alarming anyone beyond the temporary barricade.

She'd learned and memorized the sound over the previous six days of her confinement. She could tell who'd opened the door by the tone of the crying hinges. Those in a hurry brought a high-pitched squeal, while the people who moved through their appointed tasks with patience caused the creaking to sound like light, repeating clicks. The pneumatic closer attached at the top of the doorframe hissed like the sound of a sleeping child's breath and was punctuated by the awful clang of the bolt striking the jamb. The sounds were etched into her memory like the words of an old favorite song.

When Anya opened the door slower than anyone else, the hinges gave no hint of discomfort and offered only silence through the arc. The former Russian assassin peered through the narrow opening down the seemingly endless hallway, but her vision was not the chosen sense; instead, she held her breath and allowed her ears to listen for movement in the dimly lit corridor. Like the unique sounds of the hinges, she'd learned the subtle differences between the footfalls of the eleven women and seven men who rotated through shifts, day after day, in the place where minutes passed like hours and hours like weeks.

The meticulous planning had occupied her mind while her body recovered from the injuries inflicted aboard a luxurious yacht at the hands of a Russian mafia boss in Miami. He'd gained the upper hand after slipping an odorless, tasteless sedative into the hot tea that had become part of her routine.

Her mind drifted back to a time when she'd admonished Chase Fulton, an American covert operative, for always drinking from the same cup. Routines breed predictability, and predictability leads to vulnerability. That's exactly what Leo, the Russian mafia boss, used to disorient her just minutes before he'd shoved her into a mirrored wall so violently that she'd suffered lacerations to her neck, head, and shoulder. The cosmetic surgeon promised only minor, hardly noticeable scarring.

Anya's natural Eastern European beauty was a tool she learned to use to its fullest advantage. The early skills were cultivated and developed at the Sparrow School just outside Moscow, but she'd mastered the skills on the streets as an officer of the *Sluzhba vneshney razvedki Rossiyskoy Federatsii*, officially dubbed The Foreign Intelligence Service of the Russian Federation. The SVR rose from the ashes of the former KGB after the fall of the Soviet Union, but the intelligence services of the world believed there was little difference between the modern agency and the Cold War–era beast.

Just as she expected, the hallway was empty and the lights were dimmed. Confident she could make the requisite sixteen strides to the stairwell without being seen, she stepped into the corridor and applied just enough pressure to the door to avoid the hiss of the closer and the knock of the bolt striking the jamb. She moved precisely as she'd been taught, allowing the outside of her feet to strike the ground first and then rolling onto the balls and toes.

Reaching the metal door to the stairwell, she meticulously pressed the panic bar and listened as the metal bar sank into its frame. Avoiding the metallic clang would be impossible, but with motions barely above a snail's pace, she could mitigate the sound. Once through the door, she scanned the hallway again and eased the door back into place without being noticed.

Taking the stairs two at a time, she reached the landing on the roof of the building. To her delight, the door to the roof was propped ajar with a small block of wood keeping it from closing—a sign that her target was indeed on the roof.

The door swung silently as she stepped through and onto the flat roof. Instantly, her nose filled with the smell of a cigarette—the same smell she'd detected on the skin and clothing of the man who did the tasks the registered nurses would not.

She stepped from behind an enormous air conditioning unit and watched David, the LPN clad in blue scrubs, exhale a long plume of white smoke into the night sky over the Walter Reed Military Medical Center at Naval Support Activity Bethesda, just north of Washington, D.C. She'd assumed he would see and hear her coming, but the sounds of the night masked her stealthy approach.

"Could I get one of those?" she said.

David jumped and shot his eyes toward the sound of her voice, dropping his cigarette as he did. He threw his hand over his heart. "Don't do that! You scared the hell out of me."

Anya took three more strides, closing the distance between them. "I'm sorry. I did not mean to frighten you, but I would like to have a cigarette." With her Russian accent impossible to hide, she tried to overcome it with a flirtatious smile . . . just as she'd been taught.

And it worked. David produced a pack from his pocket and shook up a single cigarette through the small hole in the top.

Anya pulled the long white cigarette from the pack and placed it between her lips. She leaned in and spoke without parting her lips. "Could I have a light?"

David cupped his hand around the lighter as he moved the flame toward Anya, and she raised her hands to further shelter the flame from the night wind. In the instant when the fire touched its target, Anya clasped the man's wrists, spun him around, and shoved him face-first into the base of an antenna bolted to the roof. Blood flew from his nose and forehead on contact, so Anya roughly threw the now unconscious man to the ground. She carefully rolled the front of his shirt into a tight wad and pulled it across his bloody face, trying to keep the scrubs free of blood. Next came the pants and shoes. They were easier since there was no need for caution to avoid blood. Anya draped her gown across the unconscious man and stepped into his scrubs. The shoes were a size too big, but they were better than no shoes at all.

She felt for a pulse in David's neck and found an athletic thump. He was alive, but she didn't envy the headache he'd have when he woke up. Back through the door and down the stairs she went, ignoring the floor on which she'd been confined for days. She reached the ground floor in record time, and seconds later, she walked through an exit door and onto a concrete walkway leading from the hospital.

Escaping the hospital had been simple, but getting off the Navy base would prove to be a horse of a very different color. A grove of trees stood to the right of the sidewalk, while an open grassy area laid to the left. Crossing the open field, even under darkness, made for too many opportunities for someone to see her and start asking questions she couldn't answer.

The only logical route was through the trees, so she bent down and retied the oversized shoes, drawing them a little tighter on her feet. The desire to run was almost too powerful to overcome, but she willed herself to walk at a leisurely pace as if she belonged on that stretch of sidewalk at that hour. David's ID badge hanging from the pocket of the scrubs wouldn't withstand scrutiny. She looked nothing like the LPN, but from a distance, it was close enough to fool onlookers.

Four strides into the trees, a confident, strong voice came from beside a mighty oak. "Why do you smell like smoke, and where are you going, Anya?"

She froze and turned to the voice. Special Agent Ray White of the U.S. Department of Justice stood in the shadows, nonchalantly leaning against the solid oak.

She sighed, obviously disappointed with herself and surprised by Ray White's appearance. "You can't make me stay. You promised if I did one mission for you, I would be free."

Ray picked at his teeth with a twig he'd been whittling with his pocketknife. "That's not exactly what I promised, but it's close. The mission involves more than just one man in just one city. Phase two is waiting for you as soon as you feel up to it, and from my observations tonight, you're definitely ready for something to do. What do you say we hop in my Suburban and find an all-night diner where we can have a piece of pie and talk about what happens next?"

She eyed him with both contempt and admiration. His choice of words had been meticulous, and she'd fallen into a seemingly open-ended agreement with the man who'd likely send her to her death on the streets of yet another city and at the hands of the *Russkaya mafiya.*

2

SKOL'ZHENIYE (SLIPPING)

The 1950s-style chrome and Formica tables and vinyl-covered seats gave Capital Diner the look and feel of a bygone era. A Wurlitzer sat silent against an otherwise empty wall, and the yellowing of the ceiling tiles told the story of fifty years of fried food, cigarette smoke, and neglect.

Supervisory Special Agent Ray White slid a plastic-covered menu across the table to Anya. "Every time I come here, I always expect The Fonz to show up, punch that jukebox to life, and say, 'Aaaay!'"

The Russian frowned in utter confusion. "What does this mean?"

"Don't tell me you've never seen *Happy Days*."

Her frown continued. "My days are sad since I met you."

He shook his head. "No, it's an old TV show, and The Fonz was this guy . . . Oh, never mind. I can't explain it."

"I do not watch television."

A waitress whose apron looked worse than the ceiling tile ambled to their table. "What'll it be?"

Ray looked up at the woman and wondered if she ate exclusively at the diner, and he tried to imagine her cholesterol numbers. "What kind of pie do you have tonight?"

The waitress turned to gaze into the cooler. "It looks like we've got apple, lemon meringue, and one piece of cherry left."

Ray turned to Anya. "What's your favorite kind of pie?"

She laid her hand on his arm and twisted until she could see the face of his watch. "Coulibiac with sturgeon and salmon is best pie in all of world, but no one should eat pie at one o'clock in morning."

The waitress beat Ray to the punch. "We don't have anything like that, but I think we've got some fish sticks in the freezer."

Ray ignored her and screwed up his face. "Fish pie? Really? That's disgusting." He didn't wait for Anya to put up any further protest, and he turned to the bulbous waitress. "We'll have two pieces of apple pie, coffee for me, and I'm sure she wants hot tea."

Anya shook her head. "No, not tea. I will have only water."

The waitress scribbled on her green-and-white order pad. "Suit yourself. Ice cream on the pie?"

"Yes, definitely ice cream," Ray said. "Thank you."

As the woman shuffled away, Anya said, "Why do you think I will not kill you and walk away?"

Ray rearranged the salt and pepper shakers and picked at a damaged corner of the table. "It's not what you do."

"Is exactly what I do."

Ray drew his pistol from the shoulder rig beneath his jacket and slid it across the table. "So, do it. There are seventeen rounds in the magazine and one in the chamber. By my count, there are three people other than you and me in the diner: the drunk passed out in the corner, the waitress, and a cook. By my estimation, the drunk could sleep through a train wreck, and it's likely that neither the cook nor waitress is armed." He tapped his index finger to his forehead. "Put one right here. It'll make a mess in the booth behind me, but that's none of your concern. I'll be dead before the sound stops echoing off the walls, and you can put a pair in each of the employees. They'd probably welcome anything that gets them out of their miserable day-after-day existence in this place. If you want to shoot the bum for fun, I guess you could, but I'm betting you won't."

Anya stared down at the Glock 17 and let Ray's scenario play out in her head. He was right. She could kill them all and disappear into the night, never to be seen again, but that's not all he was right about. She pulled a napkin from the dispenser beside the salt and pepper Ray had carefully arranged, and she laid it on top of the pistol. Without touching the weapon, she slid it back across the table with one finger pressed into the napkin. "I do not need pistol. There is piece of broken metal on my chair. I could have it pulled free in seconds and cut your throat with it. You have ink pen in pocket of shirt and another in pocket inside jacket. With either of them, I could make hole in your brain through eyeball. There is knife, fork, and spoon rolled inside paper napkin. All of these are sharp enough to leave you bleeding to death on floor. Except for sounds you would make, all of these ways I could kill you would be almost silent."

He eyed the napkins rolled around the silverware. "There's no need for threats."

"Is not threat. Is only most convenient things I could use to kill you."

Ray re-holstered his gun. "Please don't use the fork. I believe that would take the longest and hurt the most. Don't get me wrong . . . I'm not afraid of dying. It's just the agony leading up to it that I'd like to avoid."

Anya stared into his soul. "I believe coming of death will be greatest peace any of us will have."

Ray ignored the philosophy lesson. "Okay, your point is taken. You *could* kill me, but you won't. At least not tonight. You're slipping."

"What does this mean, slipping?"

Ray subconsciously slid his silverware, still wrapped in the paper napkin, away from Anya's hand. They were likely the deadliest hands he'd ever seen only inches from his own, yet they were still beautiful—like the hands he might see in the full-color jewelry ads folded inside Sunday's *Washington Times*. "It means you let me predict when you'd run and what direction. You let me choose this diner and what you would eat. Worst of all, you let Leo get the jump on you in Miami. If Gwynn hadn't been there, this operation would've been over, and you'd be rotting in a pine box somewhere. These aren't the kinds of things SVR Captain Anastasia Burinkova would allow to happen."

The accusation stung almost as badly as the reminder of her days as one of the Rodina's most feared assassins. "I am not this person anymore. I am American now."

"You're American by choice and by the mercy of the American government, but"—he pointed toward her chest—"Captain Burinkova still lives in there. The skills, the mindset, the fearsome beast . . . They're still in there."

The waitress reappeared and slid two pieces of pie, a plastic cup of water, and a mug of coffee onto the table. "Will there be anything else?"

Ray White didn't take his eyes off Anya. "No, that's all. Thank you."

Anya looked up and smiled. "I think I would also like coffee, please." As she spoke, she slipped the toe of her right foot behind the waitress's left heel.

The woman sighed. "Sure, one more coffee coming up. Cream or sugar?"

"No, thank you. Just coffee."

As the woman turned to leave, she stumbled across Anya's borrowed shoe and caught herself against one of the swiveling stools mounted in front of the raised counter behind her.

As Boy Scout Ray White lurched to help the waitress, Captain Burinkova slipped the saltshaker from the table and onto her lap and then quickly spun off the top. She filled the palm of her right hand with a tablespoon of salt, and as the commotion came to an end, she slid the shaker back into place and reached for Ray's plate and mug that had been displaced when he lunged for the falling waitress. With a sleight of hand any magician would envy, she emptied the contents of her palm into his coffee and repositioned the plate and mug.

Anya offered the smile she'd been taught that could melt the coldest of hearts. "Was nice of you to try to help lady. You are gentleman, even if sometimes cruel."

He set his jaw. "Anya, I'm sorry for the things I'm forced to say to you, but—"

"Are you sorry only for lies, or also for truth?"

"I've never lied to you," he insisted. "It's true that I've skirted around the truth, but I have a job to do, and that job is to make sure you are at the top of your game and that you stay in the operation until the end."

"When is end of operation, Special Agent White?"

He let his eyes fall closed and exhaled a long breath. "I don't know."

"But is your operation. You are in command. Is your responsibility to know when operation will come to end."

He shook his head. "No, that's not how it works at Justice."

Anya raised a finger. "This word, *justice*. I think it does not mean what you think."

Ray smiled in spite of the gut-punch Anya delivered. "Have you ever seen the movie *The Princess Bride*?"

"I do not watch movies."

Ray chuckled. "There's a line in the movie. One of the characters, Inigo, a Spanish swordsman, says . . ." Ray paused. "Never mind. Maybe we'll watch it together sometime."

The waitress returned and slid a second mug onto the table.

Ray looked up. "Are you okay? That fall looked like it hurt."

She nodded, and the excess skin of her chin continued to move after the rest of her head had stopped. "Yeah, I'm fine. I don't know what I tripped over. Enjoy your pie."

Anya ignored the woman and forked a bite of apple pie into her mouth. "Mmm. Is good, but not like coulibiac."

Ray scowled. "I can't wrap my head around the idea of a fish pie."

"Maybe when we watch together *Princess Bride* movie, I will make for you coulibiac."

Ray couldn't hold back the coming smile, so he tried to mask it behind the mug as he sipped his second drink of steaming coffee. Instantly, he spat the liquid back into the mug and stared into the black abyss of his cup.

"What is wrong, Gentleman Ray White? Did you not see Captain Burinkova slip poison into drink while you were saving damsel in distress? Is maybe *you* who is slipping, no?"

"Okay, you made your point, but I'm not the one who fell for it while on an undercover op."

"No, that was me," she said. "You were not on undercover operation. This was me because your Justice Department says I am better for this operation."

He pushed his salty coffee away and lifted Anya's mug to his lips. A battle of wits at one a.m. against Anya was a terrible choice, so he said, "If you'll stay with me for another field assignment, you can call your friends and tell them you are all right."

"They are looking for me, no? And you are afraid they will find me, yes? This is why you give to me token gift of calling them. I will do this for you, but not because of meager gift. And I have demand."

Ray pushed up his sleeves. "You don't get to make demands. That's not how this works."

Anya pressed her wrists together and held them toward him. "Okay, in this case, you will arrest me, and I will tell judge about deal you made with me and how I did everything you wanted."

Ray sighed and pushed her hands away. "What's your demand?"

Anya made a show of separating her wrists. "You will give to me Special Agent Guinevere Davis for assignment so I can continue her training."

"That's your demand? You want Gwynn to come with you? That's it?"

Anya lifted the salted coffee to her lips and pretended to enjoy the taste. "Yes, this is my demand because, like me, she will soon be immune to poison."

Ray shuddered at the thought of swallowing the rancid coffee. "Fine, you can have Gwynn, but don't you want to know what the assignment is?"

3

LUCHSHIY DRUG DEVUSHKI (A GIRL'S BEST FRIEND)

With the pie plates empty but only one empty coffee cup, Anya stood from the table and extended her hand. "Is now time for me to make decision of where we go."

Ray wiped his mouth with the corner of his napkin and slid from his chair. He stepped around the Russian to put her on his left side, where he carried his shoulder holster and Glock 17. From that side, it would be more difficult for most people to draw his weapon from him. Anya could likely still pull off the feat, but it would require her leaving herself vulnerable with her arms crossed. Ray had no illusions that he was faster or craftier than the woman who was more than a decade his junior and who had thousands more hours of intensive training than the U.S. government would ever provide for an officer of the Justice Department.

"So, where are we going now that it's two a.m.?"

With her right hand laced through his left arm, she smiled up at him. "I was hoping you would maybe take me someplace having great tea and is quiet enough for mission brief."

He didn't want to smile, but suppressing it wouldn't be easy. "I think I know just the place."

"Then, this is place I wish to go."

He thumbed the key fob, unlocking his government-issue Suburban, and opened the passenger-side door. Anya climbed inside and eyed the M4 rifle wedged between the driver's seat and center console. The stack of radios mounted beneath the dash looked like enough commo gear to launch a spaceship. A PR-24 baton rested neatly in its friction lock cradle. And finally, a Mossberg riot gun stood in a locking rack to the right of the radios.

When Ray slid into the driver's seat, Anya said, "Did you think you would need all of this to capture me again? If yes, I am flattered." She let her fingertips lightly trace the barrel of the shotgun. "Are you afraid of me, Special Agent White?"

He slid his key into the ignition. "I didn't need any of my toys to catch you tonight, but a few of these things might have come in handy if you'd caused a scene."

"But I did not cause scene . . . Well, maybe salt into coffee was a small scene, but no need for striking stick or shotgun."

"That reminds me," he said. "Open the glove compartment and hand me my cuffs."

She pressed the button, and the compartment door opened as the light illuminated the interior. Two pairs of Smith & Wesson stainless steel handcuffs rested beside a snub-nosed .38 revolver. "Was wise of you to leave behind handcuffs. I think you could not put them on my wrists without being badly hurt."

He eyed the Russian. "Maybe we'll have to try that. My money's on the cop with superior size and weight."

"Perhaps we will, but being fat is not benefit when handcuffing someone like me."

"I know you didn't just call me fat."

Anya pressed the tip of her index finger into the flesh of his stomach. "You are too old to have pie in middle of night. You are soft in middle."

He groaned. "I'll have you know I can still do two miles in twelve minutes and a hundred sit-ups in two."

She ignored him and pulled the .38 revolver from its holster, then emptied the shells into her palm. "Last time I saw revolver like this one, I made it to blow up in a bad man's hand while he was trying to kill me in strip club in Key West Island."

Ray rolled his eyes and yanked the gun from her hand. “It’s just called Key West—not Key West Island. And what were *you* doing in a strip club?”

“I was there to find man who was holding friend of mine and kill him. This is what friendship means to me.”

He licked his lips, as his mouth suddenly felt like sandpaper. “Did you do it?”

She stroked the barrel of the riot gun only inches beside her. “Did I do what? Kill him? Or get back friend?”

“Both.”

“I did not kill him, but he died later in night. And yes, my friend is alive and safe.”

“This friend of yours . . . Would her name happen to be Elizabeth Woodley?”

Anya stared at the shotgun as her fingers glided across the forearm, and she shook her head.

Ray lowered his chin. “Now I think you’re lying. I think her name is Elizabeth Woodley, but you call her Skipper.”

Anya tried to hide the surprise. “You will now tell me something about you that others do not know.”

“I can’t,” he said. “It’s against the rules.”

Anya laughed. “You are now lying. I do not believe there are rules about what you are to tell Russian assassin in front seat of car with weapons everywhere. I will make with you bet. I believe you cannot put handcuffs on me. If yes, I will do for you all missions your Department of Justice wishes. If no, you will tell to me something about you. This is bet, no?”

Ray slid the revolver across the center console. “Put this back where you found it.”

She took the weapon from his palm, reloaded it, and returned it to its place in the glove compartment. “Is not wise to let me have loaded gun. I could—”

Ray held up a hand. "We've covered this already. You *could*, but you won't."

They pulled up in front of his brownstone, locked the Suburban, and climbed the stairs.

Anya gazed into the darkened sky. "Yes, this is place with very good tea."

Ray held open the door. "You said 'great tea' back at the diner.'"

"So, I did," she said. "I like when you listen closely to me."

He closed and locked the door and headed for the kitchen.

Anya watched him move through the room with the confidence of a man who is comfortable and unafraid. "You did not answer my question."

"What question?"

The whistling kettle halted conversation, and Ray produced a pair of mugs with the Justice Department seal emblazoned on them. He pulled a jar from the cupboard. "I seem to remember you like honey in your tea."

She took the jar from him and covered the bottom of her cup with the golden honey, then on tiptoes, she replaced it and closed the cupboard.

He poured the steaming water over teabags in each mug and motioned toward the living room. "Shall we?"

Without a word, Anya led the way into the next room and nestled onto the sofa.

Ray chose his recliner and lifted the mug to his lips. He blew across the steaming surface and took a tentative sip. "You were right. This place does have great tea."

Anya sipped hers and nodded a silent agreement. After several swallows, she looked up. "You are now stalling. I want to hear of next mission."

"I wasn't stalling. I was just going through the briefing in my head to make sure I don't leave out anything important."

"So, you are now ready to give briefing. I will keep questions until end."

"Articles," he said.

She frowned. "What articles?"

"*The*, *a*, and *an*. We had this talk in Miami, and you said you would start using English articles."

She looked away. "Is not easy for me, but I will try."

She repositioned to face him. "I am ready for *the* briefing."

He nodded his approval. "Diamonds are a girl's best friend." Anya's blank stare made him pause, and finally, he said, "That's an old advertising slogan, I think."

Her expression didn't change.

He held up his thumb and index finger, indicating a small object. "You know . . . diamonds, precious gems."

"Yes, I know what is diamond, but I do not think they are girl's best friend."

He waved both hands in surrender. "Okay, forget the best friend thing. We're talking about diamonds. Hundreds of millions, maybe billions of dollars' worth of diamonds. You have been to New York City, right?"

She nodded. "I have been to city once, but only to Queens and Belmont Park."

"That's about to change very soon. You're going to Manhattan. More specifically, Forty-Seventh Street between Fifth and Sixth. That's known as the Diamond District." He paused, expecting some reaction, but she didn't flinch. "You do know what the Diamond District is, right?"

"Yes, I have heard of this. Is place with many jewelry shops and diamond brokers."

He took another sip of his cooling tea. "What do you know about diamonds?"

She shook her head. "I am not typical girl. I have never had diamond—*a* diamond—but I have seen them, and they are beautiful."

He placed his mug on the table beside the recliner. "You've never had a diamond? Really?"

She appeared to find the question ridiculous. "I told you this. I would not lie about having diamond."

"I wasn't accusing you of lying. It's just surprising that a thirty-two-year-old woman has never had a diamond."

"I have never needed diamond. Does Gwynn have one?"

He shrugged. "I don't know. I've never seen her wear one, but I would think she at least has some earrings or a tennis bracelet."

Anya pinched her eyebrows together. "I did not know she plays tennis."

Ray shook his head. "We're getting off track. We'll get back to Gwynn later. There's a guy in the city. His name is Viktor Volkov, but he's known as Yuvelir."

Anya's eyes widened. "This means the jeweler."

Ray sighed. "*Pomnit'? YA tozhe govoryu po Russki.*"

"Yes, I remember you speak Russian, but do you know this word *volkov*?"

Ray nodded, an ominous look on his face. "Yes, it means hawk."

Anya returned the look. "Yes, it sometimes means this, but also any bird of prey is volkov. It is bird that kills to stay alive. Is this also true of Viktor Volkov?"

Ray stared into his empty cup. "Probably, but that's not why we want him. We don't know how, but Viktor has devised a way to plant diamonds grown in a laboratory into the inventories of legitimate diamond dealers."

Anya's expression said she was trying to hold her question, but Ray needed to know what she was thinking.

"What is it?" he asked.

"I am sorry. I said to you I would save questions for end, but this is not possible."

"What's not possible?"

"It is not possible for . . . ah, I do not know word, but it is person who studies diamonds and other stones."

Ray leaned in. "Gemologist."

"Yes, gemologist. It is not possible Viktor Volkov can put into jewelry store fake diamonds and this person, the gemologist, will not know."

"That's the kicker on this one. The diamonds you call fake are real diamonds, chemically identical to a natural diamond that took millions of years to form."

"I have heard word. I think is cubic zirconia. This looks like diamond but is not."

"So, you do know something about diamonds."

"I know very little, but this does not sound possible to me. You have wrong information."

Ray steepled his fingers. "That's what I thought, too, but I was wrong. These stones are not cubic zirconia. Even the best gemologists can't look at the diamonds and tell the difference between a natural stone and one of Viktor's that was grown in a lab."

"I must know more of this fake diamond creation, but what is mission? If you want Viktor Volkov killed, I can do this, no problem."

Ray let out the breath he'd been holding. "That's not what we want, Anya. We want to know how he's doing it . . . all of it. From the creation of the stones to the mechanism he's using to get them into inventory."

"This is what you want me to do, and this is all? I am not to kill him?"

"Yes, all we want is information. You'll gather it for us, and we'll take it from there. There will be no arrests while you're undercover. You'll be long gone before we make any moves on Viktor. It's that simple. Implant yourself into Viktor's circle, gain his trust, learn his process, and report back to me. That's it."

"Why?"

Ray scowled. "Because you don't want to go to prison for the rest of your life."

Anya shook her head. "No. Why is Viktor doing this thing?"

"Oh, *that* why," Ray said. "There are only four motivations for criminal behavior: money, power, revenge, or sex. It's always one of these or a combination. We assume it's for the money, but we can't figure out how he's monetizing the operation. He doesn't appear to be selling the stones to the dealers. They're simply showing up in shops."

"You said I can have Gwynn, yes?"

"Yes, but why is it so important for you to have her with you?"

Anya leaned back against the cushions. "Because she is girl's real best friend."

Ray stood, dangling his empty mug by a pinky finger. He reached for Anya's mug, and she took the last swallow of tea before holding up the cup for him to return to the kitchen. As she added her mug to his, he allowed them both to slip from his hand. With catlike reflexes, Anya shot both hands forward, and when the ceramic cups hit her palms, Ray lowered his handcuffs with blinding speed, clasping a cuff on each of Anya's wrists.

He lifted the cups from her palms. "I believe that makes me the winner of our bet. Goodnight, Anya."

4

VOSSOYEDINENIYE (REUNION)

The next morning, Anya stretched and slid her legs from beneath the cover. The digital clock on the bedside table read 8:24. She rubbed the sleep from her eyes and enjoyed the first good shower in over a week. As she stepped from the shower and pulled a towel around her shoulders, she saw a T-shirt, sweatshirt, underclothes, socks, and jeans lying on the counter beside the sink. She towel-dried her hair and pulled it into a ponytail. The clothes fit perfectly, and she smiled, knowing why.

As always, she rolled the towels and headed down the stairs, excited about the reunion to come. Special Agent Guinevere Davis met her at the bottom of the stairs, and the two shared a long hug.

Gwynn eyed her outfit. "Good, they fit. I heard all you had to wear was a set of stolen scrubs and a pair of clown shoes."

Anya performed a pirouette. "Yes, they fit perfectly. Thank you. When I saw them in bathroom, I knew they were from you. Is nice to see you again."

She reached out and took Gwynn's hands in hers. "I did not have chance to thank you for what you did for me. I would not be alive if it were not for you. I will never forget this."

Gwynn pulled Anya into another hug. "You never have to thank me. I know you would've done the same for me."

"Of course I would. We are partners."

"Good morning, Sleeping Beauty," Ray said as he turned the corner from the kitchen. "I thought you were going to sleep the day away."

Anya groaned. "Is your fault. You did not give to me key for handcuffs. I spent precious time picking locks while I should have been sleeping."

Gwynn glanced down at Anya's wrists. "Handcuffs? Why were you in cuffs?" She spun to face her boss. "Why was she in handcuffs?"

Ray nodded toward the dining room. "Come on. Let's eat. I think I'll let Anya tell you why she was in cuffs."

The three took their seats around the table and dug into the pancakes and bacon Ray made.

Anya said, "It was silly bet, and he tricked me. This is all."

Ray pointed a syrupy fork at Anya. "You set the parameters of the bet. Not me. There was no prohibition against trickery."

Gwynn swallowed a mouthful of bacon. "Let me guess. You bet him that he couldn't handcuff you."

"This is true, but not all of truth. I believed you would play fair, but I was wrong."

Ray paused with a forkful between his plate and his mouth. "Is that what we're doing now? Playing fair? That poor guy at the hospital last night probably doesn't think you played fair."

Anya ignored the jab. "These pancakes are delicious."

Ray nodded in satisfaction. "That's what I thought."

Anya turned to Gwynn. "Do you have a diamond?"

She pulled back her hair to expose an earring. "These are about three-quarter carat each. My dad gave them to me for law school graduation."

Anya leaned in, inspecting the solitaires. "They are beautiful. I do not have a diamond, but I think I would like one."

"I'll make a deal with you," Ray said. "If you'll include English articles at least fifty percent of the time for forty-eight hours, I'll buy you one."

The Russian placed a finger beside her mouth as if considering his bribe. "This is very nice offer, but is not necessary. I have Russian boyfriend named Viktor Volkov. He is in diamond business, and I can make him give me as many diamonds as I want. I can make him give me everything I want."

"I like the confidence," he said, "but I suspect your so-called boyfriend has no shortage of beautiful Russian women—and any other nationality he desires—hanging from his arm anytime he wants."

Gwynn jumped in. "Yes, but those women aren't Anya. I used to be the cutest girl in almost any room until"—she cast a thumb toward the Russian—"*she* showed up."

Anya rolled her eyes. "That is kind of you to say, but you are beautiful woman. If I was man, I would fight for you."

"Were," Ray said.

Anya frowned. "Were what?"

"You said 'If I *was* man.' It should've been if I *were* a man. It's one of those strange rules in English. I can't remember exactly how it goes, but if you're describing a situation that doesn't exist, the verb is were, not was, regardless of singular or plural."

"This is ridiculous arbitrary rule. There are too many of these in English language. Russian is simple language and does not have so many rules."

Ray laughed through a mouthful of coffee. "Russian is anything but simple and has even more rules than English."

Anya dismissed his argument. "Whatever you say. You are wrong, but you are in charge, so I will not quarrel with you."

"You're learning," he said. "Quarreling with me is never a good idea . . . unless, of course, you want to be wrong."

They finished breakfast without any more English lessons and moved to the living room.

Anya asked. "You have for me nice apartment in New York, just like Miami, yes?"

Ray said, "I've not seen it, but I'm sure there's no ocean view. We have an apartment near Times Square. It's a two bedroom because I knew you'd insist on having Gwynn come along."

"I cannot wait to see it," Anya said.

"That's good, because you don't have to wait long. All we need to do is outfit you with a new wardrobe and get you on a plane to New York."

"I do not need airplane ride. I have Porsche."

Ray lowered his chin. "It isn't your Porsche. It belongs to the federal government."

She scowled. "Because you tricked me with handcuffs, I also belong to federal government until mission is completed. This means the Porsche and I belong together. You will get it for me."

"It's not that simple, I'm afraid. Besides, nobody has a car in New York. The streets are too congested."

"This makes no sense. If no one has car, why are streets congested?"

Gwynn laid her hand on Anya's forearm. "Don't listen to him. He hates the city, but he's probably right. A car service is a lot better up there. The Porsche would get banged up, and it's way too sexy for that."

Anya turned to Ray. "This makes sense, but you will keep Porsche for me so Gwynn and I will have it for next assignment, yes?"

Gwynn shot a look toward Ray. "Next assignment?"

Ray pulled at the stitching on the arm of his recliner. "Yeah . . . about that. I should've told you, but you've been officially assigned to Operation Avenging Angel as a participating field agent."

Gwynn's eyes lit up like fireworks on the Fourth of July, and she grabbed Anya's hand. "Did you hear that? I'm officially assigned as a participating field agent with you."

"What does this mean?"

Ray started to answer, but Gwynn cut him off. "It means I'm going with you to New York City, and we're going to paint the Big Apple red!"

Confusion consumed Anya's face. "Uh, I do not understand this painting apple."

Gwynn giggled. "In the roaring twenties, there were more horseracing venues in New York than anywhere in the country, so everybody went to the races. The winning horses were always given the biggest, juiciest apples after the race, so a newspaper reporter referred to New York City as the Big Apple, meaning the best prize. The name stuck, and in nineteen seventy-one, the mayor signed a proclamation officially giving the city the nick-name of the Big Apple. At least that's what they taught us in school."

Anya still wore the confusion like a veil. "But why would we paint it?"

"It's just a figure of speech, girl. It means we're going to have a good time in the city."

"In that case," Anya said, "we are painters of city of New York. When do we leave?"

Ray chewed his bottom lip. "That's the thing. You leave this afternoon as long as we get everything done in time."

"Is perfect for me, but I do not have clothes or knives."

Ray held up a finger and stood. "Wait here."

He returned with a heavy canvas bag and handed it to Anya.

She set the bag on her lap and slid back the zipper. Inside rested her collection of custom-made knives Bernard Claiborne had created for her at the CIA technical services lab. She pulled out a pair of throwing knives and caressed them as if they were her own precious children. Next, a fighting knife came out of the bag, and a huge smile came over her face. "This one is my favorite. Is perfect knife, and I want more. You can do this for me, no?"

Ray eyed the glistening blade. "I'll see what I can do, but no promises."

"This means you will get for me more just like this one."

Ray sighed. "Does anyone ever get away with telling you no?"

"Sometimes, yes, but not so many. I know this operation is important for you—and also for your career—so you will give to Gwynn and me everything we need."

"I'll never understand how women do it, but you always get what you want, and there's nothing the men of the world can do about it."

Anya narrowed her eyes. "I want to go home, but I cannot because of you."

Ray closed his eyes and spent a few seconds imagining his name above the door on some prestigious law firm somewhere nice and quiet. *If I had only listened . . . Two decades practicing law surely would've been better than twenty years in D.C. as a lawyer with a badge and gun.*

He opened his eyes. "I walked right into that one, didn't I?"

Anya nodded silently. Her bitter reminder that she was no one's partner, but an indentured servant, sucked the air out of the room until Gwynn said, "The best thing about New York City is the shopping, and I think the Justice Department owes you a brand-new wardrobe."

Ray drummed his fingers on the arm of his chair. "When will you be ready to go, Gwynn?"

She directed her gaze away from him as if he'd caught her stealing cookies from the jar. "Well, to tell the truth, I was sort of hoping I'd be going along, so I'm already packed."

"Of course you are," he said. "When we collected your knives from Miami, we brought back your clothes, too, but I don't think they're exactly right for The City. Perhaps we should make a run back to the FBI's bargain basement."

Gwynn met Anya's eyes and turned to her boss. "If it's all the same to you, New York clothes should be bought in New York."

"Fine, but we don't have much time to waste. Volkov is a creature of habit. His business trips to wherever he goes always last less than a week, and he's always back in The City in time for Friday night dinner at Matryoshka."

Anya asked. "What time does he have dinner?"

"Usually about nine."

She stood. "Good. You will make for us reservations at Matryoshka at nine thirty tomorrow night. I have plan to make Yuvelir come to us, but we will need also Johnny-Mac and fake diamond ring."

5

TSELYY NOVYY MIR (A WHOLE NEW WORLD)

The three-and-a-half-hour train ride from Washington's Union Station to Penn Station in Manhattan put Anya and Gwynn in New York City just before 3:30 that afternoon. The FBI courier delivered their clothes and personal belongings and had them neatly stored in their new apartment, just off Times Square, before the duo stepped from the Yellow Cab and into the assignment that was everything their previous mission in Miami was not.

The first difference between the two operations greeted them as they climbed the five steps from the sidewalk and into the lobby of their new temporary home. "Good afternoon, ladies. I am Patrick, one of your doormen."

The sixty-something Irishman dressed in tails and white gloves held the ornate door for them, and the DOJ special agent said, "Thank you, Patrick. I'm Gwynn, and this is Anya. We're in seventeen-oh-one."

Patrick tipped his hat. "Yes, ma'am. I'm aware. Three gentlemen were here earlier to drop off a few of your things."

"Oh, good. We look forward to seeing the apartment. Arrangements were made sight unseen, so we certainly hope it lives up to the pictures."

Patrick situated his black hat back on his head. "I'm certain you'll not be disappointed." He offered each of them a card. "You'll find all of our numbers on there. If there's anything we can do for you at any hour, never hesitate to ring."

Anya spoke for the first time. "You can get for us car service, yes?"

"Of course. If you'll only give us half an hour notice when you can, we'll be Johnny-on-the-spot for you. It usually takes less than a quarter hour, but this is the city. That accent of yours . . . Might that be Georgian?"

Anya showed a look of surprise. "That is excellent guess. I am from Georgia."

"I thought so. Me brother's wife is Georgian . . . from Kutaisi, if memory serves me. Whereabouts would you be from?"

"Kutaisi is long way from my home. I live in city of Athens, about eighty kilometers east of Atlanta."

Patrick hesitated and then gave her a Santa Claus belly laugh. "You're a sharp one, ain't you?"

He was still laughing when the elevator doors closed on the Fed and the Georgian.

On the ride to the seventeenth floor, Gwynn said, "That was funny."

Anya gave one satisfied nod. "It was American humor. They say you have mastered new language when you understand jokes."

Gwynn smiled. "Yes, they do say that. Patrick was nice, don't you think?"

"Yes, he was nice, but he is not handsome man like Michael, the doorman in Miami."

Gwynn raised her eyebrows. "I'll give you that. He's more like somebody's grandfather, but I like him."

The doors of the elevator opened into a wide foyer with a long, marble-top table against one wall and a gilded mirror hanging above it.

"Push and hold button to keep door open."

Gwynn did as Anya instructed, but she didn't know why. The Russian moved slowly through the elevator car, inspecting the mirror from every angle.

"Stay here, and hold button." Anya stepped from the car and turned the corner into the hallway. Moving left and right, she eyed the mirror carefully before returning to the elevator, then slid her finger onto the hold button. "Now, you do it."

"Do what?" Gwynn asked.

"Look into mirror from every position inside elevator and remember what you see. After this, move to hallway and look back into mirror from many angles."

Gwynn did as she instructed and returned to the elevator. "Okay, I did it, but why?"

Anya stepped into the foyer. "Mirror is bending of eyes to look around corners. Your brain has now picture of everything in mirror from every angle. I hope we do not need this knowledge, but it will give to us advantage if some person comes for us in building."

Gwynn examined the foyer and hallway again. "What an amazing mind you have. I don't know if I'll ever think like you."

Anya took Gwynn's arm. "It is my hope for you that you do not have to think like me. World is dangerous place for people like me. It is better to live without such dangers in your life."

Gwynn led the way to the apartment. "I think it was Sun Tzu who said, 'The best way to guarantee peace is to always be prepared for war.'"

"This is a good philosophy, I think."

By Gwynn's count, the door to the apartment lay eleven strides from the foyer and offered no view of the mirror. The doorframe held no hairs, but the deadbolt made a scratching sound as she turned the key. The entrance hallway was seven feet long and opened into the living room with the kitchen on the left and a short hallway to the two bedrooms on the right.

Gwynn examined the space. "It's a lot smaller than the Miami apartment, but it's nice."

Anya pulled the blinds aside and looked down on Times Square. "Is more than adequate, but there is no view of ocean."

Gwynn joined her at the window. "You're right. There's no ocean, but it's still kind of pretty. I wonder how it'll look at night."

They inventoried the apartment and discovered the FBI couriers had chosen bedrooms for each of them. Anya's few clothes and knives were in the first bedroom, while Gwynn's items were farther down the hallway. It was the arrangement Anya would've chosen, but she wondered if the couriers gave it any real thought.

Gwynn stepped into Anya's room. "This is nice, and you've got a private bath. Mine has a door from my room and the hallway."

"If you like this one better, we can change, but for now, it is safer if I am closer to front door."

Gwynn peeked out the window. "No, I'm fine the way it is, and honestly, I like you being between me and the front door."

Anya sat on the edge of her bed. "You know the city, yes?"

Gwynn joined her on the bed. "Yeah. I went to college and law school at Columbia in Morningside Heights. That's near Harlem at Broadway and Hundred and Sixteenth Street."

"This is good school, Columbia?"

Gwynn chuckled. "Yeah, you could say that. I was really lucky to get in. Like I told you before, my dad was a teacher, and Mom was a paralegal, so they couldn't afford to send me to Columbia. They could barely afford to send me to a community college, so I worked really hard in high school and earned a merit scholarship to Columbia for my undergrad."

Anya thought about Gwynn's story. "This is what they mean when they say American Dream, yes?"

Gwynn shrugged. "I guess so. I mean, I got a good education by working hard and taking my studies seriously. Now, I've got the coolest job in the world."

Anya cocked her head. "You think being policeman is coolest job in the world?"

She took the Russian's hand. "No, working with you is the coolest job in the world. Honestly, my job was pretty boring before you came along."

Anya let her eyes explore the ceiling. "I think I would enjoy boring job inside office with telephone, typewriter, and a boss."

Gwynn laughed. "Yeah, right. You wouldn't last a week in an office. You'd stab your boss in the throat the first time he yelled at you."

Anya smiled. "That would make office exciting for everyone else."

"It certainly would. Speaking of exciting, how about we freshen up and go shopping?"

Patrick had the car waiting for them by the time they reached the lobby. Unlike their driver in Miami, the Town Car had an Indian gentleman in his thirties behind the wheel.

"Where would you like to go, ladies?"

Anya slid onto the rear seat. "We would like to buy clothes."

The driver eyed Gwynn, hoping for something a little more specific.

"Let's start at Bloomingdales on Lexington and East Sixtieth," she said.

"Yes, ma'am."

The remainder of the afternoon and early evening was spent collecting shopping bags and boxes and racking up points on Uncle Sam's American Express.

When their driver dropped them off back at the apartment, Anya said, "We cannot carry all of this up to the apartment. It will take two trips."

Patrick opened the door of the Town Car, and Gwynn decided to have a little fun with the Irishman at Anya's expense. "Hi, Patrick. I'm afraid we've made a huge mistake. We bought too much stuff to carry in one trip. Do you think it would be safe to leave half of it in the lobby long enough for us to make it upstairs with the first load?" She gave him a wink.

"Oh, missy, you're giving an old man another laugh. I'm going to have to keep me eye on the two of you troublemakers."

Anya sat confused by everything happening around her, so Gwynn continued the game. "You know what? I don't think I want to carry any of this stuff up there. Let's just forget it and buy more stuff some other time."

Anya stepped from the car and eyed the doorman. "I do not understand."

Patrick threw up his hands in mock surrender. "The lady said she doesn't want to do it, so I reckon you should go on up, and I'll find something to do with all of this stuff."

Gwynn took Anya's arm. "Come on. Let's go up."

The Russian looked between the car, the building, and the doorman in rapid succession, but Gwynn kept pulling her toward the door.

Completely baffled, Anya followed Gwynn into the elevator. "What is happening? Why would we buy all of those things and then leave them on the street? I do not understand."

Gwynn had carried the charade as far as she could, and she burst into laughter. "You may know everything there is to know about being an assassin, but you've got a lot to learn about being a New Yorker. I'll make a deal with you. You keep teaching me what you know, and I'll teach you about life in the city."

Anya scowled. "What are you talking about?"

Gwynn pressed the button for the seventeenth floor. "This is a whole new world for you, isn't it? Patrick will have someone bring our bags up for us. It's part of the service."

The Russian drew a blade from somewhere Gwynn hadn't noticed and bounced it against her palm. "If you do this to me again, I will pretend you are boss yelling at me inside office, and I will stab you in throat."

6

MATRYOSHKA (NESTING DOLLS)

Federal agent Gwynn Davis and former Russian assassin Anya Burinkova spent the evening putting away their trophies from the day spent shopping in Manhattan. Both were exhausted from the arduous day that had begun at Supervisory Special Agent Ray White's breakfast table and culminated with the two women settled into their new Big Apple apartment overlooking Times Square.

Gwynn joined Anya on the couch with a bottle of water in one hand and a stack of paper menus in the other. "Something just occurred to me."

Anya looked up. "What is it?"

"Do you remember the name of Viktor Volkov's favorite Friday-night restaurant?"

"Of course I remember. It is Matryoshka. This means—"

Gwynn cut her off. "I know what it means. Matryoshka are Russian nesting dolls. I think we qualify. We've been nesting all afternoon, and just look at us . . . we're definitely dolls."

The two shared a laugh, and then Anya said, "If doormen—I mean, if *the* doormen—carry our packages for us, do they also bring for us food when we want?"

"You're getting better at this English thing. Pretty soon you'll sound like a New Yorker."

Anya rolled her eyes. "I have been in New York for several hours, and I have never heard two people who sound the same. I do not believe there is a New York accent."

"Actually, you're probably right," Gwynn said, "but you'll notice some similarities over the next few days. It really depends on where you are in the city. And yes, food will magically appear whenever we want." She slid half of the menus across the center cushion of the couch. "Do any of those sound good to you?"

She picked up the menus and shuffled through them. "Where did you get these?"

"They were in the drawer in the kitchen. I guess the previous tenant left them. Do you like Chinese?"

"The people, or their food?"

Gwynn shook her head. "I was specifically asking about food, but now I'm curious about the other."

Anya pulled out a Chinese menu written in Mandarin and ran her finger down the page. "I like all of it, but this is my favorite."

Gwynn leaned toward her. "Are you kidding me? You can read Chinese?"

"Only Mandarin. Not Cantonese. And yes, I like the people, but I do not trust the government."

"Be honest," Gwynn said. "Do you really trust any government?"

Anya looked up from the menu. "Is interesting question coming from government police officer."

Gwynn giggled. "Yeah, I guess it is, huh?"

Anya extended her hand. "Give to me phone. I will make order."

Gwynn handed over her cell phone, and Anya dialed the number. Two minutes later, Gwynn was even more amazed at her partner's ability to not only read Mandarin, but also her apparent ease in speaking the language.

"Okay, that's pretty impressive," Gwynn said.

"Is only order for dinner. I did not negotiate a peace treaty."

The delivery arrived, and the two devoured the dishes as if they hadn't eaten in days.

Gwynn laid down her chopsticks. "I've waited as long as I can. I need you to tell me the plan for tomorrow night."

Anya finished her dinner and spent twenty minutes explaining every detail of how, with Johnny-Mac's help and a fake diamond, they would lure Volkov right into their hands.

Gwynn listened intently. "That's a brilliant plan, but what if he doesn't take the bait?"

"I am great actress. I will make certain he not only takes bait, but also he will swallow my hook."

"If anybody can pull it off, it'll be you. I can't wait to see the performance."

"You will brief Agent McIntyre, yes? He doesn't like me, so it will be better for you to do it."

Gwynn frowned. "What do you mean he doesn't like you? Everybody likes you. He's just intimidated by you, that's all."

"Not everyone likes me. I have told you of the man who once loved me, yes?"

"Yeah, Chase Fulton."

Anya let the memory of the man consume her momentarily. "Yes, him. He has now wife. Her name is Penny. She does not like me."

Gwynn huffed. "Well, that's kind of understandable, don't you think? You're a threat to her. She probably thinks she's competing with you for Chase's affection."

"If this is what she thinks, she is wrong. In some ways, he is a simple man. He loves her and will not hurt her for me or anyone else. He is loyal to his friends and to her. This is admirable thing. Sometimes people talk of how they would change their past if this were possible. I would do this. I would be loyal to him, and I would love him if I could turn back hands of clock."

Seeing one of the deadliest warriors on Earth open her soul and share such personal emotion left Gwynn mesmerized. "Does he know?"

"Does he know what?" Anya asked.

"Does he know you'd, you know, change things if you could do it all over again?"

"I do not know. I have never said this to him, but more than this, I have secret I can never tell him. But every day I want to so badly it hurts inside me."

Gwynn watched the Russian fight back the tears welling up in her eyes. "Secrets can eat at us like cancer. I know it's not the same, but you can always tell me."

"This I cannot tell anyone. You have responsibility to government, and you could not keep secret. This is burden for me to carry alone."

"I understand, and you're probably right. If I learn something about you that might affect the operation, it's my duty to report it. I hope I never have to make that choice, though."

Anya wiped away the single tear that escaped the corner of her eye. "I hope this, also." A few seconds later, the Russian's face showed no sign of ever having been in turmoil. "There is not fighting training tonight. Maybe we will do this tomorrow. For now, I must sleep."

After Anya closed her door and slid beneath the cover, Gwynn stood at the living room window, admiring the scene below. Times Square bustled with people who looked like tiny scampering ants. Countless people went about their lives, never looking up to see who was looking down on them. Gwynn and Anya were tasked with the awesome responsibility of stopping a criminal element so violent and so contemptuous of law and civility that it would eat away at the very foundations of the moral and financial stability of the United States until those foundations crumbled beneath their feet. No one would ever know the sacrifices they made to rid the world of such parasites. Turning from the window, Gwynn ached to know Anya's unspoken secret.

* * *

As promised, Patrick had their car on the curb twenty minutes after Gwynn's call the following evening. The Town Car had been replaced by a black Lexus LX-570. They slid onto the back seat, and someone closed the door behind them.

"What's up, ladies? I'm Geno, and I'll be doin' the drivin' tonight. Where we headed?"

Gwynn excitedly pointed toward the driver and whispered, "*That's* the New York accent I was talking about."

Anya nodded and appeared to be taking mental notes of the dialect. "We would like to go to Matryoshka at eighty-eight Fulton Street."

"Sure, no problem. You ladies just sit back and relax. I'll have you there in no time."

No time turned into forty minutes in the Manhattan traffic.

Anya said, "Now it makes sense why no one has car in New York."

The driver shot a look into the mirror. "Yeah, the problem is them that do got cars don't know how to drive, and then there's no place to park. So, that being said, you're better off without your own car."

Gwynn whispered, "Yep, that's definitely pure New York accent."

Once inside Matryoshka, just past nine thirty, the hostess greeted them and led them to a table near the front. Anya scanned the room. Every table except theirs was occupied, but Viktor Volkov was nowhere in sight.

Anya turned to the hostess and spoke in Russian. "It is very noisy here. Is there a quieter part of the restaurant? We don't mind waiting if we have to."

Pleased to hear her native language, the hostess beamed. "Give me a minute, and I'll find you someplace nice and quiet."

Anya and Gwynn moved to an alcove near the kitchen to watch the hostess go in search of a more suitable table—hopefully, one in full view of Viktor's table.

The hostess returned and motioned for them to follow. "*Poydem so mnoy.*"

"She wants us to follow her."

"Yes, I caught that," Gwynn said. "I'm learning."

As they were led through a curtain into a smaller dining room in the back, Anya spotted Yuvelir immediately in the back corner of the room with his back to the wall.

The hostess turned to Gwynn. "This is good table for you, yes?"

Gwynn nodded. "Much better. Spasibo."

Anya had a brief conversation with the hostess in rapid-fire Russian before sitting down facing Volkov. Once in her seat, she leaned toward Gwynn. "She says the stroganoff is no good, but the baked salmon with vegetables is perfect."

Gwynn continued her study of the menu. "I guess there are advantages to speaking Russian, even in New York City."

"Only inside Russian restaurant."

Gwynn perused the menu a little longer. "There are some nasty-sounding dishes on here. Boiled veal tongue with mushroom sauce? Are you kidding me?"

"You should maybe try it. You might be surprised with both flavor and texture."

"Yeah, and I might throw up. I think I'm sticking with something a little less disgusting."

"We will start with appetizer," Anya said.

Gwynn slid her finger up the page and shivered. "Oh, my God. Cow feet and chicken. How can that even be a thing, let alone an appetizer? There's something seriously wrong with anybody who eats cow feet. I can't even imagine what part of the chicken comes with it."

Anya tried not to laugh. The night's plan of action required that she be distraught, angry, and brokenhearted. "Maybe for you, just a salad and no appetizer."

She let her finger slide down Gwynn's menu until it reached the salad list. Gwynn actually gagged when she read cod liver with lettuce, eggs, and onion. "No wonder you wanted to be an American so badly. Nobody eats cod liver."

Their waitress arrived and looked as if she could've been Miss Russia or right off the pages of the Victoria's Secret catalog. Anya ordered for them in flawless Russian, just loud enough for Volkov to hear. When he looked up to meet Anya's eyes, she gave him a polite, slightly flirtatious smile. He didn't return her smile, but instead offered a barely perceptible nod and then didn't look away.

"I swear to you, Anya, if you ordered me something nasty, I'm catching the next train back to D.C., and you're on your own."

She let her eyes drift away from Volkov's. "I ordered for you mussels in white wine sauce, pork-stuffed dumplings, and grilled Norwegian salmon."

"Thank you. Now, please tell me you're not having veal tongue or cow's feet. Cows don't even have feet. They have hooves."

"I am having buzhenina. Is roasted pork, smoked eel salad, and sausage with sour cabbage."

Gwynn sighed. "The eel sounds disgusting, but I might want a bite of the buzhenina."

The appetizers arrived, followed shortly by the salad and dumplings. Anya stayed in character and shot occasional glances toward Volkov. To her delight, he was staring back at her every time she looked up.

The main courses arrived, and the portions were enormous.

"I'll never be able to eat all of this," Gwynn said.

Anya whispered, "Do not worry. We will not be here long enough to finish. It is time to call in Johnny-Mac."

7

PREDSTAVLENIYE (THE PERFORMANCE)

Gwynn thumbed the send button on her phone, launching a two-word text message to Special Agent Johnathon McIntyre.

Outside the restaurant, Johnny-Mac felt the vibration and pulled his phone from his pocket. The screen displayed the message he'd been waiting to see for over an hour:

It's Showtime!

Four minutes later, he waded through the sea of tables inside the Russian restaurant. When he spotted Special Agent Gwynn Davis, he moved quickly to the table and faced Anya with Gwynn at his right hip.

Anya barked in heavily accented English. "How dare you come to table. You are worthless, terrible little child. You will leave now!"

Johnny-Mac put on an Oscar-worthy performance. "After everything I've done for you, I'll not be treated this way. You're an ungrateful, selfish bitch."

Anya wasn't expecting his words to sting, but it appeared he was blending his actual feelings with his performance. She took a few seconds to brush off the reality in his tone, then turned to Gwynn with an outstretched hand. "Give to me ring! Give to me!"

Gwynn suddenly felt the heat of the moment and almost believed it was far more than acting. She fumbled through her bag and pulled out the worthless ring.

Anya yanked it from her hand and held it up in Johnny-Mac's face. "This is what you call being good to me? Huh? This is worthless piece of trash. Is not real diamond! Did you think the poor Russian girl was too dumb to know difference? Is this what you really think of me?"

Agent McIntyre shoved a finger into her face. "Look at you. You're making a fool of yourself in front of all these people."

"I am no fool!" she roared. "If I were fool, I would believe your lies, but I am finished with you. Get out of my face, and *YA bol'she ne khochu tebya videt', ublyudok!*"

The switch to angry Russian had been part of Anya's plan all along, but she didn't expect the raw emotion that came along with it. Her pulse pounded in her neck as her face turned blood red. She shoved the ring toward Johnny-Mac's face again. "This is what I think of you and your phony ring!" She hurled the piece of jewelry across the room, bouncing it off the wall behind Viktor Volkov, who'd been watching the show with great interest. From the corner of her eye, she saw Volkov lift the ring from the floor and shove it into his pocket.

Anya rose from her seat and screamed, "You are dead to me!" Before she finished the verbal attack, she landed an open-hand slap on Johnny-Mac's right cheek, sending him stepping away after the blow.

He lunged for her and grabbed her wrist. The heated exchange took a dark turn as the agent's grip dug into Anya's flesh. She raised a foot in preparation to send a heel kick crashing into his shin—or perhaps his knee—but she never delivered the blow. Instead, Viktor Volkov laced his powerful right arm around Johnny-Mac's neck from behind and lifted him from his feet. With the agent kicking and flailing, the beefy Russian dragged him through the kitchen and deposited him in the alley behind the restaurant.

Ninety seconds later, Volkov returned to the dining room and lifted his jacket from the chair beside his table. As he slid an arm back into the jacket, a soft round of applause rose from the room.

Anya looked up and said, "Spasibo."

Volkov motioned for a waitress, and she scampered to his side. He pointed toward Anya's table. "Move their meal to my table. They will be sitting with me for the rest of the evening."

His Russian accent was unmistakable, but a gentleness emanated through his words that neither Gwynn nor Anya expected. The waitress moved their plates and pulled a pair of chairs to Volkov's table.

Anya and Gwynn joined the man as Anya whispered, "I told you he would take bait and also swallow hook."

"I'm sorry your dinner was ruined by that man, but I assure you he will not bother you again. I am Viktor Volkov."

Anya wiped a feigned tear from her face. "Did you hurt him?"

Viktor narrowed his eyes. "Did you want me to hurt him?"

She nodded, a look of desperation on her face.

"I was a little rough with him, but I did not hurt him . . . this time. But I did make him understand I will kill him if I hear he has disturbed you again. He is your husband, no?"

Anya shook her head. "No! He is not husband. Only person I have been on date with a few times. I thought he was a good man, but I was foolish. He is liar and has terrible temper."

Volkov sighed. "Well, as I said, he won't bother you again. I'm afraid I did not get your names.

"I'm Gwynn, and my friend is Anya."

He offered a slight dip of his chin. "It is a pleasure."

He pulled the ring from his pocket, along with a jeweler's loupe. He pressed the loupe to his right eye and moved the ring into focus in front of the magnifying loupe. "You were correct. Ring is *fugazi*. You know this word, *fugazi*?"

Anya shook her head. "It means two things. First, it means fake piece of jewelry in the business, but it means also situation that turned bad very quickly. I think both are appropriate for tonight."

Gwynn squeezed Anya's trembling hand, and Volkov noticed.

He placed a finger beneath Anya's chin and raised her face to look into his. "You have *nastoyashchiy drug,* a true friend, to hold your hand, and now you have me to protect you from that horrible little man."

Anya gazed toward the ring and Volkov's loupe resting on the table. "How do you know it is *fugazi*?"

Volkov motioned for another waitress. When she arrived, he spoke in Russian. "Bring a meat tenderizer from the kitchen."

She returned seconds later with a stainless-steel hammer with triangular protrusions on one surface and a smooth, rounded finish on the other. Volkov produced a piece of folded white paper from his interior jacket pocket. As he unfolded the paper, a glistening, loose diamond appeared in the creases. He pulled back the tablecloth and placed the diamond on the heavy wooden table. "A diamond is the hardest of all stones. Nothing can cut diamond except other diamond. Is magnificent thing. Watch closely. This is two-carat diamond and is IF clarity and E maybe F, but is colorless. Do you know what this means?"

Anya shook her head.

Volkov said, "Two carat means the stone weighs point four grams. Is bigger than average stone. Clarity means what you see when you look deep inside diamond. Anything you see inside is bad. Cloudy areas or dark spots, these are called inclusions, and they lower value of diamond. FL means flawless. This means perfect diamond. These are rare and are most expensive diamonds in all of world. This one is IF, internally flawless. This means there is nothing inside stone but may have almost invisible mark on outside of stone. I say this one is flawless, but I am not final authority. Finally, the color. This means how clear is diamond. D, E, and F are colorless. This scale goes to Z, which means yellow or brown. This diamond is E in color."

Anya's feigned anger and fear melted into feigned admiration.

Volkov handed her the loupe and produced a pair of locking jeweler's tweezers. He positioned the stone in the prongs of the tweezers and placed them in Anya's left hand. "Place loupe against your cheek and look inside." She did as he instructed, and he laid his hand across hers, then slowly moved the tweezers closer and closer to the loupe. "Stop when stone is in focus, but do not move loupe." He pulled his hand from hers as she slowly moved the stone into focus.

She gazed into the nearly invisible diamond. "It is beautiful."

"Yes, it is," Volkov breathed. "Allow Gwynn to see."

Anya offered the loupe, and Gwynn pressed it to her cheek. Just as Volkov had done, Anya placed the tweezers in Gwynn's hand and positioned them closer.

Gwynn moved the stone too close and then backed it away until it came into focus. She gasped. "It is astonishing."

Volkov smiled. "You have eye for beautiful things. This could be why you are true friend for Anya. The two of you are the only things inside restaurant more beautiful than this diamond."

Anya blushed at the compliment, but Gwynn couldn't look away from the stone. She finally surrendered it back to Volkov, and he lifted the meat tenderizer in his left hand while holding the diamond against the table in the prongs of the tweezers. With a powerful blow, he sent the hammer into the stone. Dishes and glasses clattered and leapt across the table. When he lifted the hammer, the stone had escaped the grasp of the tweezers and had been driven into the surface of the table. He dug it out with the pointed tips and repositioned it between the prongs. He handed the tweezers to Anya. "Look again, and try to find mark from hammer."

Anya inspected the stone through the loupe for a long moment and then handed the stone and loupe to Gwynn. After several minutes of searching, they gave up.

"It didn't do anything to the diamond," Gwynn said. "That's amazing."

He lifted the tweezers from her fingers and handed her the ring Anya had thrown across the room. "Now, look at this one."

Anya and Gwynn took turns staring through the loupe at the *fugazi* until Gwynn said, "It looks almost better than yours. How do you know it isn't real?"

Volkov leaned back in his seat. "You have heard phrase that if something seems too good to be true, it probably is, yes?"

Both women nodded.

"This is why I know that it is not real diamond. It is too good to be real. This stone would be worth thirty thousand dollars U.S. if it were real. No one would mount a stone so valuable in setting so cheap. It is probably real gold, but only maybe ten-karat gold. This means only ten parts gold for every twenty-four parts of alloy. It is gold, but cheap gold."

He took the ring from Anya's fingers and laid it on the table. "Watch what happens when I hit with hammer, but this time, not so hard. Only soft hit."

He tapped the mounted stone without disturbing anything on the table, and the *fugazi* crumbled into a dozen shards of glass. Volkov tossed the ring without its stone onto a plate of scraps and replaced the tablecloth. He folded the real diamond back into its paper carrier and tucked it back into his pocket.

Anya leaned forward. "How do you know so much about diamonds?"

Volkov smiled. "I'm in the business. I get paid to know more about diamonds—especially fake diamonds—than everyone around me."

The three ate and talked for an hour. Anya told the story of coming to America to become a model or maybe an actress, but neither dream became reality. Gwynn described how she practiced law in New Jersey but couldn't get into one of the big Manhattan firms she so desperately wanted to join.

Viktor listened intently to both women as they enjoyed the dessert of chocolate cake and port. When they finished, he pulled up his sleeve to reveal his Patek Philippe wristwatch. He checked the time, reached inside his jacket, and produced the folded paper containing the diamond. He slid the paper into Anya's hand. "This is for you. As you saw, it is not a *fugazi*."

Anya protested. "I cannot take this. It is too much."

He folded her fingers around the envelope and squeezed her hand. "It is yours, but I have only one condition. You must come with me tomorrow to the Diamond District, and we will find for you a setting for the stone, yes?"

Anya shot a look toward Gwynn, who was bobbing her head up and down. "Yes . . . yes, I will do this. I will come with you, but you cannot be serious. Surely I cannot keep diamond."

He gave her hand another firm squeeze. "The diamond is yours, and my number is on the paper. Call me tomorrow, and I will pick you up. Of course, friend Gwynn is welcome to come along, also."

They stood, and Volkov kissed each of their hands in turn. He said, "It would be my pleasure to have my driver take you home if you would like."

Anya laced her arm through his and looked up at him with affection pouring from every inch of her face. "We would love that, but we have a driver waiting for us. It is benefit of Gwynn's job. I will call you tomorrow."

To his delight, Anya raised herself on tiptoes and pressed her lips to his skin, just beneath his ear. "Thank you for being real Russian man and not terrible American child."

8

OGLYANIS' NAZAD DVAZHDY (LOOK BACK TWICE)

Anya and Gwynn found their SUV waiting on the curb, just where the driver promised it would be. What they didn't find, however, was the driver who'd delivered them to the restaurant. Instead, they discovered a woman in her late thirties perched behind the wheel.

As they approached the Lexus, Gwynn made eye contact with the female driver, which caused her to shove open the door and leap from the car.

Gwynn raised a reassuring hand. "It's okay. We can get our own door. No worries."

The driver sprinted around the back of the car. "Uh-uh! You don't get your own door when momma's drivin' you." She held open the door as both passengers slid onto the back seat.

The driver hopped back into her position behind the wheel and pulled the transmission into drive. Without checking over her shoulder or in the mirror, she cranked the wheel hard and accelerated into traffic to the sounds of horns and shouts.

Gwynn gasped. "That's one way to merge into a traffic lane."

"It ain't for you, girl. It's for blondie back there. I seen what you did to that fine-ass man. And you walked away, workin' it! And you listen to momma when she tells you that man turned and looked back at you not once, girl, but two times. You hear me? Two times that man looked back at you. I hauled ass outta there so you could roll down that window and blow that fine man a kiss on the way by."

Without argument, Anya followed momma's direction, rolled down the window, and puckered up. Volkov offered the slightest nod and turned the corner.

Back at the apartment, they'd barely gotten through the door before Gwynn said, "That was a master class in how to have a man eating out of your hand. Holy Russian seduction, Batman. How do you do that?"

Anya kicked off her heels and set the teapot on the stove. "All men are cavemen inside. I play with caveman with my eyes, my hands, and sometimes my body. Soon he tells me if he will disobey caveman inside of him. If this happens, I have ways to break through shell and let the caveman come out to play. I will teach to you also this after you learn to stay alive when people want to kill you."

Gwynn kicked out of her heels and leaned against the refrigerator. "Seriously, that was awesome to watch. I've got so much to learn. Maybe I should've been born in Russia, and then . . ."

Anya turned and glared at her. "Never say this. You do not know what you're saying. The things I was forced to learn and also things I was never permitted to do as child in Soviet Union, I never want these things for you. I will teach to you everything you want to learn, but I will never be cruel to you because I care for you. Cruelty can never be undone. You are lucky to be American at birth. Never forget this."

"You care for me?" Gwynn whispered.

"Yes, I care deeply for you. I sometimes let myself pretend you are not doing all of this because it is your job, but because you are my friend."

Gwynn wrapped Anya in her arms. "Stop it. You're going to make me cry, and big bad federal agents aren't supposed to cry. Yes, it's my job to work with you, but even if it weren't, I'd still want to do it. I'm having the time of my life, and no matter what happens next, I'd never take away the time we've had together. I just wish it could've been under different circumstances."

Anya returned Gwynn's hug. "I wish for this, also, but I am afraid my life will always be less than the lives other people get to have."

The whistling teapot terminated the moment, and minutes later, the two were curled up in opposite corners of the couch.

Gwynn eyed the Russian through the steam leaving her mug. "What would you have done if Volkov didn't grab Johnny-Mac when he did?"

Anya took a sip. "I would have put Johnny-Mac onto floor. Sometimes Russian men like strong women. I was playing for him damsel in distress, first, but I had alternative idea if plan number one did not work."

Gwynn laughed. "I would've loved to have seen that, but for Johnny's sake, I'm glad you didn't have to do it. What do you think Volkov did to him in the alley?"

Anya shrugged. "I think maybe he just frightened him. Volkov's hands were smooth and soft with clean nails."

"What does that have to do with anything?"

"Men with hands without scars are not fighters. He is businessman. Volkov is strong, but he has hands of man who lives in safety and comfort. This kind of man does not make fights when it is not necessary."

"That's what you noticed about him? His manicured nails and soft hands?"

Anya took another sip of the steaming tea. "I notice everything about him, from feet to head."

Gwynn placed her mug on the end table. "Okay, then, let's hear it. Give me the whole rundown."

Anya cradled her mug. "It is from foot to head, as I told you. His shoes were Italian, and bottoms were smooth. This means one of two possible things. He does not walk on sidewalk too much, or he recently bought new shoes. Wrinkles on top of shoes say to me they are not new, so he probably has a driver who drops him off everywhere he goes."

"Okay, I'll buy that. Keep going."

"His watch was on right arm. This probably means he is left-handed. All of his whiskers are same length. Hair does not do this naturally, so he cuts whiskers with cutter designed to leave stubble."

"Why is that important?"

"This means he is vain about appearance, and we can use this to make him feel self-conscious sometime in future to break his confidence and focus."

"You would've made a great cop, you know that?"

"I made even better assassin."

Gwynn cocked her head. "But I thought you said killing always hurts."

"Yes, this is true, and pulling splinter from finger also hurts, but is better after. I never kill innocent people—only splinters in the world, and world is always better after."

Gwynn allowed the smile to come. "Sort of like Leo in Miami?"

"Exactly like that."

Gwynn stared down at her toes. "You know . . . I have a confession about what happened that morning in Miami."

"A confession?"

She traced the rim of her mug with her fingertips. "Yeah, when I saw you lying there, I thought he was really going to shoot you."

"Yes, of course. This is what he would have done if you were not there to kill him."

"Yeah, that's the thing," Gwynn said. "I didn't mean to kill him."

Anya sat immediately upright. "What?"

"Yeah, when that shard of glass left my grip, I was throwing at his gun hand, not his neck."

Anya frowned. "This is thing they teach to you at Academy?"

"No, we were never taught to throw knives at the Academy."

Anya shook her head. "No, I know this. I mean, you were taught to use nonlethal force to stop someone from killing your partner?"

"No, not really. I'm authorized to shoot in defense of myself, fellow agents, or bystanders, but I wasn't shooting. I was throwing a piece of broken glass that slightly resembled a knife."

"This is same thing. You sent projectile toward my attacker with the intention of stopping him from killing me. Is same if shooting or throwing broken glass."

"I guess you're right," Gwynn said. "But anyway, what I was trying to tell you is that I missed my target."

Anya reached for her hand. "You saved my life. I had lost too much blood to fight, and he would have killed me."

Gwynn's attention fell to her feet again. "There's something I've been wanting to ask you, but I'm a little afraid."

"Do not be afraid. Ask me anything. I will always answer if I can."

Gwynn didn't look up. "It's just that . . . I've been wondering . . . you know . . ."

"No, I do not know. Please just say question."

"It's not like I'm questioning your ability or anything. It's just that I've been trying to figure out what happened. I mean, how did Leo get you in that position?"

It was Anya's turn to stare at her feet. "I must now tell confession. I made terrible decision. When Leo confronted me, I should have attacked him, but I made decision to be affectionate to calm him. This was worst plan. I reached for him, and he took my hand. At that moment, I thought my plan was working, but he jerked my arm and spun me around. I think then he kicked me into glass wall. I was cut from thousand pieces of glass and almost unconscious. This is when you saved me."

Gwynn squeezed Anya's hand. "I hope I didn't upset you by asking. I just couldn't piece it together."

"Is always fine for you to ask. I made terrible mistake I will never make again, but I am thankful you were there."

"I'm glad I was there, too. I don't ever want anything like that to happen again, but I'll always have your back."

"And I will always have yours. Now, we must go to bed. We have date tomorrow to find setting for my diamond."

"Yes, we do," Gwynn said. "I know it's not really your diamond, but you have to be at least a little bit excited."

"I am very excited, and yes, it is my diamond."

Gwynn raised an eyebrow. "Uh, this is a criminal investigation, and that diamond will become evidence when all of this is over. That's how it works."

"Perhaps that is how it works if Volkov gave to you first diamond, but I am not police officer."

Gwynn let out an uncomfortable laugh. "Yes, but there will be a trial, and we'll have to prove chain of custody on every piece of evidence, including that diamond."

"This will only be necessary if there is trial, yes?"

"Well . . . yeah. I mean, if there's no trial, there won't be any chain-of-evidence issues."

Anya gave a sharp nod. "This is good. I will keep diamond, and you will throw broken glass at Volkov's hand, and maybe again you will miss and hit him in neck, just like Leo. There is no trial when defendant is dead."

9

DRUGAYA ZHENSHCHINA (THE OTHER WOMAN)

New York is often called The City That Never Sleeps. That may be true, but there are times when it's more awake than others. From seven to nine a.m., Monday through Friday, the streets and sidewalks of Manhattan are nearly invisible beneath the hordes of drivers, riders, walkers, and homeless former drivers, riders, and walkers. Saturdays, however, are an entirely different story.

After a breakfast of bagels, cream cheese, and jam in Times Square, Anya and Gwynn strolled side by side down 7th Avenue on the edge of the Garment District. Shops, restaurants, and construction scaffolding lined the street.

Anya grabbed Gwynn's hand and pointed with excitement toward a double-decker bus filled with wide-eyed tourists. "We must do this."

Gwynn pulled away, "Uh, no. I lived here for eight years. If you want a tour, I'll be your guide, but we're not getting on that nasty thing."

"But we do not have car."

"But we do have a car service, and they can do the driving while I play tour guide. What do you want to see?"

Anya beamed. "Everything."

Gwynn gave a chuckle. "Well, that might take a while, but we can do the tourist stuff like the New York City Library, the Statue of Liberty, and Central Park all in one day."

"I want also to see Empire State Building."

"We can do that right now." Gwynn motioned southward. "It's right down here on Thirty-Third. Come on, I'll show you, but I don't want you to be disappointed. There's no giant monkey with airplanes circling overhead."

Anya stared in bewilderment.

"You know . . . King Kong."

"I do not know this king."

Gwynn palmed her forehead. "If you're going to be an American, we've got so much work to do and so many movies to watch."

A left on 33rd led them to one of the most famous buildings in the world. They stood across the street, looking up like tourists at the massive structure.

"Believe it or not, this was the tallest building in the world for forty years, and it was designed, planned, and built in just twenty months."

"How do you know this?"

Gwynn laid an arm across Anya's shoulders. "I told you, I was a great tour guide."

"Yes, you did. We can go to the top, yes?"

Gwynn checked her watch. "We can go to the eighty-sixth floor to the observatory if you want, but we have to buy a ticket. What time did you plan to call Volkov?"

Anya took Gwynn's arm and dragged her across the street to the chorus of protesting horns. "We have plenty of time for him. We will buy tickets and see the top first."

Anya peeled off two crisp one-hundred-dollar bills to cover the cost of riding the elevator to the observation deck eighty-six floors above Midtown Manhattan, and she thought the view was worth every penny. Anya raised her head from a pair of coin-operated binoculars and pointed south in wide-eyed wonder. "There is Liberty Statue!"

Gwynn followed her finger to the iconic gift from the French, and although the statue was barely visible with the naked eye, she said, "It sure is. That's the Statue of Liberty."

Anya pinned her face back against the shiny, coin-eating binoculars and froze. A minute later, she hurriedly shoved her hand into her pocket, then turned to Gwynn. "You have coins?"

"Yeah, sure. Here you go."

Anya, seemingly undeterred by the string of tourists waiting for their turn, fed the machine until it consumed the contents of their pockets. When the scene went dark for the last time, she stepped down from the perch and turned to Gwynn. "A man once promised to show me the statue and Disney World and White House, but this did not come true until now."

"Chase, again?"

"Yes, he made this promise to me in Honeymoon Harbor near Leo's house in Bimini."

"You've got to get that man out of your head, you know."

"This is not possible. He is the kindest man I have ever known, and he is brilliant leader and loyal friend to his men."

A pair of tourists pushed their way past and stepped up to the binoculars.

Gwynn led Anya away from them and found a quieter corner. "I don't mean you have to forget about Chase, but you get this look on your face when you talk about him. It's like you're a teenaged girl swooning over the star quarterback."

"No, this is wrong. He was catcher, not quarterback. He took me to see baseball game at University of Georgia, and this is where I had my first chili dog. It is a wonderful story. I must tell you."

Gwynn raised a hand. "Anya. Stop it. How old are you?"

"I am thirty-two, and you are twenty-eight."

"Yes, but you're acting like . . ." Gwynn hesitated, afraid that what was about to come out of her mouth would be more hurtful than beneficial.

"When was first time you kissed a boy?" Anya asked.

Gwynn blushed. "I was twelve or thirteen, but what does that have to do—"

"The boy you kissed . . . Was he thirty-five-year-old KGB instructor?"

"What? No, his name was Billy Anderson. He was a math geek, and I needed help with pre-algebra."

"My first kiss with boy was lesson about how to kiss correctly to make Americans tell me everything they know. When was your first time doing sex with a boy?"

Gwynn checked over her shoulder in fear of someone overhearing their conversation. "That's not really something I want to talk about up here with all of these—"

Anya interrupted again. "He was maybe fifty years old, or maybe older, and smelled of vodka and cigarettes. I was gift to him from Communist party because he was loyal to Mother Russia. It was sweaty, and rough, and horrible."

Gwynn looked away as the sickening picture came into focus in her mind's eye.

Anya continued. "The first time I kissed Chase was in ocean on island of Saint Thomas, and the first time he made love with me was first time I learned men could be kind and caring for me. This is a time I will never forget, so please do not say to me I must take him from inside my head. I will not do this."

Gwynn swallowed hard. "I'm so sorry. I didn't know."

"Yes, you did," Anya said. "You know everything of my past. Agent White used the things your government knows of my past while he was interrogating me."

Gwynn took the Russian's hand. "Anya, I'm really sorry. We didn't know the things you just told me. There's no way we could know details like that, and I didn't mean to imply that you should forget the good memories you have with Chase. I was only trying to say . . . I'm just, sorry. I don't know what I was trying to say. Come on. Let's go see that Liberty Statue of yours."

They left the observation deck, but not before Anya had one more long look around at the Big Apple spreading out in every direction beneath them.

As the elevator doors opened to the lobby, Anya said, "I think we should see statue tomorrow. It is now time to work."

"Whatever you say, but if you think my Empire State Building trivia was good, just wait 'til you hear my Statue of Liberty spiel."

Anya pulled her phone from a pocket and dialed Viktor Volkov's number from memory. Gwynn listened as her partner spoke in her soft, flowing native tongue. She wondered why Russian sounded so harsh on the tongues of men, but when spoken by a woman, it was more beautiful than the language of the men and women who built the statue Anya so longed to see.

Anya pocketed the phone. "He will pick us up in front of building in fifteen minutes."

Volkov was early, and he held the door for the two beautiful women who were sworn to destroy him, although that thought was still days from entering his mind. To him, Anya was a woman scorned by a man who tried to pawn off a *fugazi* as the real thing, and a woman like her clearly deserved nothing but the finest of everything New York, and the world, had to offer.

Viktor shot his cuffs and checked his watch. The Patek Philippe of the night before had been replaced by a Cartier of significantly lower value, but a far more chic design. "Good morning, just barely, ladies. I hope your day has been good so far. I promise your afternoon will be unforgettable."

Anya laced an arm through his and raised herself to gently kiss his cheek. "Our morning was great, and I got to see Statue of Liberty from the Empire State Building."

"The view from way up there couldn't possibly be as beautiful as the two of you. Please make yourselves comfortable, and I will show you the most valuable city block in the world."

Anya followed Gwynn into the back seat, and both were surprised to see another woman sitting with legs crossed on the rearward-facing seat. She had a flute of champagne in one hand and a jeweled clutch in the other.

Viktor nestled into the back of the limousine beside the woman, and introductions were made. "Anya, Gwynn, this is Veronique. She works with me in getting my stones placed in the finest shops. I thought perhaps you would enjoy meeting her."

Anya assessed the woman from foot to head, just as she'd done with Volkov. The glamour of the red soles of the thousand-dollar Louboutin heels didn't stop at her ankle. The skin of her lower legs was flawless and disappeared beneath the hem of a designer dress that must have cost even more than the shoes. She wore her hair and makeup like the crown of a princess atop the elegance of her body.

Gwynn suddenly felt like Cinderella's stepsister and shrank into the plush leather seat.

Anya, unthreatened by the woman, leaned forward and offered her hand. "*Ravi de vous rencontrer, Véronique. Je suis Anya.*"

Apparently unimpressed with Anya's French, the woman squeezed her offered hand and responded in flawless Russian. "*Kak priyatno poznakomit'sya, Anya.*"

Viktor closed the door, and the unseen driver pulled into traffic. Minutes later, the limo came to a stop at the corner of 47th Street and 5th Avenue. Viktor's driver held open the door, and the four stepped from the car and onto the sidewalk. Gwynn stepped into the shadows near the buildings, as if trying to hide.

Anya noticed and turned to Veronique. "Don't you hate women like my friend Gwynn who are beautiful the moment they wake every morning?

The rest of us must spend hours to look so nice. I am certain you know exactly what I mean."

Gwynn smiled, stepped from the shadows, and forgot all about the glamorous lady from France, regardless of her countrymen's generosity with the statue.

10

SVOP
(THE SWAP)

Veronique slid her manicured hand inside Viktor Volkov's left arm as the foursome made their way west on 47th Street. To Anya, the scene was nothing short of chaos, where cars, taxis, and delivery trucks flowed continually down the one-way street. But the constant noise rising from the single city block came from the throngs of hawkers, speaking in dozens of languages, pleading with passersby to step inside and buy one of the world's most precious lumps of carbon.

Anya's eyes traced the movements of the men of faith. "There is synagogue here?"

Volkov laughed. "Yes, over two thousand of them, but not synagogues to the God of the Torah. Another god is worshipped here. His name is Mammon. Do you know this god?"

Anya shook her head. "No, but how can he have two thousand synagogues here inside city and I do not know of him?"

Volkov led them into an alcove away from the crowded sidewalk. "Mammon is the demon of greed. His power is so strong that he can lure innocent men to him and consume them with endless desire for more wealth. This is the god of Forty-Seventh Street."

Anya laid her palm against his chest. "You are here. Are you one of these innocent men lured by Mammon?"

Volkov looked away and then back. "Sometimes, I am, but not always . . . and certainly not today. Today is about you and finding a beautiful setting for a beautiful diamond for the finger of a beautiful woman."

They pressed by the hawkers and into a small shop with a U-shaped glass counter filled with hundreds of pieces of magnificent jewelry.

A young, used-car-salesman-type reached across the counter. "Viktor, my friend. How are you? Where have you been? It's been too long since you've been in my shop."

"I have been out of town, my friend, but I'm here now, and we must find the perfect setting for my friend's diamond."

The car salesman tilted his head. "Out of town? Where?"

Volkov leaned toward the man. "I do not ask where you go when you leave your shop. I expect the same courtesy, my Hebrew friend."

The man behind the counter turned to face Anya. "I'm Levi. Tell me about your diamond."

"Is beautiful diamond of color E, IF clarity, cut round, and two carats."

Levi shot a look at Volkov and back at Anya. "That's quite a stone. Would you happen to have it with you?"

Anya reached into her pocket. "Of course. You could not put in setting if I do not have with me."

"I love your accent," Levi said. "You must also be from Russia like my friend Viktor."

"I was born in Russia, yes, but I am now American. You would like to see diamond, yes?"

Levi laid a black, cloth-covered board on the glass in front of Anya, and she unwrapped the diamond from its *brivke*, the folded white paper containing her stone. Levi pulled a pair of long locking tweezers from his pocket and rolled the stone across the cloth until it was facedown. He slid the tweezers around the diamond, squeezed, and locked the stone into the tool. Raising it to his eye, he peered through a loupe, twisting and turning the diamond as he examined every facet. Still squinting into the magnifier, he asked, "Who told you it was IF? I can't find a flaw, and I have perfect eyes."

Anya looked up at Volkov, who said, "I agree, but it was graded by the GIA. What can you do?"

Levi continued searching. "I think the gemologist was having a bad day. I'd definitely grade it as flawless. I'd like to have a basketful of stones just like this one."

Anya was anxious to move the process along. "Show to me settings."

Levi lifted a tray from the case and placed it on the glass. Every setting in the tray was breathtaking. He pulled a ring from the back row and dropped the diamond into the center. Two rows of small diamonds surrounded the much larger stone, and Gwynn gasped.

Anya glanced over her shoulder at her partner and then back at Levi. "I want something simple and elegant, like my friend."

Gwynn grinned, and Levi looked at Volkov.

The Russian showed the Israeli his palms. "It's her diamond. Mount it in the setting she wants."

Levi lifted the stone from the elegant setting. "Are you sure you want something simple? This stone is so beautiful, I think it deserves some glitter around it."

Anya brushed her hand against Gwynn's. "My diamond is beautiful without glitter. I am sure I want white gold solitaire setting."

Levi watched the dollar signs blow away. "Okay. If that's what you want." He produced an oversized keyring with sized rings hanging from a metal loop. "Which finger?"

Anya peered down at her hands and finally stuck out the index finger of her left hand. "This one."

Levi slid sizing rings across Anya's finger until he found the perfect size. He then stepped through a curtain into the back of the shop and returned with two rings. They were identical except for the number of prongs. "If you plan to wear the ring every day, I suggest the six-prong setting, but if it will only be worn on special occasions, four prongs will show off more of the stone."

"Yes, of course I will wear every day. Is my first diamond, and I wish to see it on my finger every time I look down."

"Six-prong it is," he said as he lifted the stone and headed for the back room."

Viktor said, "Leave open the curtain so she can see how you set the stone, or better yet, let her come back there with you."

"I'll leave the curtain open so you can make sure I don't switch the stone, but she can't come back."

"Good enough," Volkov said.

Anya asked, "What does this mean, switching stone?"

"There are some less-than-reputable jewelers who will trade out a similar but less valuable stone when they have your diamond behind closed doors, but my friend Levi knows I never forget the details of a stone, so he would never try doing this to me."

With the curtain pinned back, giving an unobstructed view of the workshop, Levi clamped the setting in a small vise, slid on his jeweler's glasses, and gently placed the diamond in the setting. Working with the skill of a master craftsman, he drew the prongs into place, securing the stone in the setting. When he finished, he gripped the diamond and tugged at it, making sure it was firmly seated in place.

He buffed the ring, restoring its brilliance, and held it out toward Anya. She extended her index finger, and Levi slid the ring across the knuckle. Anya stared down at the gorgeous ring and momentarily lost herself in amazement.

When she held it up for Gwynn to see, she was disappointed but intrigued that her partner seemed to have no interest in the ring. Instead, she was intently watching Veronique inspect a collection of loose diamonds on the other side of the shop.

Anya turned back to Levi. "How much?"

He stared at the ceiling for a long moment. "Two seventy-five."

Viktor slid a pair of one-hundred-dollar bills across the counter, and Levi stared down at the bills. "It's two seventy-five."

Volkov huffed. "Today, it is two hundred, and that means you doubled on your investment. You forget that I have eyes and ears everywhere. I know exactly how much you paid for that setting, and two hundred is generous."

Anya followed Gwynn's gaze as she watched Frenchie skillfully clamping stone after stone into her tweezers and bringing them to her eye. When she found exactly the diamond she'd been searching for, she loosened the tweezers, allowing it to drop into her palm. She quickly covered the diamond with her thumb, and using the tweezers, grasped the replacement diamond she'd been palming for twenty minutes. Loaded with the new stone, Veronique handed the tweezers back to the sales associate, and the woman returned the stone to its *brivke*.

As if mesmerized by the brilliance of her first diamond, Anya held the ring up to the light and watched the colors dance from the prism as she tilted and twisted her hand. She leaned toward Volkov and pressed herself against him. "It is more beautiful than anything. I do not know how to thank you, Viktor. Is it really mine?"

He slid his hand across her shoulder and down her back, and in their native Russian, said, "It is yours forever."

"I'm happy you like the setting," Levi said. "If you ever need anything else, please come back, but don't bring him." He motioned toward Volkov. "Every time I see him, I lose money. He's bad luck."

Volkov leaned across the glass and gave Levi a playful shove. "I've put more money in your pocket than you've ever put in mine, so stop whining."

Levi grinned. "Get outta here."

Volkov motioned toward Veronique. "If she wants anything, let her have it, and you and I will haggle over prices later. *Mazl un brokhe*, my friend."

Back on the street without Veronique, the three continued through the crowd, and Anya couldn't take her eye from the diamond resting on her finger. She took Volkov's arm and squeezed. The smile that had melted hearts and resolve all over the world didn't garner the same reaction from Viktor Yuvelir, the jeweler. His reaction was more like that of a father happy to see his daughter pleased with his gift.

"Why did you give to me such a beautiful diamond?"

As if the question were absurd, he looked down in confusion. "I did not give the diamond to you. I gave you to the diamond. It was lonely without you. Now you can make the diamond happy every time you stare at it in admiration, and the diamond can make you happy every time you catch a sparkle of light from a facet."

Anya slapped his arm. "How many times have you given this speech to women?"

He shrugged. "It's a good speech, no?"

"Is very good speech, Viktor, but you must not buy for me expensive things. I feel obligation to you after such gift."

He raised an eyebrow. "An obligation, you say? In that case, you will have dinner with me tonight, and the obligation is fulfilled."

She laid her head against his shoulder. *Perhaps my smile hasn't lost its magic after all.* "What about Veronique? She will be jealous, no?"

Viktor shot a look across his shoulder at Levi's shop. "You have the wrong impression. She is neither French, nor is her name Veronique. She and I are business partners. Nothing more."

Anya raised her eyebrow. "Is this so?"

"It is, and perhaps after dinner, maybe you would like to discuss a little business, as well."

Anya pulled away. "I do not understand. I am actress, not businessperson. There is nothing I can do for you in diamond business."

"That's where you're wrong, my beautiful Russian princess. You have no idea how perfect you are for this business."

She pulled herself tightly against his arm again. "In this case, yes to dinner, and maybe yes to business talking after, but what about my friend?"

Viktor gave Gwynn a glance. "Surely, she can find something to do in the big city, but if not, I have a young man—a scientist—who works for me and would love to join the three of us for dinner."

Anya turned to Gwynn. "Did you hear this? A scientist. You will come, yes?"

"He doesn't wear taped-up glasses and a pocket protector, does he?"

Viktor laughed. "I think you will be pleasantly surprised. It is settled. I will pick you up at eight."

Anya nodded. "We will be ready for you at eight, but we must not go to Russian restaurant. Gwynn does not like to see cow's feet on menu."

"No cow's feet," Viktor said, "although they are delicious. One scientist, one businessman, and two beautiful women. It will be a perfect night."

11

AKH, KAPITALIZM (AH, CAPITALISM)

At precisely eight o'clock, the telephone rang, and Anya lifted the receiver. "Da."

The voice on the other end faltered for a moment. "Uh, hello . . . This is, um, Edward, downstairs. Your limousine is here."

"Spasibo, Edward. Please tell driver we will be down in five minutes."

"Yes, ma'am."

The elevator doors opened to the lobby, and Edward was even more tongue-tied in person than on the phone.

Volkov's driver stood just inside the double-door entrance. He watched Anya and Gwynn step from the elevator and offered a slight bow. Then, he pressed his index finger against Edward's chin, closing his mouth. "It is not polite to stare."

The driver held open the door as Edward remained frozen in place.

Gwynn whispered. "I hope your jeweler and my scientist are as impressed as young Edward."

Anya giggled. "How could they not be? Just look at us. We are most beautiful girls in all of Big Apple."

Once inside the limousine, Gwynn smiled with enormous sincerity and relief as she offered her hand to the gentleman sitting beside Viktor. "Hi, there. I'm Gwynn."

The young man took her hand and kissed it lightly, just behind the knuckles. "I am Sascha, and I am charmed. Viktor did not tell me you were an angel—only that you were without a date for the evening."

She almost blushed as she withdrew her hand. "It's nice to meet you, Sascha. Viktor says you're a scientist. What do you study?"

He waved a dismissive hand. "It is all so boring. I wouldn't want to put you to sleep. What do you do?"

Gwynn gave the man a long review from foot to head, and she liked everything she saw. "My work would definitely put you to sleep. I'm a boring lawyer. Nothing glamorous, I assure you."

Sascha leaned forward. "Fascinating. In what area of the law do you practice?"

The slightest hint of an Eastern European accent rolled from his tongue, but his English was flawless.

"Contracts mostly," she said. "It's certainly not what I thought it would be."

"And what were your ambitions prior to settling for contract law?"

The sting of the word *settling* didn't sit well with Gwynn, and she laughed to herself that she'd been offended by an affront on her make-believe job. "Oh, I thought I'd be a big-city trial lawyer, but I've never been inside a courtroom since I passed the bar."

"I'll wager a month's salary you passed on the first attempt."

Gwynn looked away. "Well, you'd win that bet, but if I had it to do all over again, I think I may have done something different."

"Fascinating," he said. "And what would you become if you could undo all those years of college and law school?"

She ran a finger across his knee. "I don't know. Perhaps I would've been a great research assistant for a scientist who's too shy to brag about his work."

Sascha leaned back in the luxurious seat. "You'd quit on day one. Besides, it's not like I'm curing cancer or putting men on Mars. I'm a geologist and physicist. Basically, I study why rocks don't move on their own."

Viktor laid a hand on the man's shoulder. "My friend is being modest. He is a double PhD in physics and geology. Without him, I would be a peasant on the streets of Leningrad, begging for bread and coins."

Anya said, "Is Saint Petersburg now."

Volkov sent her an icy stare. "Is Leningrad to those of us who knew it in the glorious days of the Soviet Union."

Anya returned his stare. "Those days were not so glorious for me. This is why I am now American capitalist."

Volkov laughed. "Ah! Capitalism, indeed. I am also one of these." He turned to the minibar and poured flutes of champagne for everyone. "To capitalism!"

Glasses were raised, and rims were touched.

Anya playfully bumped Volkov's shoulder with hers. "And also to Leningrad!"

"Leningrad!"

When the limousine stopped, the foursome stepped to the sidewalk in front of the former Mayfair Hotel on Park Avenue and into Daniel, New York City's premier French restaurant.

Before offering his arm to Anya, Viktor leaned down and whispered to Gwynn. "No cow's feet. I promise."

She gave him a wink. "I'm holding you to that promise. And you were quite right about my date. I am absolutely pleased."

They were immediately seated at an elegant, quiet table with silver service spread to perfection.

The maître d' approached and offered a respectful bow. "Mr. Volkov, how nice it is to see you again. I see you've brought the two most beautiful women in the city along with you this evening."

Volkov lifted a butter knife and exhibited swordplay toward the man. "How dare you insult my guests like this. Their beauty cannot be contained within a city of only seven million. It is possible they are the two most beautiful women in all the world."

"My apologies, sir, but—and I have no reason to doubt this fact—if they are the most beautiful women in all the world, would that not also make them the most beautiful in the city?"

Volkov grabbed his chest. "Touché. Now, champagne."

"Only the finest, of course." The man bounded away as if sent by the king himself.

Soon, champagne flowed, and servings of Golden Ossetra caviar were delicately placed in front of each of them.

Gwynn glanced at Anya for the briefest of moments and remembered her saying, "I am terrible Russian. I do not eat caviar, I do not drink vodka, and I detest cold."

Perhaps Anya was a better actress than Gwynn knew. She devoured the fish eggs as if they were sumptuous manna from Heaven.

Next came Maine lobster salad, celtuce, shiso bavarois, lemon crème fraîche, and crispy yuba.

Gwynn suddenly came down with a case of the nervous giggles, and all eyes turned to her.

Sascha leaned in. "Are you all right, my dear?"

She covered her mouth with a linen napkin. "I'm so sorry. It's just that I've never eaten a meal like this."

"It's not a meal yet," Sascha said. "This is only starts and appetizers."

The giggles continued. "No, that's not what I meant. I mean, I've never been to a place like this. I'm lucky to have Chinese takeout twice a week. This is utterly amazing."

Viktor laughed, Sascha relaxed, and Anya smiled at her friend and partner.

"Food is life," Viktor said. "And life should be celebrated. After all, this is why we work so hard at being capitalists." He slapped Sascha on the back. "Right, my friend?"

The scientist raised his glass. "Absolutely!"

The meal continued for two hours and culminated with a dessert the waiter described as Apurímac coconut finger lime sorbet, dark chocolate crémeux, and cajeta sauce.

No waiter appeared with a weighty check, expecting someone to offer an American Express; however, the maître d' made a final tableside appearance. "I hope everything was perfect."

"As always," declared Viktor.

"I shall pass your compliments to the chef."

Viktor tucked more than a couple folded one-hundred-dollar bills into the man's cupped hand. "This is for you and the waitstaff."

"Please do come again soon. It has truly been too long."

Viktor led the way back onto Park Avenue, where the limo waited, and they climbed inside. Ten minutes later, they pulled through an open garage door and into a warehouse on the Upper East Side.

The door immediately closed behind them, and Anya scanned the interior of the building, memorizing everything she saw. "What is this place?"

"This is my shop. I told you we would talk about business tonight."

They filed from the back seat, and Volkov entered an eight-digit code into a cipher lock beside an oversized, heavy steel door. A pair of electronic tones sounded, followed by a series of clicks. Volkov turned the handle and pulled open the door. The hunk of steel looked more like something that would be found sealing a vault than a shop door in a vacant warehouse.

Inside the space, a collection of fashionable sofas, chairs, tables, and lamps was arranged perfectly upon an Oriental rug that probably cost more than the limousine. A pair of French doors, also with cipher locks, opened at Volkov's touch, and the doorway revealed an interior room much less formal than the previous. Industrial carpet covered the concrete floor, and straight-backed chairs lined the wall. The only other door in the space was, unquestionably, a vault door. Volkov entered a ten-digit code that Anya immediately memorized and then pressed his thumb to a small, oblong glass window. A few seconds later, an electronic voice said, "Identification verified," and Volkov spun the spoked wheel and pulled the massive door from its jamb.

Lights flickered on inside the vault, and the Russian led the three of them into the space. Colored velvet bags, perfectly spaced five feet apart, lay on a thick wooden counter. Volkov lifted a black bag, freed the string, and dumped the contents onto a lighted glass section of the counter. As the light played through the dozens of diamonds dancing their way across the glass, the prismatic effect sent showers of purple light pouring onto the ceiling and around the room. When the gems finally came to rest, Anya and Gwynn gasped in unison.

Sascha lifted a blue bag and poured its contents onto a second lighted glass panel. He produced two pairs of clamping tweezers from a nook in the back of the counter and clamped the jaws of each around a diamond from each of the two lighted panels. He pulled a loupe from his pocket and placed it in Anya's palm. "Please compare the two diamonds."

Anya stared down at the loupe. "But I don't know anything about diamonds."

Volkov cleared his throat. "This is not true. You know far more than most people. Perhaps you simply don't realize it. Last night, at dinner, after your unfortunate encounter, we discussed the four Cs of diamond grading. I'm certain you remember."

Anya said, "Yes, I remember, but . . ."

"No but," Volkov said. "Simply look into each diamond, and tell me the differences."

Anya pressed the loupe to her cheekbone and closed her left eye. Pulling the first diamond into focus, she admired the clarity with one tiny exception. She pulled the stone away. "It has small black spot, deep inside."

Sascha studied the stone. "You are right. That black spot is called an inclusion. That is one of the things that lowers the value of a diamond. Now, take a look at the other."

Anya lifted the second stone and studied it carefully. "This one has also inclusion but is maybe larger."

Sascha looked and agreed.

Volkov asked, "How good is your memory?"

Anya stared into his eyes. "One-zero-four-seven-two-two-nine-six-three-one."

Volkov took her face in his hands and kissed her forehead. "You are perfect, my beauty. You have the face of an angel, the body of a fashion model, and the mind of a chess master."

"Thank you, I guess," Anya said.

Volkov continued. "Remember the first diamond you studied with the tiny black inclusion?"

"Yes, I remember this."

He motioned toward the first pile of diamonds. "Now, find its twin in this collection."

One by one, she clamped each diamond into the tweezers and studied it through the loupe until she found the perfect match. She handed the gem to Viktor, and he passed it to Sascha.

The scientist pulled the stone into focus and studied it for several seconds. When he was satisfied, he said, "She's done it."

Volkov grinned. "Try four."

Sascha pulled four stones from the second pile and had Anya study each of them. "Now, find their twins in the first pile."

Anya used the tweezers to separate the stones she'd memorized and slid them beside the four she'd just seen. "These four are the closest matches."

Sascha cast a doubtful look toward Volkov, and the Russian said, "This is not possible. No one can memorize that many stones."

Anya stuck the tweezers toward him. "See for yourself."

He lifted each pair of diamonds and examined them closely. After the fourth perfect match, he wrapped Anya in his arms. "You are my angel sent to me just when I need you most."

12
KOMMERCHESKOYE PREDLOZHENIYE (THE SALES PITCH)

Viktor Volkov returned the diamonds to their velvet homes, and Sascha did the same with his collection. With the bags back where they'd been when the foursome walked in, Viktor led them from the vault and back into the lavishly appointed sitting area. "You said you are an actress, yes?"

Anya glanced quickly at Gwynn and then let her gaze settle on Volkov. "Yes, I am actress."

Volkov inspected his fingernails for a long moment. "And acting . . . Does it pay well?"

Anya felt the warm, familiar feeling of her prey falling perfectly into her talons. "Sometimes, yes, and sometimes, no. When I have part in commercial or television show, I am paid far more than back in Russia."

Volkov crossed his legs. "And when you're paid for a role, how many nights could you afford dinner like we enjoyed earlier?"

Anya feigned embarrassment. "I think maybe only once, and I would then be hungry until next time I have job."

Volkov watched the toe of his shoe as he made figure eights in the air. "Do you ever take private acting jobs, or is all of that done through an agency?"

Anya's curious smile turned to stone. "Are you asking if I am *devushka legkogo povedeniya*?"

Volkov waved a defensive hand. "No, no, of course you're not a prostitute. I would never suggest such a thing. I'm only asking if you would like to have a part-time job working with Sascha and me during the times when you don't have an acting job. A little extra spending money is never a bad thing, in my experience."

He took the bait, but I cannot jump immediately into his boat. I must put up at least small fight.

"I will have to consider this offer, but I must first know what you will ask of me and how much is 'a little extra spending money'?"

Volkov uncrossed his legs and leaned forward. "The money depends on how good you are, and what I will ask of you is that you continue to do exactly what you did inside my vault tonight."

Anya wrinkled her forehead. "You want me to match diamonds to others? This is child's game of *ob"yem pamyati.*"

He nodded and leaned back in his chair. "Yes, indeed it is a game of memory, but you're better at it than anyone I've ever seen."

"I have very good memory, but this thing you ask, it is not acting job. It is merely tedious work inside prison cell with good lighting."

That spawned a chuckle from the jeweler. "We've not gotten to the acting portion yet. First, you must memorize your lines."

Anya turned to Gwynn. "This is not against laws, is it?"

Gwynn offered her palms. "How should I know? I'm a contract attorney, not a prosecutor."

Anya turned back to Volkov. "This is not illegal?"

Volkov scoffed. "How could it be illegal to memorize stones? You're just helping me match diamonds for earrings or multi-stone pieces where symmetry is important."

"This is all we are doing? Matching stones?"

Volkov gave Sascha a half smile. The hook was set, but Viktor Volkov believed he was the angler. "Yes, of course. This is all I want. You have a beautiful mind and a perfect memory for diamonds."

Anya frowned. "I can do this for you, but is not a performance. Is only remembering."

Volkov took her hand in his and gently kissed just behind the first diamond she'd ever worn. "We will get to the performance in time. You saw Veronique on stage this afternoon, and you, my angel, you are going to be twice the actress she could ever dream of becoming."

Anya feigned embarrassed humility. "I do not know. She is very beautiful."

Volkov snapped his fingers and shot a point toward the former Russian assassin. "And that is exactly why you are perfect for this."

Still playing the frightened child, Anya said, "There is payment for me if I do this for you, yes?"

Volkov couldn't douse his grin. "How much did you make on your last acting job?"

Anya bowed her head as if humility hindered her response.

"Just tell me. There's no reason to be shy now."

"I am not shy," she said. "It is just that it sounds like I am bragging, and I do not do this."

"You're not bragging, my darling. You're merely telling the truth. So, let's have it. How much?"

One of the world's deadliest assassins stared at the fibers of the rug between her feet. "I have small role in Canadian television show, and I am paid ten thousand dollars for three episodes, six days in preparation, and seven days in filming."

Volkov drummed his fingertips against the pad of his thumb. "That is roughly five thousand dollars per week. I will pay the same five thousand dollars per week, but the workweek is only three days of four hours each day. No one can stare at diamonds longer than that without having each of them begin to look identical."

Anya's eyes became fascinated orbs of disbelief. "This is four hundred dollars every hour. This cannot be true."

"Oh, I never tell lies about money. Never."

Anya bounded from the chair and threw herself around Volkov. "I am a thousand times, yes. I will do this for you, and when this is done, you will teach to me next job, like Veronique."

Volkov reveled in the affection from his beautiful comrade. "I feel you will need no lesson of any kind to outshine her. When would you like to start?"

Anya kissed both of Viktor's cheeks and embraced him again. "I have already started. I found seven matching diamonds tonight."

As Volkov encouraged her to stand, he allowed his hand the liberty of exploring the curve of Anya's hip. "That, you did, my dear. That, you did."

She gave him the glancing brush without resisting, but only for a moment before she stepped away.

He rose from his chair and returned to the vault. When he emerged again, he placed a banded stack of one-hundred-dollar bills in Anya's hands. "This is ten thousand dollars because I trust you to keep your word. I think you and I understand the meaning of the word *trust* better than most. Wouldn't you agree?"

Anya offered up a perfect smile and tossed the cash to Sascha. "Trust can never be a river. It must flow in both directions. I will do for you what you ask, and you will pay to me what you promise. You trust I will do this, and I trust you will also keep promise to me."

Sascha picked up the stack of bills and tossed it from hand to hand, then he gave Volkov a nod. "See . . . I told you."

Viktor sighed. "You did, and you were right."

Anya glanced back and forth between the men. "What did he tell you?"

Viktor Volkov leaned forward and snatched the cash from his partner. "He said you wouldn't take the money up front, and he was obviously right."

Anya stared at the bills as if she were desperate for cash. "How did you know I would not take money, Sascha?"

"You are a proud Russian woman. I told this to Viktor, but he said you had become an American."

Anya smiled. "I am both of these things, so I can now choose best of both worlds. It is true I am Russian at my birth and proud woman when I left Soviet Union, but now I am living here in America and is very good country. I am American when is appropriate and Russian when is necessary."

Volkov slammed his hand against the arm of his chair. "If you will not take my money, at least accept my invitation to the ballet tomorrow night. The prima ballerina is the finest dancer in all the world, and you make me think of her every time I see you."

Anya narrowed her eyes. "Why would I make you think of a ballerina? I am far too heavy to be a dancer."

Volkov's eyes slid across her body. "You are perfect, inside and out, and I will not have you believing anything less. But it is not how you look that reminds me of the ballerina, although, like you, she is stunning. It is another of your attributes that keeps her dancing into my mind whenever you are near."

"I do not understand."

Volkov stood and reached for Anya's hand. She gave it to him, and he brushed a strand of hair behind her ear just as Chase Fulton had done so many times. "Do not worry, my pet. It will all make sense tomorrow night. It is an early performance. I will pick you up at six, and we will again have dinner after this beautiful young ballerina brings tears to your eyes."

The actress put on her smile. "I love the ballet, and tomorrow night I will be on the arm of the most handsome man in the Big Apple."

"It's settled then. It is, of course, black tie, and you will need a dress." Volkov replaced the stack of bills into Anya's palm. "Tomorrow should be your first day at your new job, but since you have shopping to do, you can start the day after."

Anya leaned in and kissed his cheek. "Spasibo. And I will make sure you are the envy of every man in attendance at the ballet. It is too bad we cannot go to the Bolshoi."

He ran the back of his hand down the curve of her flawless face. "Perhaps one day we shall."

Anya beamed. "Perhaps."

The trap had indeed been set, and the bait had been swallowed.

Sascha and Volkov shared a glance, and the Russian Jeweler cleared his throat. "Yes, well, I am sorry to end our beautiful evening, but, unfortunately, I must. My driver will take you home or anywhere else you'd like to go. Consider him and the car to be yours for the night. Enjoy New York, and I will see you tomorrow at six . . . in your new gown."

Gwynn and Anya slid into the back of the car, and the driver closed the door behind them. After taking his place behind the wheel, he threw an arm over the back of the seat. "Where may I take you, ladies?"

Gwynn turned to Anya with anticipation in her eyes, but the Russian said, "Home, please. We have a big day tomorrow."

Gwynn's hope deflated, and she reached for the bar. She made short work of pouring a pair of drinks. The two touched glasses, and Anya said, "We are luckiest girls in Manhattan."

The driver held open the door in front of their building on the edge of Times Square. "Good night, ladies. It has been my pleasure."

Without looking back, Gwynn and Anya climbed the stairs and glided through the door held open by the gloved attendant.

Once inside the elevator, Gwynn's eyes lit up. "You really are an actress, and you deserve an Academy Award for your performance tonight. That was amazing."

Anya pressed the button for their floor. "It is easy to give men what they want because they always want the simplest of everything."

"What does that mean?"

Anya opened her hand and held out her palm. "Veronique obviously replaces diamonds, one at a time, with whatever these are."

Gwynn stared down at the pair of gleaming stones. "You lifted two of Volkov's diamonds! You are amazing, but don't you think they have every stone counted? You're going to get busted."

"I was already busted by your boss in Saint Augustine. That is why I am here, remember?"

Gwynn turned the lock and opened their apartment door. "No, you're here because you chose to be. You could've run at any moment while we were in Miami, and escaping from Walter Reed Hospital would've been a piece of cake. You *want* to be here. Otherwise, you'd be halfway around the world in some place no one's ever heard of."

The Russian pressed the door closed behind them. "Do you really believe I would choose to be here if I could go back to my life before you and Agent White apprehended me in Saint Augustine?"

Gwynn grimaced. "No, I'm sorry. That's not what I meant. It's just that—"

"My choices are not to be here or be free."

Gwynn shook her head. "No, that's obvious. But I mean, you kind of like doing this with me. That's all I'm saying."

Anya stepped toward Special Agent Gwynn Davis and let their bodies touch gently. She tilted her head barely perceptibly to the right and slowly continued moving toward her federal government babysitter.

Gwynn's mouth grew instantly dry, and her pulse raced. She bit her bottom lip in anticipation as Anya closed both eyes and the distance between them. As the Russian's breath fell across Gwynn's skin, she palmed the wall behind her, bracing for the instant Anya's lips would meet hers.

Suddenly, the deadbolt in the apartment door slammed into the jamb with a metallic thud, and Gwynn flinched as she threw her eyes open.

Anya playfully kissed the tip of Gwynn's nose and laughed. "What is wrong? Did you think I couldn't resist you, Special Agent Guinevere

Davis? Did you believe I would press you against wall and kiss you like long-lost lover? Is this what you thought?"

Gwynn swallowed hard. "No . . . I . . . I mean . . ."

Anya pressed her finger to Gwynn's lips. "Shh. I know what you mean, but you must remember. I am well trained to make anyone believe anything I want. If you believe I choose to be here, this is only because it is what I want you to believe. I am actress. Just ask Viktor Volkov."

13

VASH LICHNYY UBIYTSA (YOUR PERSONAL ASSASSIN)

Gwynn shoved past Anya but turned after a few strides through the foyer. She threw an accusatory index finger toward the Russian. "You told me you'd never do that, and I trusted you."

"I told you I would never do what?" Anya demanded.

Gwynn scowled. "I swore I would never lie to you, and you swore you'd never seduce me. I'm not your enemy!"

Anya's gaze fell to the floor as Gwynn stormed away.

Fifteen minutes later, the teakettle whistled, and Anya balanced two mugs in one hand as she lightly tapped on the door to Gwynn's bedroom.

"What?" came the harsh reply.

"I made for you tea, and I would like to talk with you."

Gwynn sat up in bed. "I'll take the tea, but I'm not in the mood to talk."

Anya twisted the doorknob and crossed the floor without a sound.

Gwynn reached up for the steaming mug, and Anya sat on the edge of the bed. "If you do not wish to talk, this is okay. I will tell to you what I have to say, and then I will leave you alone."

Gwynn blew across the steaming tea, ignoring her intruder.

Unfazed, Anya said, "I'm sorry. I did not mean to be unkind. I was only making point about how it is easy for me to make others believe something that is not true. I know you are not my enemy. You are the only girlfriend I have ever had. I need for you to know one important thing, and this thing is absolute truth."

She paused to take a sip, and Gwynn couldn't hold her silence any longer. "How can I trust you, Anya? How do I know whatever you're about to tell me is the truth and not just part of your whole ruse to fool everyone around you, including me? Huh? How can I know?"

Anya set her mug on the nightstand. "You will know it is truth because you can test me, and you will know instantly if I am telling the truth."

In spite of her anger, Gwynn listened intently as Anya continued. "I am not doing this of my own will, and you know this is true. But you didn't have to arrest me and threaten for me to go to prison for rest of my life to get me to do these things for you."

Gwynn lowered an eyebrow. "What are you talking about? You said you weren't here by choice."

"This is true, but I was given no real choice. Prison or this thing we are doing . . . this was my choice. No one would choose to go to prison, even if it is American prison."

"Then what are you saying?"

Anya licked her lips. "If you had come to me with tea and asked me to help you stop Russian mafia, I would have said yes without threat of prison."

Gwynn placed her mug beside Anya's. "Are you telling me you would've volunteered for this assignment if we'd asked?"

She nodded. "This is exactly what I am telling you."

Gwynn curled her legs beneath her and leaned toward the Russian. "That's easy for you to say now, but there's no way to go back in time and test this claim of yours."

Anya took Gwynn's hand in hers. "Is not necessary to go back in time. To test my words, you only have to free me from Agent White's threat to send me to prison, and then ask for my help. If I walk away, I have failed test, but if I stay with you to finish job, you will know my words are true."

Gwynn stared in wonder at Anya, weighing her words carefully. "You do understand that I don't have the authority to free you from this agreement with the Justice Department, right?"

Anya nodded. "Yes, I know this is not something you can do alone, but you can take offer to Special Agent White."

Gwynn flattened a wrinkle in the sheets around her legs. "Anya, if I do this, and it gets approved, and then you disappear, my career is over. They will bury me in the basement of the DOJ, and I won't see the light of day until I retire in thirty years at the same pay grade I am now. That's if they don't charge me with collusion for helping you escape."

Anya sucked her bottom lip. "I know you do not have reason to trust me, but I believe we are doing something good. I have no loyalty to my former country and especially none for the criminals like Leo in Miami and Viktor Volkov. I am not sure exactly what Volkov is doing yet, but we will know soon. Whatever it is, I think he is criminal and should be stopped."

Gwynn lifted her mug. "I don't know, Anya. You just put on a performance about how you could make anyone in your world believe whatever you want. You're a con artist—maybe the best in the world at it. I can't tell the difference between sincerity and performance art from you. I will tell you this much, though. There's no way I'm taking this crazy offer of yours up the chain until we're finished with this assignment. Volkov is committing fraud to the tune of millions of dollars per year. We may not know exactly how he's doing it, but there's no question it's happening. When this is over and Volkov is behind bars, you and I will have this conversation again, but I'm not making any promises tonight. It's not happening."

Anya stared into the air above Gwynn's bed. "Okay. Thank you for listening. I will leave you alone now, just as I promised."

Gwynn laid a hand on Anya's knee. "Spasibo for the tea."

Anya covered Gwynn's hand with her own. "You are welcome for tea. Good night."

Anya pulled the door closed as she crept back into the hallway. For most of her life, sleep had come easily for the Russian, but the lingering regret of what she'd done to Gwynn left her restless, though that wasn't the only thought pouring through the assassin's mind. Having claimed to be willing to continue working with the Department of Justice, even without the threat of prison hanging over her head, a bevy of questions danced in her mind.

How much truth lay in that off-the-cuff admission? How many of these missions can I survive? When would the DOJ finally run out of Russian mafia kingpins to unleash me on? And most important of all, would Special Agent Guinevere Davis take my offer seriously enough to send it up the chain of command?

The sun burned through the morning fog before Anya's eyes enjoyed the solace of sleep, and she dragged herself to the kitchen for morning tea. As the teapot belched its shrill report minutes after nestling over the flame, Anya turned to see every piece of furniture in the living room pushed against the walls. Gwynn sat in the middle of the room, stretching like an Olympic hurdler preparing for a race.

Anya motioned toward the displaced sofa. "What is all of this?"

Gwynn looked up from her stretch. "I thought it was time for another fighting lesson. The teakettle isn't the only thing in this apartment that needs to blow off a little steam."

Anya poured the scalding water across a teabag. "I did not get much sleep. I think this is not best time for lesson."

Gwynn hopped to her feet. "I'm sorry to hear that, but I wasn't making a request. I was giving instructions. Now, get out here, and let's fight."

The first sip of tea warmed its way into Anya's stomach, and she stepped from the kitchen in her T-shirt and shorts. "This is terrible plan, Gwynn. You will not feel better after trying to hurt me."

Gwynn rolled her head, feeling the muscles in her neck and upper back loosen with every rotation. "Who says I'm trying to hurt you? I just want to learn everything I can before you disappear."

"I am not going to disappear. I told you . . ."

Before the remainder of the sentence left her tongue, Gwynn lunged toward her with the speed and agility of a cat, sending a right jab toward

Anya's chin. She deflected the blow and stepped aside as Gwynn's momentum carried her past. Raising her right foot in a side kick, Anya tapped Gwynn's kidney with little more than enough pressure to feel it. Gwynn turned, planted one foot, and thrust toward the Russian again. This time, she lowered her head and sent her shoulder crashing into Anya's stomach with the intention of leaving the former SVR officer flat on her back and fighting out of her guard. Instead of allowing the force of the charge to propel her backward, though, Anya leaned forward and lifted her feet, placing all of her weight on Gwynn's back and shoulder. The DOJ agent couldn't support the weight in her precarious position and fell-face first with Anya pinning her to the floor.

Gwynn's breath came hard and deep, but her foe's heart rate hadn't risen above eighty beats per minute. Undeterred, she scampered and twisted her body in a wasted attempt to escape. Anya easily retained her superior position, keeping Gwynn pressed to the floor.

As the muscles in Gwynn's body relaxed in exhaustion, Anya said, "Are you finished?"

Gwynn let out a sigh of submission, and Anya planted a knee on the carpet. The Russian's mistake sparked Gwynn's resolve to thrust her hips skyward, sending her foe forward, leaving Anya on her side and Gwynn standing in the perfect fighter's stance three feet away.

"Get up," Gwynn demanded.

Anya slowly stood. "This is only going to get one of us hurt. We should stop."

Gwynn sighed. "Of course you're right." She lowered her head and stepped toward her teacher with arms outstretched.

Anya reached out to accept the coming embrace and apology, but the instant the Russian relaxed, Gwynn exploded upward with a powerful knee strike to her abdomen, followed by a pair of elbow strikes to the base of Anya's neck. The unexpected attack left Anya with almost no air in her lungs, but the elbow strikes were little more than annoyances as she regathered herself and wrapped both arms around Gwynn's legs. With a powerful thrust from Anya, the special agent landed flat on her back with a burst of air exploding from her lungs. Anya pressed her body against Gwynn's supine form, pinning her arms to the floor.

With her lips only inches from Gwynn's ear, she whispered, "I am starting to think you enjoy rolling around on floor with me."

Gwynn's resolve finally cracked, and she let out a hint of laughter. The chuckle quickly grew into full-blown belly laughter from both women until Anya rolled off her victim and leaned back against the displaced sofa. "Do you feel better now?"

When Gwynn caught her breath, she said, "Yeah . . . a little. Please tell me the knee strike hurt at least a little bit."

Anya glanced down, examining every inch of her body and frowned. "Did you land a knee strike? I did not feel it if you did."

"Next time, I'll just shoot you in your sleep."

Anya rolled her eyes. "What fun would that be? At least wake me up so I do not have to go into afterlife never knowing who killed me."

"You've got it," she said, offering Anya her hand. "I promise to let you know I was your personal assassin."

Anya took the offered hand, and the two pulled each other to their feet.

"I made for you English breakfast tea with honey, but is probably cold now."

"You Russians think tea makes everything better, don't you?"

"Not everything, but most things. You are no longer angry with me?"

Gwynn brushed the hair out of her face. "Oh, I'm still angry, but some retail therapy will take care of that. We have to find our little Russian Cinderella-ovna a dress for the ball tonight. You have to look good for your Eastern Bloc jeweler."

14

SOBYTIYE CHERNOGO GALSTUKA (I'M NO HERO)

After morning rituals, the doorman called to announce the arrival of the car service. Anya adjusted her long ponytail as she lifted the receiver. "We'll be right down."

"Did you hear that?" she asked as Gwynn shouldered her bag.

"Did I hear what?"

Anya threw her hands onto her hips. "I used the contraction *we'll*, and I used it correctly on telephone."

Gwynn pulled open the door. "Don't get so excited. You may have used a contraction, but you left off the article *the* before telephone."

"English is hard."

A man, clad in a driver's cap, held the door as they slid onto the back seat. Once behind the wheel, the driver asked, "Where to, ladies?"

Gwynn wasted no time. "Let's start at Barney's on Seventh Avenue at Sixteenth Street."

"As you wish," he said as he pulled into the midmorning traffic of Times Square.

After battling the Manhattan mayhem, the driver finally pulled to a stop in front of Barney's and turned to face his customers. "I'll be nearby. Here's my card, so just call when you're ready, and I'll pick you up right here."

Gwynn slid the card from his hand and dropped it into her bag. "Let's go. Somebody might be buying your dress right now. What would you do then?"

Anya cocked her head. "I would choose another one."

"You're missing the point. Just get out."

Ninety minutes later, Anya emerged from the dressing room and onto the mirrored platform.

Gwynn tugged at the waistline and made tiny adjustments to the fabric of the eleventh dress. She stood back and twitched her nose. "You look amazing in it, but you're perfect, so you make every dress look terrific. I really hate you."

Anya sighed. "I really hate trying on dress after dress. Please choose one so we can go home."

Gwynn ignored her. "No, this one isn't exactly right. Let's go to Bergdorf's."

The saleslady rolled her eyes. "We have a much more expansive selection than Bergdorf's. I think I have just the dress for your friend. I'll be back in a flash."

Anya laid a hand on the lady's shoulder. "If you have perfect dress for me, why did you waste all of this time showing me the first eleven dresses?"

She pulled away from Anya's grasp. "I was developing an eye for your style."

Anya turned, and Gwynn unzipped the latest dress. She stepped from the gown, leaving it piled on the floor behind her. Curious eyes glared as she stood barely clothed before the mirrors, but Anya ignored their stares as she stepped into her jeans and pulled on her shirt. As the Russian stepped from the raised platform, the saleslady returned with yet another gown.

Anya brushed past her. "I cannot try on another dress. Can't you please just pick one?"

Gwynn pulled her friend toward the door as she dialed the driver's number from memory. "We're ready to go."

The driver stammered. "Uh, wait. You must stay inside. The police are . . . I mean, there's a . . . just stay inside! I'll call you when it's safe to come out."

Noticing the look on Gwynn's face, Anya asked, "What is it?"

"The driver says there's some sort of disturbance on the street outside, and the police are involved."

Without a word, Anya sprinted toward the Sixteenth Street exit. The same instinct sent Special Agent, albeit undercover, Davis charging for the exit only steps behind her partner. A uniformed guard at least a hundred pounds overweight stood between a bevy of curious onlookers and the locked exit doors.

Gwynn parted the crowd and stopped inches in front of the shocked guard. "I'm a federal agent. What's going on out there?"

"I don't know, ma'am, but the doors are locked, and you'll have to stay inside until NYPD says it's safe."

"You're not listening. I said I'm a federal agent. Now, get out of my way."

The guard held up both hands. "Until you show me some ID, you're nobody, so calm down and let's see your badge . . . federal agent."

Gwynn drove her hand into her bag where her credential pack should've been but felt only an empty interior compartment—just as it should've been for any undercover officer. The realization hit her at the same instant she saw her favorite Russian slip behind the guard and twist the lock on the door.

A collective gasp rose from the bewildered crowd, and the guard spun to see the previously locked door swinging closed. He gave Gwynn a shove. "Get back, lady. I don't care who you are."

He propelled his formidable heft toward the door, pulled on the handle, and resecured the locking bolt.

Gwynn's heart raced, and her mind exploded as thoughts of what Anya might do on the street rushed through her head. As much as she didn't want to lose a cooperating participant, which would end Operation Avenging Angel, her greatest fear was having video of the beautiful Russian on every cable news show as she sliced off the head of some unsuspecting criminal in Downtown Manhattan.

Growing more desperate to see the action outside the doors, Gwynn ran from the crowd and pressed her face to the heavy glass of a nearby floor-to-ceiling window. The vantage point gave her a terribly obstructed view of the scene unfolding outside. Four NYPD police cars blocked the intersection of Seventh Avenue and Sixteenth Street while a collection of unmarked cars rested at various positions around the scene. A pair of ambulances awaited the outcome, their crew standing by with gloved hands and gurneys poised. Whatever was happening, Gwynn knew all too well the outcome had little chance of ending peacefully. Every fiber of her being screamed for her to be on that street with her sidearm in one hand and a bullhorn in the other.

Well out of Gwynn's line of sight, Anya took cover behind a stone pillar and leaned outward, inch by inch, taking in the scene on the street. A boy of perhaps three dangled from a man's left arm, tears streaming from his terrified face. The man's right hand trembled, and his knuckles turned white from gripping the handle of a chef's knife.

The ubiquitous roar of the New York City street was hushed, leaving an eerie silence hanging in the air, punctuated only by the cries of the child and the frantic yelling of his captor.

"Na im vordin e! Na im vordin e!"

Anya scanned the crowd of mortified bystanders and the faces of the police officers peering across their pistols. No one, except her, knew the man holding the screaming child was speaking Armenian and declaring the child to be his son. A wave of conflicting thoughts and emotions poured through her head as she tried to develop a strategy to end the standoff without the child being hurt. Fearing the dozens of cameras and cell phones trained on the scene, she pulled her shirt over her head, leaving only her eyes exposed to the lenses. In confident, calm Armenian, as she approached from the sidewalk, she repeated, "Give the boy to me. I promise no one will hurt him."

The man locked eyes with her as she continued her approach. The indecision in his face mirrored the emotion she felt about inserting herself into a situation that was never hers. Her calm tone continued as she repeated the phrase with every step until the man let the boy slide from his arm. Simultaneously, with the boy's feet striking the ground, Anya's fist struck the knifeman's bicep. The blow shocked the man and left his arm incapable of raising the blade. A second and third hammering blow from the Russian's well-trained fist sent the knife clanging to the filthy asphalt between the two parked cars that had served as the man's cover.

Instinctually, the man glared down at his only weapon as it bounced across the pavement. As he leaned forward to reclaim the weapon with his left hand, Anya fired a side kick to his knee, folding the leg backward and sending the sickening sound of bone, ligaments, and muscle tearing and separating. The agony of the kick sent the boy's kidnapper to the ground in a fog of Armenian profanity.

Anya sensed, more than saw, the police officers closing on her with pistols raised. The terrified boy trembled in shock and disbelief as one of the officers scooped him up and continued sprinting, putting distance between the boy and the scene. Anya leapt over the man and picked up speed as she crossed Sixteenth Street and turned east. Reaching full stride, she dared a glance over her shoulder to discover two uniformed police officers in pursuit. The larger of the two wouldn't have the stamina to continue more than another minute, but the leaner, younger officer was slowly closing the distance. He would be an issue if Anya couldn't find an alternative route before reaching Sixth Avenue.

Still running as fast as her legs would carry her, the exit she so desperately needed appeared as if God Himself had placed it just for her. A massive stone church stood on her right, but the church wasn't her escape. It was the alley beside the church that called to her. She had a mere fraction of a second to make the decision to turn down the alley or continue east on

Sixteenth. Many of New York City's alleys ended with the brick backside of a building. If the alley beside the church was a dead end, she'd be caught with no possibility of escape, short of fighting and potentially killing the pursuing NYPD officer. By her estimation, Sixth Avenue was another five hundred feet away—more than enough ground for the cop to chew up the distance between them. Fighting a police officer in the open streets of Manhattan was an immeasurably worse option than standing toe to toe with him in the back of an alley with no witnesses.

With her feet pounding the sidewalk, she slowed just enough to make the turn into the alley. Two dumpsters, piles of garbage, and wooden pallets greeted her as she accelerated into the shaded corridor. She passed the pallets and sacrificed two seconds to scatter them across the greasy alley, hopefully creating enough of an obstacle to build a few more second's separation between her and the sprinter in blue behind her. Just as she'd feared, the alley ended fifty feet ahead against a block wall extending into the sky.

With her heart pounding and her lungs chugging as much air as she could take in, Anya focused her attention between the pallets behind her and the two doorways to her left and right. The silhouette of the officer filled the opening of the alley, diminishing what little lead she had, but where others would've panicked and possibly surrendered, Anya's years of training and survival gave her the fortitude to focus on the options and make a decision. She sidestepped and grabbed the handle of a door on her right, but it resisted as she rattled the heavy steel against its bolt. Abandoning door number one, she shot to a second one across the alley. Her hand met the handle simultaneously with the officer leaping across the pallets like a hurdler. He was only seconds away when Anya gave the door a yank. To her delight, it gave way, and she stumbled backward into the center of the alley with the broken handle still in her fist. An instant glance told her the door hadn't opened; instead, the handle had separated from its base.

With precious seconds wasted, Anya mentally measured the distance to the sprinting cop.

Why hasn't he drawn his gun yet?

A quick examination of the broken handle revealed a rusty, jagged edge. It wasn't the perfect weapon but certainly an option. Anya stepped back into a fighter's stance and surveyed her environment one final time. Seizing the only remaining option, she bolted forward toward the oncoming officer and launched the broken handle toward him. Her aim was better than she'd dared to hope. The spinning missile arced through the air directly toward the officer's head, startling New York's finest and causing him to change stride and brush off the weapon. This gave Anya part of a second—exactly the time she needed—to leap into the air, plant her left foot on the rim of a filthy dumpster, and propel herself skyward toward an open window on the second floor of the church.

She caught the sill with her fingertips and scampered up the hundred-year-old wall, sending debris pouring from beneath each of her feet as she begged for purchase on the decaying surface.

The officer yelled from below. "Hey! Stop! I'm not going to arrest you. I just want to talk to you. You're not in trouble. You're a hero."

The last thing Anya wanted was to be a hero, and the second to last thing she wanted to be was someone having a conversation with a New York City police officer.

Finally, the toe of her left shoe found the hold she'd wanted so badly, and her long, toned body shot through the open window like an arrow from an archer's bow. She hit the floor in a shoulder roll and came up on the balls of her feet, her eyes scanning every inch of the room. A woman in an apron with a broom in one hand and a dustpan in the other screamed as if she'd seen the devil himself. The woman belted out a prayer in Spanish and crossed herself as the broom she'd been holding fell to the floor.

Anya searched the depths of her mind for any Spanish phrase she could create to calm the woman. With nothing else coming to mind, she calmly said, "*Dios te bendiga*," hoping God's blessing would keep the woman from panicking any further.

With no time to stay and catch the woman if she passed out, Anya pressed through the door, glancing both directions down the long corridor. She turned right, away from Sixteenth Street, and picked up speed as she sprinted the length of the hallway. A ninety-degree turn to the left told Anya she'd reached the rear of the building, and the time had come to find an exit. As massive as the church was, she would be a trapped animal if the NYPD dispatched a team to search the building. Getting back outside was her best chance of escape.

The instant she rounded the corner, the echo of the woman's second scream pierced the otherwise silent corridor. Anya sighed as the reality reached her. The determined cop had obviously made his way through the open window, as well. The maid was going to need another blessing to keep the heart attack at bay.

The policeman was a problem, but not the immediate concern. At least a dozen seconds separated him from Anya, giving her plenty of time to form a plan. Still running, she saw a mop bucket with the long, rigid handle of a commercial-grade mop protruding from the soapy water. As she sprinted past the bucket, she yanked the mop from its rest, spilling the water across the floor and creating a minefield of the slickest substance the cop would ever try to run across. With the mop in her hand, she turned another corner and kicked open a heavy wooden door. Behind the door was exactly what she'd hope to find: a stairwell leading down to the first floor and up to whatever waited above.

As the door closed behind her on its pneumatic arm, she shoved the mophead against the first step and the tip of the handle beneath the handle of the door. It wasn't an impenetrable obstacle, but it would certainly add a few more precious seconds to the distance between her and her pursuer.

She took the descending stairs six at a time and slowly peered into the hallway. A man wearing the dress of a man of the cloth strolled nonchalantly down the hall with a book in one hand and a cup of coffee in the other. Confident the man presented no threat, Anya pulled the elastic band from her ponytail and drew her long hair forward, hiding most of her face. She stepped from the stairwell with her head low and her face mostly obscured by her hair.

Walking unhurriedly, she passed the man without a word and continued down the hallway toward an illuminated exit sign hanging above the door to her freedom.

15

CHELOVEK OKHOTA (MAN HUNT)

Back at Seventh Avenue and Sixteenth Street, a pair of EMTs loaded their gurney onto the waiting ambulance. The gurney's occupant, Razmik Sahakyan, an Armenian immigrant, writhed in pain and struggled against the handcuffs holding his wrists to the rails of the bed. His right leg lay twisted, destroyed at the knee.

Finally outside the store, Special Agent Gwynn Davis stood at the edge of the crowd, listening intently to the chatter over the NYPD radio. Her interest had nothing to do with the Armenian who'd never again walk without a limp. She was only interested in the other Eastern European immigrant who'd made a hit-and-run appearance on the scene. The fear she'd experienced the previous night over the possibility of losing the Russian and spending the rest of her career locked in the basement of the Justice Department reared its ugly head again. The perfect avenue to escape had presented itself, and Anastasia Burinkova had taken it. As much as she dreaded the call to her boss, Supervisory Special Agent Ray White, the thought of never seeing Anya again tore at her very soul.

Protocol and standard operating procedure dictated that she must immediately report Anya's escape, but the lingering hope that Anya may simply be well hidden and biding her time until the melee ended was too much to resist. She watched as, one by one, the police cars, both unmarked and otherwise, pulled away from the scene. One patrol car remained, and leaning against the trunk, stood a middle-aged officer with a few too many pounds hanging over his gun belt.

Gwynn approached the officer, who still looked as if he'd just tried to run a marathon. "Excuse me, officer. I'm Special Agent Davis with Justice. Were you able to apprehend the person who ran?"

The officer didn't look up to check the DOJ agent's credentials. Instead, he caught his breath and said, "No, she was too fast. My partner continued the foot pursuit, but she escaped through the church down the block." After panting for thirty seconds, the cop finally looked up and tilted his head. "What does the DOJ have to do with any of this? I thought the FBI handled kidnappings."

"They do, but I just happened to be in the area. Did you get a good enough look at the runner to give me a description?"

The officer held up one finger and pulled a water bottle from inside his cruiser. After a long drink, he said, "I didn't get a good look at the guy, but whoever he was, he had his shirt pulled up over his head, and he was wicked fast. Hang on a minute, and I'll call my partner."

Gwynn pulled a small pad and pen from her bag in an attempt to appear more official. Without her credentials, she was treading on thin ice by sticking her nose any deeper into an NYPD chase.

Regaining his composure and catching his breath, the officer pressed the push-to-talk button on his shoulder mic. "Sixty-six fifty-four to sixty-six fifty-five, say location."

The reply came, not over the radio, but through the air. "I'm right here, you fat moron. What do you want?"

The officer turned to see his partner jogging to a stop on the sidewalk fifteen feet away. "Oh, yeah, whatever. This is Special Agent . . ." He pointed toward Gwynn. "What did you say your name was?"

"It's Davis. Special Agent Gwynn Davis with Justice."

He turned back to his much younger partner. "Yeah, Davis. That's it. She don't care nothin' about the perp with the busted leg. Alls she wants to know is if we got a description of the rabbit."

The younger officer eyed her thoughtfully. "I didn't get a good look at her face."

"Her?" yelled the first officer. "You mean that guy was a girl?"

"Yes, she was a blonde female, probably five feet nine or ten and a hundred thirty-five pounds. That's the best I can do, but why does the Justice Department care about a runaway good Samaritan?"

Gwynn put on her government-issue stern face. "I'm sorry, officer, but I'm not at liberty to say. Where did you last see the subject?"

He gave her a frown before pointing down the block. "She ran out the back of the church right down there. After that, she was in the wind."

Gwynn pretended to make a note on her pad. "Thank you, officers. You've been very helpful."

Before either man could protest, Gwynn tucked her pad and pen back into her bag and headed east on Sixteenth. At the top of the stairs to the church, she checked her watch and sighed. It had been eighteen minutes since Anya sprinted from the scene. She could've been three miles away on foot by then, and God only knew how far she could be if she'd stolen a bike or a car.

Gwynn pulled her cell phone from her bag and dialed her boss's number, but she couldn't garner the strength to press the send button. Still torn, she shoved the phone back into her bag and pulled open the old oak doors to the church. Inside, a smattering of parishioners milled about, some of them praying while others whispered to each other. The massive church would take a team of agents hours to adequately search, but the police officer hadn't said Anya was hiding in the church. He said she'd escaped out the back. If out the back was, indeed, where Anya had gone, then there was no place Gwynn would rather be. Wasting time searching a massive church would only give the former SVR assassin more time to vanish.

The courtyard behind the church was massive on a scale Gwynn had not imagined possible in Manhattan. Other than Central Park, open-landscaped real estate was almost unheard of. The southern edge of the courtyard was walled by numerous shops with signs threatening anyone who dared trespass. If Gwynn didn't find her favorite Russian before Washington, D.C. found out she was missing, trespassing would be the least of her concerns. Homelessness and prosecution would claim the top two spots on that list.

Trying to think like an assassin, she scoured the area, hoping against hope that Anya was only hiding from the NYPD and not running from the Justice Department. She concluded that hiding, even doing so in a courtyard of this magnitude, would be a terrible plan in case the police continued their search for the mysterious leg breaker. At that point, searching the courtyard became a search for exits from the courtyard.

All of the shops could serve as an escape route if the doors weren't securely locked. Anya likely didn't have a set of lockpicks in her pocket, so she'd have to rely on the absentmindedness of a shopkeeper to make use of one of the back doors. Gwynn ran along the row of shops, pulling on every door, but none budged.

A gazebo, with a collection of smokers huddled beneath, rested on the only high ground in the courtyard. Gwynn trotted toward the structure, leapt to the rail, and propelled herself onto the roof. The height gave her ten feet of advantage over the ground, so she scanned the area in all directions. There was no exit from the space except through its surrounding building. Gwynn stood exasperated on the roof of the gazebo as the collection of smoke-filled onlookers beneath fired questions and curses toward the crazy woman on top of their shelter.

Resigned to press send on her cell phone, Gwynn let her legs hang over the edge and sat on the sloping, octagonal roof. With her phone in hand, she cast one final look around the courtyard and caught a glimpse of something that didn't quite fit its surroundings. She pocketed the phone and slid from the roof, landing like a cat beside a filthy cigarette butt can. The thirty-second sprint that delivered her to the site of what she'd seen from her previous perch felt like it took hours. Finally standing at the base of a tree six feet from the low-roofed shops, she gazed upward at the broken tree limb with its splintered joint at the trunk, glaring white from the interior wood that had never seen the sun.

Imagining where the limb would've reached before being broken, she drew a line with her eyes to the edge of the roof over the shop. The gutter was bent into itself as if the knee of a fleeing Russian had landed there only minutes before. She scampered up the tree to the next higher limb and made her way to its limit toward the shop. With a powerful lunge, she launched herself through the air and performed a perfect parachute-landing fall on the metal roof, just as she'd been taught at the Academy. Back on her feet, she ran to the front edge and peered downward onto the sidewalk some fifteen feet below. Not even Anya was crazy enough to attempt that fall. Broken ankles have a way of becoming the premature ending of an escape. Glances left and right provided the answer she'd been seeking. A construction scaffold was secured to the roofline fifty feet away. Gwynn covered the distance before she'd realized she was moving. Seconds later, she was on the sidewalk in a crowd of ecstatic tourists and disgruntled New Yorkers. If the courtyard and church were too large to search efficiently, the borough of Manhattan might as well have been the surface of the moon. The Russian was a ghost—a spirit on the wind—and forever gone.

Instead of dialing Agent White, Gwynn redialed the last call made from her phone, and the car appeared in minutes.

The driver stepped from the car and held open her door. "How did you get all the way over here?"

"It's a long story."

The driver closed the door and took his place behind the wheel. "And where's your friend?"

"That's an even longer story. Just take me back to the apartment, please."

They pulled from the curb and crawled along with the snail's-pace traffic.

The driver checked the mirror. "You missed all the excitement outside Barney's. Apparently, there was a guy who stole a kid or whatever. I couldn't see it all from where I was sitting, but somebody said a dude ran out of the crowd and kicked the guy's ass. The kid is okay, but they carried the dude out in an ambulance. Can you believe that?"

"Yeah, I can believe almost anything in New York City."

The driver huffed. "You can say that again, lady."

Throughout the ride back to Times Square, Gwynn eyed her phone as if it were her ticket into Hell. Perhaps it was, but the longer she waited, the worse the repercussions would be.

Soon, the massive stories-tall electronic billboards filled the windshield, and Gwynn stepped from the car and climbed the stairs into the building where she'd likely never again sleep down the hall from her partner and friend.

16

SOBYTIYE CHERNOGO GALSTUKA (BLACK TIE)

After practicing the conversation a dozen times, Special Agent Gwynn Davis finally gained the courage to dial the phone and press the green button.

A confident, almost perturbed voice filled her ear. "Special Agent White."

"Uh, Agent White, it's Davis. We've got a problem."

"*We've* got a problem, or *you've* got a problem?"

"Both, sir."

His exasperated sigh sounded like the cold north wind. "Let's hear it."

"She's missing, sir."

"Quit with the sir, Davis. Who's missing?"

"Uh, Anya, sir."

The sound of White's feet hitting the floor and the creaking cry of his office chair thundered through the phone. "What? What do you mean Anya's missing? Where is she?"

"I don't know, sir. You see, there was a kidnapping outside Barney's this morning, and—"

"Are you telling me someone kidnapped Anya?"

"No, no, sir. It wasn't Anya. It was a little boy. There was a standoff with police, and Anya snuck out behind the guard at Barney's and saved the boy."

White's palm landed with a smack against his forehead. "Why didn't you stop her, Davis? You know we can't let her face hit TV screens. That's the worst possible outcome."

Gwynn cleared her throat. "Well, there's one thing that could be worse."

"Yeah? What's that?"

"She escaped from the scene. The NYPD chased her, but she was too fast for them."

"Escaped? I'm not following. Slow down, and tell me exactly what happened."

Gwynn told the story, play-by-play.

Ray White's head didn't explode, but the pressure was building. "You let her get away, and you didn't immediately report it to me?"

"Well, I was trying to find her, sir, and . . ."

White roared, "You were *trying* to find her. You, fresh-out-of-the-Academy, Junior Agent Guinevere Davis, were trying to find one of the most highly trained Russian assassins on the planet, by yourself, in New York City. Is that what you're telling me?"

Determined to keep the tears at bay, Gwynn gritted her teeth. "I found her trail across the top of some shops and down a scaffold, but I couldn't make any more progress."

White leaned back in his chair and tried to calm himself. "We'll deal with your transgressions—multiple transgressions—later. For now, let's cover the background. Did she say or do anything to make you believe she was going to run?"

Gwynn replayed the previous night's feigned attempt at a kiss by the front door and the morning's sparring match in the living room. "No, sir, she didn't. In fact, quite the opposite. She told me she would've helped us if we'd simply asked. She said we didn't have to arrest her and threaten her. She believes what we're doing is the right thing. I mean, that's pretty much exactly what she said."

White let out a long, pained breath. "She was setting you up, Davis. She was trying to get you to talk me into changing the terms. Let me guess. She said if you'd get her a deal that didn't include the threat of prison, she'd volunteer to stay on as long as we needed her. Does that sound familiar?"

Gwynn's heart sank into her stomach. "How could I have been such an idiot?"

White slammed a hand onto his desk. "Would you look at that? CNN already has footage of your little train wreck. No, wait. It's not a little train wreck. It's a train wreck of nuclear waste in the streets of Manhattan."

Gwynn protested. "I didn't mean to—"

"Shut up, Davis. Just shut up. I'm listening to the report."

"A bizarre event on the streets of New York City today. Thirty-four-year-old Razmik Sahakyan, an Armenian immigrant, is accused of kidnapping his son early this morning from Hell's Kitchen in west Manhattan. A brief standoff with police on Seventh Avenue and Sixteenth Street in front of Barney's, a person who is now being called "Barney Badass," ran from the world-famous department store, assaulted and disarmed the kidnapper who was wielding a large knife, and saved the child, whose identity is being withheld at this time. After saving the child, the good Samaritan ran from the scene and evaded police, but the . . . excuse me for saying so . . . badass can be seen clearly in this video CNN acquired from a bystander at the scene. If anyone knows the identity or whereabouts of this do-gooder, NYPD asks that you notify them as soon as possible. It is likely a reward is in order for this brave citizen. From Manhattan, I'm Jodie Bellacourt, reporting live for CNN."

White said, "I don't know how much of that you heard, Davis, but it may not be as bad as I feared."

Gwynn breathed a sigh of enormous relief. "That's good to hear."

"Oh, your part in this is still as bad as it gets, and you're going to pay for it, but at least there are no pictures of Anya's face flooding the airwaves."

"I'm really sorry, Agent White. I had no way to know—"

"Stop apologizing, Davis. You're not making things any better."

"So, what do you want me to do now?"

Ray White almost chuckled. "I want you to do exactly what you've been doing all day—absolutely nothing. I want you to sit your ass down in that apartment, and don't get up. If my hunch is correct, Anya needs at least a few things she left inside the apartment, and she'll be back to get them. So help me, God, Davis, if you let her leave that apartment again, I will hang you out to dry, and I'll use your badge as a coaster. Do you understand me?"

"Do you really think she's coming back to the apartment?"

"What's wrong with you? Weren't you listening? Yes, I think she's coming back, but not while she thinks you're there, so you'll have to make sure the doorman knows you're not home, even if it takes all the cash you own. Got it?"

"Yes, sir. Pay off the doorman, and hole up in the apartment. I've got it."

The line went dead, and Gwynn sat in disbelief as she stared down at the black screen of her cell phone. The trip to pad the doorman's pocket took less than five minutes, and she was back inside the apartment locking the deadbolt behind her. As she stood staring at the chain hanging from the lock, it occurred to her that the chain could only be in place if someone were inside the apartment, and Anya would know the same thing, so she left the chain hanging free and turned off every light inside the apartment. The urge to stare out the window was almost too much to overcome, but she managed to stay clear of the glass overlooking the street below.

Gwynn's mind alternated between exploding and imploding as the minutes passed like hours inside the darkened space. Every sound from the hallway was magnified and seemed to penetrate the door as if it were an echo chamber.

If she comes back and I capture her, will I still have a career?

How did I ever let this happen?

Why would she do this to me?

Questions without answers ricocheted inside her skull, growing louder with every passing second. As she pondered just how bad the coming days and weeks would be, the ding of the elevator stopping on her floor yanked her from the well into which she'd fallen.

Moving with every ounce of stealth she could muster, Gwynn moved into the kitchen behind the narrow dividing wall between the entrance foyer and the rest of the apartment. Her only chance of subduing her prey would come in the form of sheer surprise.

She pressed the cold stainless steel of her handcuffs behind the fold of her knee as the ratcheting mechanism clicked through its cycle, leaving the cuffs poised for quick application. Scenes from the morning's fight in the middle of the living room flooded Gwynn's mind. The speed and strength of the Russian were all but impossible to overcome. If she got one cuff on a slender wrist without the second one locked in place, Anya would have a swinging, jagged weapon hanging from her wrist. A weapon of any style in those hands was more than Agent Davis wanted to face.

The footsteps, if they existed, were silent in the hall. Gwynn had listened for the sounds of Anya's movements for weeks and never heard her make a sound. It was as if she floated just above the ground with every move of her feet. The question of how long she would have to wait was answered by the rattle of the key sliding into the lock. When the deadbolt receded, it sounded like a freight train roaring through Gwynn's head. She subconsciously reached for her Glock, but the reality of her inability to draw and fire on the Russian overtook her, forcing her to leave the deadly weapon secure inside the leather binding of its holster.

The knob turned, and the door moved a few inches inward and then froze. The expectation of the chain had stopped the door's swing, but when the gold chain revealed itself to be hanging uselessly against the jamb, the door continued its arc into the foyer. The key slid from the lock just as Gwynn imagined the damage a key could do to a human body in the hands of a fighter like Anya. The mental picture of the crooked, torn, bloody flesh left her unable to quench the thirst in her throat.

Finally, the door closed, and Anya Burinkova continued through the foyer and toward the hall. Gwynn sprang from her concealment and landed one step behind the Russian with her handcuffs poised for use against the bones of her wrists, but instead of the tall, lean form in jeans and a sweatshirt she'd expected, the sight froze Gwynn in her tracks.

Hearing Gwynn move behind her, Anya spun, raising both hands into a defensive position. She adjusted her feet into a modified fighting stance—as much as the dress would allow.

As the two women faced each other, both shocked by what they saw, Anya was first to speak. "Why do you have handcuffs?"

Answering a question with a question always perturbed Gwynn, but she had no choice. "Why are you wearing an Alexander McQueen?"

Anya relaxed, lowering her hands. "I like it. It fits. And I could afford it."

Gwynn tossed the cuffs onto the kitchen counter. "No, that's not what I mean. I mean, why are you here . . . in that dress? I thought you were gone."

"I am here because I have date with Viktor Volkov to see his favorite ballerina."

Gwynn couldn't stop staring at every inch of the silk chiffon dress. "You look breathtaking. I've never seen anyone except models wearing that, but . . . wow."

Anya offered a somewhat awkward turn, giving her partner a full view of the dress from every angle. "You can have it after tonight. I will never need dress like this one again."

Gwynn stood wide-eyed and mouth agape. "How much did it cost, and where did you get it?"

"It was very expensive, but Volkov gave to me money to buy dress. It would be rude if I kept money and bought cheap dress, no?"

"Oh, yeah. That would be way rude. He's going to die when he sees you."

Anya ignored the flattery and let the dress fall from her shoulders. "I cannot wear ponytail tonight, so I must change my hair. You will help me with this, yes?"

"Yeah, of course, and I'll do your makeup."

Anya offered the slightest of frowns. "I do not wear makeup. You know this."

Gwynn helped her from the dress. "Tonight, you do. Let's get to it."

The next hour was spent turning one of the world's most classic beauties into the princess of New York City.

Halfway through the process, Anya caught Gwynn's attention in the mirror. "Why did you have handcuffs when I came inside door?"

Gwynn's shoulders dropped in embarrassment, coupled with disappointment in herself. "I thought you had escaped, and I was going to arrest you when you snuck in to collect your things."

Confusion consumed the Russian's face. "Escaped? From what?"

"I thought after you ran away from the thing with the kidnapper, you weren't coming back. I even had to report it to . . ." Gwynn dropped her brush and ran from the bathroom. After dialing frantically on her cell phone, she shoved the device to her ear.

"Special Agent White."

"Agent White, it's Davis. She's back!"

White lowered his tone. "Do you have her secured? I'll send a team to—"

"No, not like that. I mean, she never ran away. She was just shopping for a dress, and now she's back."

"Slow down, Davis. What are you talking about, a dress?"

Gwynn took several deep breaths. "She ran from the scene of the kidnapping, I guess to get away from the media and the cops, but she didn't leave the mission. We were shopping for a dress for her date with Volkov when it all happened. I guess she thought she should continue the mission, and she bought a killer dress. It's an Alexander McQueen, and it is gorgeous. You should see her in it, Agent White."

"Davis, I don't care about the dress. Are you telling me she's back on board?"

"No, I'm telling you she was never *not* on board. She wasn't running from us at all. I was way wrong about all of that."

"Wait a minute. She came back voluntarily as if nothing happened?"

"Yes, exactly. I think she was sincere last night when she said she'd work this mission even if we weren't threatening to send her to prison."

"Not so fast. It could all be a ploy to get our guard down. Maybe she didn't run when she had the perfect open door to make us believe she wasn't ever going to run. I don't know, but listen to me. You keep that girl in your sights, and don't let anything like this happen again. Am I making myself clear? You're responsible for her in the field. Everything she does is on you. Got it?"

"Yes, sir, I understand. But I think you're wrong—uh, I mean with all due respect—you may be incorrect about her. I don't think she's going to run."

"You better hope she doesn't."

Gwynn laid her phone back on the arm of the sofa and turned to see Anya standing behind her. "You and Agent White thought I was not coming back, no?"

"No, not exactly. He thought you'd come back to get your things and then disappear again, but he doesn't know you like I do."

Anya cocked her head. "And what did Special Agent Guinevere Davis think?"

"Junior Special Agent Davis was scared, and she thought her boss might be right, but your friend, Gwynn, knew you wouldn't do that to her."

Anya glanced at the handcuffs on the kitchen counter. "So, it was Special Agent Davis who was going to handcuff me?"

Gwynn smiled. "Yeah, I guess it was. But, hey, I'm really glad you came back, and I'm sorry for any doubt I had."

Anya checked the time. "I was never really gone unless you call Bergdorf Goodman a place a runaway former Russian spy would go to hide."

"You went to Bergdorf's and didn't take me? You should be ashamed."

"I have confession," Anya said. "I did not want you to go. Shopping with you is exhausting."

Gwynn stuck out her lower lip. "You just need to learn how to properly shop. That's all."

Anya lifted the dress from the back of a chair. "I think I can properly shop, and this dress agrees with me. Now, help me put it on. I have date with handsome Russian jeweler, and it is black-tie date."

17

DRUGAYA ANYA (ANOTHER ANYA)

The apartment telephone rang, and Gwynn snatched the handset. Hello."

"The car has arrived for Miss Anya," came the doorman's pleasant tone.

Gwynn gave her friend and partner the once-over. "She'll be down shortly."

Anya looked as if she just stepped from a runway in Paris in the Alexander McQueen dress. "Please do not worry. I will be back."

"I believe you, but I won't expect you until after breakfast. If you're not home by noon, though, I'm calling out the cavalry."

The Russian frowned. "I will not go home with Volkov."

Gwynn blushed. "I would . . . if he asked."

"I must go. I will be home after dinner."

"No!" Gwynn demanded. "You can't go down yet. Make him wait."

"Why would I do this?"

"Because trust me, girl. You and that dress are worth waiting for."

Anya stepped from the apartment and into the hallway, and Gwynn locked the door behind the deadliest woman in Manhattan.

As the elevator doors opened, Viktor Volkov stood in a bespoke tuxedo, looking every bit the dashing millionaire he was, but his stone-faced demeanor melted when the Eastern European beauty stepped from the elevator like an angel with a brand-new pair of wings. Volkov's mouth dropped open, and his eyes turned to saucers. Without a word, Anya crossed the floor as if floating and laced her hand inside his offered arm.

In his native Russian, he said, "You look more beautiful than any diamond."

Anya offered a tiny smile and answered in formal Russian. "You know all too well that Russian women are the most beautiful in the world."

"True, but if angels exist, tonight, I have their queen on my arm."

Volkov installed Anya in the left rear seat of the black Bentley Flying Spur and took his seat beside her. After a long, admiring look, he asked, "So, how much did that dress cost me?"

Anya lifted his hand from the seat and placed it on her thigh. "Do you really care how much it cost?"

"Touché"

They pulled away from the curb, and Anya stared through the moonroof. "It is sometimes difficult to know where city lights end and stars begin."

Volkov reclined his seat and joined her in stargazing. "Indeed, it is, but tonight you will see the brightest star in the city dance with all of her heart."

Anya gave him a look. "Perhaps I should be jealous of this ballerina."

Volkov let out a roar of laughter. "Perhaps you should, my dear."

The driver brought the Bentley to a stop in front of Lincoln Center and stepped out, opening Anya's door. Every head turned as she stepped from the quarter-million-dollar luxury car in her designer evening gown showing a perfectly toned leg. Hardly anyone noticed the stunning blonde had only nine toes . . . Well, hardly anyone.

Volkov seemed to be drawn to the wound. "I hope you will share that story with me soon."

Anya glanced down, remembering the night off the beach in Charlotte Amalie, St. Thomas, when she'd pinned the American operative, Chase Fulton, to the sandy bottom of the shallow water in an effort to subdue and ultimately interrogate him. The operative had other plans and got off a shot from his Makarov pistol from inside his dry bag. The irony of having her toe shot off by a weapon made by her Russian countrymen had never been lost on her, but that was a story Volkov could never hear. Instead, she said, "Is part of reason I am now American girl. I do not wish to relive the pain of incident that took my toe."

Volkov offered his arm. "In that case, I'll never ask again. Shall we go inside?"

Her hand landed inside his elbow, and they climbed the steps to the stares of onlookers who weren't wearing ten-thousand-dollar dresses and custom-made tuxedos.

Volkov pulled the gilded invitation from his inside pocket and presented it to the hostess.

"Thank you, Mr. Volkov. Please enjoy the ballet."

They rode the elevator to his private box overlooking the stage, and Anya took in the surroundings. "These are wonderful seats."

"They certainly should be," he said. "I am a platinum-level sponsor of the Bolshoi."

Anya raised an eyebrow. "The Bolshoi?"

Volkov, pleased his self-aggrandizement had not gone unnoticed, nodded once. "Yes, my dear. You are in for quite an evening."

When the dancers took the stage, Anya leaned forward, completely mesmerized by their strength and grace. Accomplished dancers are athletes of the highest order with unrivaled stamina and control of their bodies. Memories of hours upon hours in the bitter cold training to hone her body into the perfect killing machine for the Rodina flooded through Anya's head as she imagined the pain the dancers had endured to become what they were.

Four minutes into the first act, a ballerina adorned in perfect white descended a narrow staircase at center stage, performing a flawless pirouette en pointe as her tortured toes hit every step. Her technique and strength astonished everyone in the theater, and the crowd rose as one in uproarious applause and shouts of "Bravo! Bravo!"

The ballerina continued to the front of the stage and performed the traditional reverence as the crowd continued their admiration.

Anya had seen dozens of performances, but what happened next was unheard of in the ballet. As the ballerina bowed with the same elegance she had displayed throughout her entrance, a disembodied voice rang through the theater. "Ladies and gentlemen, the youngest prima ballerina in the history of the Bolshoi National Second Company, Ms. Anya Volkovna."

The applause heightened, and Anya turned to Viktor in disbelief. "Anya Volkovna? She is your daughter?"

Volkov bowed slightly. "My niece. My brother's only daughter."

As the applause waned, the orchestra played on, and the performance continued. At the end of the final act, while the audience poured their praise and applause toward the stage, Volkov stood, took Anya's arm, and led her from the box. A tuxedoed young man placed a bouquet of roses in Volkov's hand just outside the box and motioned toward the private elevator to the stage. When the small door of the elevator car opened, Viktor motioned for Anya to step out first. She did, and he followed two steps behind.

Anya, the ballerina, bowed and curtsied as flowers landed at her feet from the throngs of adoring attendees. As she turned to leave the stage, her dark eyes lit up in delight, and she was immediately transformed from the most elegant prima ballerina imaginable to a delighted child at seeing her favorite uncle. She flew into his arms, crushing the roses between them. When the embrace finally ended, he placed his niece back on the ground and turned to his date. "May I introduce your namesake, Anya Volkovna. The former assassin took the ballerina's dainty hands in hers, and they kissed cheeks. "*Ty byl velikolepen*!"

Young Anya blushed at the compliment and spoke in Russian. "You are too kind. Thank you, Ms. Anya. I see that my uncle has, once again, adorned his arm with the most beautiful woman in the city."

Anya corrected the dancer. "Only possibly the second most beautiful as long as you are in the city."

The reunion of uncle and niece continued as dozens of adoring girls begged for pictures with young Anya.

The ballerina leaned close to Anya's ear. "Sometimes I pretend I do not speak English."

Anya whispered back, "Me, too."

Back in the Bentley, Volkov's smile could not be erased. "I so love seeing her dance. Isn't she perfect?"

Anya laid her head on his shoulder. "She is, and she obviously adores her uncle."

He put his hand over his heart. "And I love her. Since her father was killed, I see that the family has whatever they need. Even though the wall fell, Russia will never be as comfortable as America for broken families."

"I'm sorry to hear about your brother, but you are so very kind to care for his family."

"It isn't kindness. It is responsibility. I fear I may have been the reason for his murder."

Anya gasped. "How could this be?"

"It's a long and terrible story I won't tell on a night like this. This is a night only for celebration."

The driver pulled away from the curb but circled into a private parking area near the back of the theater.

Anya asked, "Are we not going to dinner?"

Volkov patted her arm. "Patience, my dear. We are most certainly having dinner, but we must wait for the guest of honor."

Almost before he finished the line, an obscure door opened from the theater, and a teenaged girl with a bobbing ponytail ran from the door, directly to the Bentley, and slid onto the front seat as if escaping the scene of a crime.

In hurried Russian, the girl spoke to the driver. "Go! Go! We must go before I am discovered."

The heavy car accelerated nearly as impressively as Anya's Porsche, and soon, Lincoln Center was well in their wake.

Young Anya turned to Volkov. "Thank you, uncle. I so love New York, and especially dinners with you. How lucky I am to dance for you and to have a magnificent dinner."

Viktor laid his hand across the seat, cupping her tiny shoulder. "I'm the lucky one. Tonight, I have two beautiful dates for dinner, and both are Anya."

Young Anya swooned. "Oh, uncle, stop it. Please tell me we are going to One if by Land."

The girl turned to Anya. "Has he taken you there? It is the best restaurant in the whole world."

"He has not, but he promised me tonight would be the first."

Volkov rolled his eyes. "I see I've been handled by two beautiful women. If it is One if by Land, Two if by Sea you want, then who am I to say no?"

Viktor reached across the seat and tapped the driver, but the cell phone pressed to the man's ear told him arrangements were already being made. The driver glanced into the mirror, meeting Volkov's gaze. "A table for four will be waiting when we arrive, sir."

The ballerina grinned and mouthed, "*YA lyublyu tebya*."

Volkov matched her grin. "I love you, too, my niece."

The promised table was not only available but also the best in the house. It was quiet, secluded, and perfectly lit. The maître d' held chairs for Anya the elder as well as Anya the junior and took Viktor's overcoat.

When the waiter materialized tableside, Volkov said, "Three vodkas to begin."

The waiter immediately turned his attention to the ballerina, and Volkov snapped his fingers above the table and demanded, "Me. Look at me! Three vodkas."

He motioned with the back of his hand for the waiter to go, and obediently, he did. Moments later, three tasting cordials arrived on the table, two in front of Volkov and one before the only Anya at the table who could rip the soul from anyone in the room with nothing more than the butter knife beside the bread plate. Without hesitation, Volkov slid the stemmed cordial to the only Anya who could pirouette down a staircase, and glasses were raised.

In unison, the three cheered, "*Zdorov'ye*" and emptied the petite glasses.

Conversation flowed, as did the wine. When they were on dessert, Volkov shot his cuff, revealing his Rolex, and checked the time.

Anya's dark, beautiful eyes fell. "Oh, uncle. Please do not say I must return to the company. I so want to stay here with you . . . and with her." She clung to Anya's arm as if for dear life.

Volkov's eyes moistened as he tried but failed to meet his niece's gaze. "It is not possible just now, my Anyechka. But someday."

"Everything is possible with you, uncle. You are wealthy and powerful. You can do everything. Why can't I stay?" She turned to her namesake. "Tell him. Tell him he can make anything possible. He'll listen to you."

The assassin's heart melted. "I'm sorry. I cannot. This thing you want, it is very difficult, but not impossible. Perhaps someday soon you can come to America for good."

In typical form for a teenager from any country, she set her jaw and teetered on the edge of a tantrum.

The drive to the hotel near Lincoln Center was silent and cold. When they pulled beneath the awning of the hotel, Anya threw open the door as Volkov called out, "I love you, my only niece."

Standing beside the car and leaning back inside, she glared at the jeweler. "If you loved me, you wouldn't make me go back."

She slammed the door and stormed through the ornate entrance of the hotel.

Volkov stared between his feet and shook his head, barely perceptibly.

Anya took his arm. "She is only a girl. She will understand someday."

He pulled his arm from her. “No, she won’t. She can never know the truth of her father’s death, and I cannot bring her here to be with me. You will soon understand, but she never will.”

18

S MENYA KHVATIT
(I QUIT)

The ride to Anya's apartment was as quiet as the ride to the ballet company's hotel, but not as cold.

Before stepping from the Bentley, Anya leaned close to Viktor, pressed her lips to his cheek, and whispered, "She knows you love her, but she is girl child. You cannot understand because you have never been. I have. Good night, my beautiful man. I will begin matching diamonds on Monday, yes?"

"Thank you, my dear. I am sorry for the way this evening must end, but—"

Anya pressed her finger to his lips. "Shh. It was wonderful evening, and niece Anya is perfect. I will be ready for driver on Monday morning."

Volkov silently nodded, and Anya slid from the car.

As she walked through the apartment door, Gwynn rose to meet her. "Tell me everything. Where did you go? What did you do? Spill it, girl." Gwynn's excitement waned as she studied Anya's expression. "That doesn't look good. What's wrong?"

"I am no longer certain I can do this. I think I must quit."

Gwynn shook her head and grabbed Anya's hand. "Come, sit down. I'll make you some tea, and you can tell me everything."

The Russian pulled from Gwynn's grasp and ambled down the hallway toward her room. By the time Anya returned, dressed in flannel pajama pants and a University of Georgia baseball jersey, the tea was ready, and Gwynn was curled up on the end of the sofa.

Anya nestled into the plush cushion and cupped the mug in both hands. "Thank you for the tea. It smells delicious."

"You're welcome. Now, tell me what's going on."

Anya blew across the mug and took a tentative sip. "Viktor Volkov has a niece, and her name is Anya."

Gwynn slammed her mug onto the end table and leaned toward Anya. "Shut up! You're lying."

Anya shrugged. "It is true. She is prima ballerina of Bolshoi second company. I saw her dance tonight at Lincoln Center, and she is beautiful."

Girlfriend Gwynn was instantly transformed back into Special Agent Davis. "How did we not know he had a niece? We have to tell Agent White."

Anya laid a hand on Gwynn's arm. "Yes, of course I know this, but I must tell you everything before you call him."

Gwynn continued ignoring her tea and listened intently as Anya spoke. "He said Anya is daughter of his murdered brother, and he is responsible for the murder."

"He told you he killed his own brother?"

"No, he only said he was reason for his brother's murder—not that he killed him."

Gwynn grabbed a pen and Chinese restaurant menu from the end table drawer and flipped it over. The pen flew across the paper as she furiously took notes of every word. "What was his brother's name?"

Anya took another sip. "Also Volkov."

Gwynn slumped. "Yeah, I kinda figured that since they're brothers. I meant, what's his brother's first name?"

"I do not know."

"Okay, so, tell me about the niece."

"I know only that she has my name and is wonderful dancer. She had dinner with us, and she demanded that Viktor let her stay with him in America, but he refused."

"Why?"

"I suppose like most poor Russian children, she believes America would be better."

Gwynn let out a groan. "This is getting painful. It's like you've forgotten how to communicate with me. Of course the girl wants to come to America, but why did Volkov refuse."

"This is meaningful part of conversation. He said, 'She can never know truth of her father's death, and I cannot bring her here to be with me. You will soon understand, but she never will.'"

Gwynn stopped writing. "What does that mean?"

"I do not know."

"So, why do you think he feels responsible for his brother's murder?"

"This I do not know, either, but his heart is broken for his niece. He loves her, and she believes he can do everything."

"This is great stuff. I can't wait to tell Agent White."

Anya paused and dived into her tea. After two long swallows, she said, "Do you believe Viktor is dangerous man?"

"We don't know yet. We know he's practically printing money, and now that we've seen his girl Veronique switching diamonds in a shop, it's starting to come together that he's stealing high-quality diamonds and replacing them with lesser stones."

"But he is not killing anyone, and he is not bringing into country bags of cocaine, yes?"

"We don't think he's involved in any of those things, but that doesn't mean he isn't breaking the law."

"I realize this, but this little girl, Anya, she is without father and will be without uncle if we send him to prison."

"That's what happens to people who break the law in this country."

"Not always. Sometimes people break laws for many years and do not go to prison."

Gwynn sighed. "Are you suggesting we lay off of Volkov simply because he has a niece with your name?"

"No, this is not what I am suggesting. I only want to know what he is doing to break laws. Maybe he is not doing something so bad that his niece should suffer for the crimes of her uncle."

Gwynn closed her eyes and sighed. "What you're experiencing is common among law enforcement officials. It's called criminal sympathy, and we simply can't let ourselves fall into that trap. Think of it like this. How many people did you kill on the orders of your superiors while you were an SVR officer?

Anya bowed her head. "I do not wish to tell you this number."

Gwynn nodded. "Okay, that's fine. Just tell me if it's a one-digit or two-digit number."

Anya looked up. "Is two digits, but when I put with it the number I have killed while working for American government, it is three digits."

Gwynn swallowed the uncomfortable lump in her throat in an effort to continue making her point. "Okay, three digits. So, anyway, how many times did you disobey and not kill a target because they had children or family who would suffer because of their loss?"

Anya's face turned pale. "This is very different thing."

"No, it isn't. It's the same thing. We're a nation of laws, and without those laws, anarchy would destroy us."

"Yes, of course, I understand this, but this little girl wants to be American. She is brilliant dancer who will one day be famous in Russia, but she doesn't care about that. She only wants to come to this country."

"You're projecting, Anya. You're seeing yourself in this little girl, and you believe you can undo the wrong of what you were forced to endure as a child by protecting Anya Volkov."

Anya groaned. "This is not true."

"Yes, it is. That's exactly what's happening."

"Yes, of course, you are right about this, but you are not correct about girl's name. Is Anya Volkovna. Volkov is name for boy, and Volkovna is name for girl."

Gwynn almost laughed. "Here we go with the failed communication thing again."

Anya swallowed the last of her tea and stood.

Gwynn cleared her throat. "You can't quit."

"Yes, I can. This is agreement with Agent White."

"No, Anya. Agent White never said you had the option of quitting when you wanted."

"Yes, he did. He told me I would do this thing or go to American prison. If I go to prison, Anya Volkovna will not suffer, but if her uncle goes to prison, this will mean she has lost both men—you call them father figures—in her life, and that is terrible for a little girl. Good night, Special Agent Davis."

Gwynn bit her jaw. "Good night, Captain Anastasia Burinkova."

Anya glared at her partner before making her way to her bedroom.

* * *

When she awoke the next morning, Anya heard the familiar voice of Supervisory Special Agent Ray White, and she suddenly dreaded what lay ahead.

A shower did little to relieve her dread, but she'd postponed the inevitable as long as possible. She pulled her hair into a ponytail as she stepped into the living room. "Good Sunday morning, Ray. I think you should be at church, no?"

"Oh, so it's Ray and not Agent White now?"

"Is only my attempt to make this morning comfortable. I know why you are here."

"If Agent Davis is correct, I'm here to arrest you. How comfortable does that sound?"

Anya held out her hands as if ready for the handcuffs, but Ray motioned to the sofa. "Sit down, and tell me what's going on."

She did as he ordered and laid out the story just as she'd done for Gwynn the night before.

White listened intently, then leaned toward the Russian. "Listen closely, Anya. A guy we'll call Bill Smith had his brother killed in cold blood and then fled Canada for the United States. He became the biggest car thief in Chicago and sent piles of cash back to Montreal to his murdered brother's widow and child out of guilt for what he'd done. I caught this bastard eighteen years ago while I was based out of the Chicago field office and sent him to prison for ten years. After he served his sentence here, he was deported back to Canada, where he was tried and convicted for the crime of having his brother slaughtered. He's now serving a life sentence under the watchful eye of the Canucks. Should I have patted him on the ass and let him go instead of arresting him?"

Anya let her eyes fall shut and sighed. "This is not real story. There is FBI field office in Chicago, but no Department of Justice field office there."

"DOJ agents often find themselves temporarily assigned to the FBI."

"This is also lie," Anya said, "but it does not have to be true to make your point."

White lowered his chin and focused on Anya. "My point isn't what you think, but you interrupted before I could finish. If my story about Chicago had been true, I would've told you how I made arrangements with the State Department to have Bill Smith's brother's widow and orphaned child brought to the States and set up in a great little house on the edge of the Rocky Mountains, where the child learned to ski and won two Olympic gold medals wearing the American flag on her shirt."

Anya felt the edges of her lips turn upward in the slightest hint of a smile. "Does this mean Anya and her mother can come to America and she can dance with New York Ballet Company?"

White sat back in his chair. "No, that's not what it means. It means if you and your girlfriend in there put Viktor Volkov in prison and figure out what he did to get his brother killed, ballerina Anya can dance with any company she wants right here in America, and maybe you can give her one of those little plastic American flags you love to carry around."

A suspicious look of doubt came over Anya. "Do you have power to do this thing?

Ray shook his head. "No, I can't get that girl a spot on a ballet company, but I can get her and her mother here and on a path to citizenship. But only if you and your tea wench do your job and put Volkov where he belongs . . . in a federal prison cell.

Anya said, "I will do this for you, but only on one condition."

White scowled. "You don't get to make conditions, especially now that you've gone all softhearted on us."

She smiled. "I think this is acceptable condition. I am hungry and would like to have pancakes. The kind of pancakes you made for me in your home in Georgetown."

19

MY IDEM NA RABOTU (OFF TO WORK WE GO)

Monday morning dawned to find Anya Burinkova, the belle of the ball at Saturday night's performance at Lincoln Center, dressed in blue jeans, a T-shirt, and a hooded sweatshirt. Her driver held open the car door at precisely eight thirty, and she slid inside, anxious to send Viktor Volkov to the New York Metropolitan Correctional Center, the federal administrative detention center in Lower Manhattan. If he were truly guilty of federal crimes as the Department of Justice believed, that's where he'd be held until he was convicted, and sentencing was handed down by the U.S. District Court for the Southern District of New York.

The same garage door she and Gwynn had been driven through the previous week rose as the driver approached and promptly closed it behind them. The building looked the same, but the feeling of the place was different. Something left the fearless former SVR officer with a sense of dread.

The car came to a stop, and Viktor Volkov stepped from the inner sanctum of the bland, dark building with his arms outstretched. "Ah! The queen of the angels has returned to me." He threw his arms around her and drew her body against his in a long embrace. "Have you eaten?"

Anya nodded. "I have, and I am ready to go to work."

"I'm sure you are, but we have a bit of ugly business to attend to before we get started." He held the door for her, and she discovered Sascha waiting in the lavishly appointed interior of the space. He wore an expression she'd never seen on his boyish face. It was a look of determined accusation—the same look Ray White wore the day he first questioned her.

"Good morning, Sascha. Is everything all right?"

The scientist bored holes through her with his eyes. "Starting a relationship with a lie is a dangerous beginning. Diamonds are rare and beautiful things, just like trust. The only thing worse than lying to us is stealing from us."

Anya's mind reeled with a thousand questions, and she scanned the room for both weapons and exits as she palmed the two diamonds she'd "borrowed" from the vault.

Have they found out I am working with the Justice Department? What will they try to do to me? Must I kill both of them? Would that be good enough for Supervisory Special Agent Ray White to bring Anya and her mother to the States as he promised?

In an effort to delay the coming storm, she said, "I do not understand. What is problem?"

Sascha wasted no time in answering. "The problem is someone stole a pair of diamonds from the vault, and you and your girlfriend are the only two people who've been inside the vault since we last saw the missing pair of stones."

"This cannot be true," she said. "If my friend and I were the last ones inside the vault, how do you know the stones are missing?"

"Because I counted them myself this morning," Sascha roared.

Anya tilted her head, glanced at Volkov, then back to Sascha. "If this is true, then you were last person inside vault since missing stones were seen, no?"

Sascha threw a finger into Anya's face. "Are you saying I stole two diamonds from myself?"

"No, of course not," she said. "I am saying your statement about my friend and me being last ones inside vault is an intentional lie because you knew truth."

Sascha's pupils narrowed, and he ground his teeth together. With no external indications, Anya smiled inside her head. The Russian scientist with soft hands and obvious anger issues was about to take a swing at her, and when he did, she would be justified in removing his head.

Volkov had stood in silence as long as he could bear and stepped between the two, placing his palm in the center of Sascha's chest. "Perhaps it is simply an error in counting. Let's have a look, shall we?"

He opened the vault door and motioned for Sascha and Anya to follow him inside. The two velvet bags rested on the spotless table, and Volkov poured the contents of the first bag onto a black padded surface and withdrew a long pair of jeweler's locking tweezers from a drawer. Anya leaned in, eyeing the pile of stones closely and pretending to count.

She stood erect. "Sascha is correct. There are only forty-nine stones in that pile."

Volkov turned to her. "How could you possibly count fifty stones so quickly?"

"I did not count fifty stones," she said. "I only counted forty-nine."

Sascha growled, "Viktor, I warned you. She's playing us."

Volkov held up a hand and slid the stones aside. He poured the contents of the remaining bag onto a separate surface and motioned toward the hundreds of thousands of dollars' worth of flawless carbon.

Anya leaned in, ran her index finger through a small pile of stones and skillfully allowed the palmed diamonds to slide from her hand. When she'd spread the stones adequately, she frowned and pretended to count again. When she finished, she turned to face her accuser. "It appears Viktor is correct this time, Sascha. There are fifty-one stones in this pile."

Sascha shoved her aside, ripped the tweezers from Volkov, and quickly counted the stones twice. When he finished, he turned, his face blood red, and he shook a finger toward Anya.

She smiled. "You may be brilliant scientist, Sascha, but you are not so good at counting."

Volkov stifled a laugh, pulled a loupe from his pocket, and tossed it to Sascha. "Find it," he ordered.

The scientist, adequately scolded, went to work inspecting every stone in the pile of fifty-one.

"Come with me," Volkov said softly, and Anya followed him from the vault. He led her through a barely visible door and into an office even more lavishly furnished than the sitting room outside the vault. "This is your office. You will work here. If you do not like the light, the chair, or anything else, you have only to tell me or Sascha and we will remedy the problem immediately."

Anya took in the room, memorizing every detail, and then cast a glance back through the door. "Thank you, Viktor. The office is beautiful, and I will be perfectly comfortable here, but I fear Sascha feels I should not be here at all."

Volkov smiled. "Do not worry, my darling. Sascha works for me, and I will see that he understands what is important is what I want, and I want you here."

She stepped toward him and extended her arms, but he held up a palm. "Not here. Here we are in business, and only business. I'm sure you understand."

Anya offered a small bow. "Of course."

Viktor turned for the door. "Make yourself comfortable. Sascha will be in with two bags of stones for you. Make as many matches as possible, but always keep the stones from each bag separate from the others. They are not to be mixed. Simply identify matches and place the pairs aside, keeping the two bags separate. Do you understand?"

She gave a quick, wordless nod, and he left her alone in her first office with her first diamond still gleaming on her finger.

Moments later, a soft tap came on her door.

"Please come inside," Anya said.

The door opened, and Sascha pushed through with a pair of bags in his hand. He set them on Anya's worktable and slid the blue bag well to the left of the black one. "Viktor explained the importance of keeping the bags separate until a match is made, correct?"

"Yes, he did."

Sascha took a step back. "Look, I'm sorry about this morning. This is my life's work, and I take it very personally as well as seriously. I was wrong, and I shouldn't have blamed you. It won't happen again."

She rose from the table and stepped to within inches of the man. She leaned in and kissed his cheek innocently just in front of his ear. "Do not worry, Sascha. I am not threat to you. I am only simple actress with very good memory."

He let out the breath he'd been holding and stepped away. Anya was left almost alone in her new office. The six cameras she'd already detected left her believing there were at least six more, and her claim to be an actress was being put to the test. Her performance for the cameras would have to be flawless.

She pulled the sweatshirt over her head, providing camera number-one a perfect view of her toned stomach and delicate lace of her bra as her T-shirt rose with the hoodie. After straightening her clothing, she sat at the worktable and adjusted the articulating arm of the light.

An hour later, she'd made six matches and devised a system of four columns on the edge of her table. The two left columns were reserved exclusively for stones from the blue bag. If a pair was made and both diamonds came from the blue bag, they would rest side by side in columns one and two. Columns three and four were exclusively for black bag diamonds. If a pair was made with one diamond from each bag, column two held the blue bag stone, and the black bag stone rested in column three. Just like columns one and two were reserved for the blue bag, columns three and four were exclusively for black baggers.

The system proved efficient and effective until the ninety-minute mark when every stone began to look like every other one. She stood from her seat, stretched, and turned for the tea service she'd noticed after only seconds in her office. The break and tea kept the coming headache at bay, and she returned to her table.

A solid rasp at the door startled her, and she almost knocked the stones from their columns. Without an invitation, Volkov came through the door and leaned against the corner of her table. "How are you doing on your first day in the diamond mine?"

Anya rubbed her temples. "It is harder than I thought, but I am making progress. I have so far only six matches. I fear this is terrible, but I am trying."

"Six? You've made six matches in two hours?"

She sighed. "Yes, I am sorry, but this is all I could do so far. I will get better and faster in time. I am still making process." She pointed toward the paired diamonds and explained the column system she devised.

Volkov laid his hand on her shoulder. "It takes seasoned gemologists hours to make a single match, and you've made six already. You're a gift from God."

Anya feigned embarrassment. "I am not gift from God. Only lucky find for you this time." She motioned toward the columns of paired stones. "I would like for you to look closely at diamonds and tell me if you agree they are matching. You will do this for me, yes?"

He pulled a loupe from his pocket. "I'll take a look, but I'm sure they're perfect."

He clamped the first two stones in a pair of tweezers and alternately inspected each stone, switching several times. After carefully placing the stones back in the appropriate columns, he repeated the procedure with two more pairs and replaced each to their previous positions. "Stay here, and don't touch anything. I'll be right back."

She did as he instructed and sat with her hands folded neatly in her lap, just as the cameras would expect. Moments later, Volkov returned with

Sascha in tow. "Look what she has done. In less than two hours, she claims to have made six pairs. See for yourself."

Sascha leaned down, lifted a pair to his loupe, and thoroughly examined the stones. Without a word, he returned the stones to the table and lifted a second pair. After meticulous inspection, he stood up straight. "Remarkable."

Anya moved the stones Sascha had misplaced and aligned them with her column system.

Volkov said, "Explain the columns to Sascha."

Anya did, and he was adequately impressed.

"Six matches in less than two hours is unbelievable. The computer can't match them so quickly."

Anya looked up. "You have computer to do this job?"

"We do."

"If this is true, why do you need me? I can only work ninety minutes before I must have time to relax, but you could have computer working constantly and never needing tea."

"This is true," Sascha said. "But with one hundred stones, the computer matches one pair every six hours and has only sixty percent accuracy, so that means, mathematically, considering the erroneous matches, it would take the computer sixty hours to make the six matches you made in ninety minutes. That's why Viktor is right . . . again. You are a gift from God straight to us."

Anya shot a thumb toward the door. "Go away. There are at least two more matches, and you are interrupting my work."

Viktor and Sascha went the way of the thumb and pulled the door closed behind them.

When they were well out of earshot, Viktor turned to the scientist. "How many matches are in those bags?"

Sascha held up his palms. "I found only five in two weeks of searching."

20

DRUG DRUGA (FRIEND OF A FRIEND)

When Anya stepped through the apartment door, she discovered Special Agent Gwynn Davis with a cell phone pressed to her ear and a finger pressed to her lips. Anya obeyed the instruction to remain silent but sat on the overstuffed chair and stared at her partner. The look on Gwynn's face said she was shoulder-deep in official business.

"Yes, sir, that's correct . . . Supervisory Special Agent Ray White . . . Thank you. I would greatly appreciate a callback today after you speak with my supervisor . . . Yes, sir, I realize that, but this is an active Justice Department investigation with agents in the field." Gwynn pulled the phone from her ear and stared into the dark screen. "That S-O-B hung up on me."

"Who?" Anya asked.

"A guy over at the State Department. I'm working on background for Volkov's brother. I learned that his name is—or was—Konstantin Dmitrievich Volkov, but that's as far as I've gotten."

Anya slowly shook her head. "Have you not read *Anna Karenina*?"

"No, why?"

"Someone is playing games with you. Who told you Volkov's brother was Konstantin Dmitrievich?"

"A guy Johnny-Mac knows at the U.S. Embassy in Moscow."

"This person is lying to you. Konstantin Dmitrievich is a character from Leo Tolstoy's greatest novel, *Anna Karenina*. Why have you never read this book?"

"I don't know. I mean, I've heard of it, but . . ."

"I will buy for you this book, and you will read it each night before falling asleep."

Gwynn sank into the cushion of the sofa. "Why do people have to make everything so hard?"

Anya moved from the chair to the sofa. "There is one thing the government is great at, and this is screwing everything up. It is different, but sometimes same in Russia and America. When the government is involved, everything takes too long and is too complicated. It is same at grocery store. In Russia, we have two kinds of crackers, but here in America, the shelves are full of crackers—hundreds of them. It is too much and too hard to choose."

Gwynn raised an eyebrow. "How does that have anything to do with some low-level diplomat in Moscow playing games with me?"

"It is simple. This person in Moscow is probably nothing more than clerk or maybe errand boy, and he does not know anything about Volkov's family. Maybe other option is this. Maybe he is higher-level diplomat and knows everything about Volkov, but he is not willing to tell secrets. If this is true, you have started avalanche inside embassy, and everything you want to know is now buried beneath a pile of large rocks, and you will never get truth from them."

Gwynn sighed. "Then what am I supposed to do? If I can't get the answers I need, we'll never be able to prove Volkov's connection to his brother's murder. If we can't make the connection, we'll never be able to get little Anya and her mother to the States."

Anya cast her eyes to the ceiling, and the wheels began to spin. After what felt like an eternity to Gwynn, her partner said, "There are two ways to find information we need from inside Russia."

Gwynn leaned forward. "Come on, don't make me wait. Let's hear them."

"First way is to go to Moscow and find the information ourselves."

"That's not going to happen. First of all, there's no way the Justice Department would approve the cost. Second, you're still persona non grata over there. Even if we got in the country undetected, you'd be back in prison the second we approached an official with any information we need. So, that's out. What's the other option?"

"Skipper."

Gwynn cocked her head. "What's Skipper?"

"Skipper is excellent analyst who can find almost anyone with only her computers."

A ray of hope shone in Gwynn's eyes. "So, all we have to do is have Agent White call up the CIA and get this analyst you know assigned to our operation."

Anya frowned. "No, Skipper does not work for CIA."

"Who, then? DIA? NSA? It doesn't really matter because we can get him temporarily assigned no matter who he works for."

"No, this is not possible. Skipper is a woman, not a man, and she does not work for government."

Gwynn scratched her head. "A female analyst who doesn't work for the government?"

"Yes, she works exclusively for Chase's team."

Gwynn sank back against the sofa. "Him again, really?"

"No, not *him*. *Her*."

"So how do we find *her*?"

Anya held up her phone. "We call her."

"I can't authorize that call, and you know that."

Anya smiled. "Yes, but you do not have to know."

"Don't do it, Anya. Agent White will have both our heads on pikes if you make that call without his approval."

"What do I have to lose?"

"Your freedom, for one thing. If you screw this up, you know Agent White will keep his word and send you to prison."

Anya pressed her lips into a thin horizontal line. "Agent White has not forbidden *you* from calling Skipper."

"No! I've screwed up enough on this operation already. I'm not going to push it any further. What I will do, though, is talk with Agent White about it. Maybe he'll approve you calling her. If not, maybe—and this is much more likely—he'll approve me to make the call."

Gwynn spent the next half hour briefing and begging her boss. She laid out what she'd found on her own, as well as the roadblock she'd encountered with the U.S. Embassy in Moscow. Saving the best—or perhaps the scariest—for last, the final five minutes of the conversation was spent explaining Skipper and hoping for his blessing to make that call.

When she hung up, Gwynn turned to Anya and shrugged.

"What did he say?"

"He's thinking about it, and that's weird. I've never known him to not be able to make a decision on the spot."

"This is big decision," Anya said. "One of the major concerns he has is my contact with my friends. He doesn't call them friends, though. He calls them people from my previous life. I do not like this name for them."

"I know this is going to sound cold, but I don't think Agent White cares what we like. He's going to do what he thinks is best in every situation, regardless of what anybody else has to say about it."

"When will he be finished thinking?"

"How should I know? Why don't you tell me about your day while we're waiting for a callback?"

"It was not a pleasant start. Sascha counted the diamonds in bags and found two missing."

"Oh, my god. He caught you?"

"No, he did not catch me. I made him look like fool by slipping the diamonds I 'borrowed' back into second bag, and Viktor made him apologize to me."

"Made him apologize? Are you serious?"

"Yes, I am. I think even he believed he'd miscounted. It was fun for me."

Gwynn shook her head. "That's amazing. So, what else happened?"

I found nine pairs of matching stones in the two bags, and I learned there is computer to do same job as me."

"Articles, Anya. You've got to learn to use English articles. You're killing me."

"I am sorry. I will try harder, but is difficult for me."

Before Gwynn could continue English class, her phone chimed, and she held it up. "It's Agent White. That was fast."

Anya motioned toward the phone. "Answer!"

Gwynn chuckled and stuck the phone to her ear. "Davis."

"Davis, it's White. Give me her phone number."

Gwynn recoiled. "What?"

White scolded. "Give me a phone number for this Skipper character. I'll make the call."

"Hang on a second." Gwynn covered the mouthpiece with her palm and turned to Anya. "Agent White wants Skipper's number so he can call her."

Anya let the long list of what could go wrong run through her head before reciting the number. Gwynn relayed the ten digits to her boss, and he hung up without another word. Gwynn was left, once again, staring at her silent phone.

"Is everything okay?"

Gwynn looked up. "Everybody's hanging up on me today."

Anya ignored the complaint. "I am concerned about what will happen when Agent White calls Skipper."

"Why?"

"The people on the team are very close. They are more than friends and what you would call coworkers. They are like a family. Skipper will tell everyone on the team about the conversation with your boss, and they will try to find me."

Gwynn shook her head. "Agent White won't let that happen. He'll make sure Skipper understands the nature of this operation, and he'll insist she keeps the information limited to those who have a need to know."

"I think you do not understand. I am part of this team, and knowing where I am, and if I am safe, is something every member of team—*the* team—needs to know. If Agent White wants her help, Skipper will demand to know where I am and if I am hurt."

Gwynn sucked a breath through her teeth. "Making demands with Agent White is never a good idea, no matter who you are."

* * *

Department of Justice, Washington, D.C.

Supervisory Special Agent Ray White stared down at the ten digits scribbled on his desk blotter and ran his hands through his graying hair. The initial graying had purely been a function of the number of years he'd spent on Earth, but the most recent additions to the field of gray could be directly tied to Operation Avenging Angel, specifically Gwynn and Anya.

Ray silently rehearsed the conversation before dialing the Silver Spring, Maryland, number.

Three rings later, a young woman's unmistakably Southern accent filled his earpiece. "This better be good. I'm busy, and whoever you are, you're interrupting me."

Ray shook off the unexpected tone. "Is this Skipper?"

"Who's calling?"

"I'm Special Agent Ray White with Justice, and I'm trying to locate an analyst named Skipper."

"Well, you've got the wrong number, Agent White . . . as if that's really your name. Now, leave me alone. I told you, I'm busy."

It was Ray White's turn to find himself staring at a phone with no one on the other end of the line.

Seconds later, Gwynn's phone rang, and she answered on speaker so Anya could listen in. "Yes?"

"Davis, it's White."

"Yeah, I was expecting your call."

"Listen, I called the number you gave me for Skipper, and I got a woman who'd never heard of anyone by that name."

Gwynn looked to her partner and shrugged.

Anya said, "You're being vetted, Agent White. Skipper—this is not her real name, by the way—will determine if you are who you say you are, and if she thinks you're important enough, she'll call you back."

"Do you have me on speakerphone?"

"Yes, sir," Gwynn said. "Anya suspected you'd be calling back, so I answered on speaker."

"Next time, let me know. Will you?"

"Yes, sir. I'm sorry."

"Don't be sorry, Davis. Be better. Now, Anya, what makes you think she's vetting me?"

"This is what she does. If she wants to talk with you, she will call you back."

"I'm afraid that'll be impossible. All calls leaving this building are routed through a switchboard that eliminates caller ID tags, so your Skipper doesn't have my number."

Anya covered her mouth to keep White from hearing her chuckling. "Trust me, Agent White, if Skipper wants your number, she already has it."

"We'll see about that," he said. "In the meantime, what is this woman's real name?"

"I am sorry, but I do not know. She is always only Skipper."

"Yeah, sure. Look, I'm only doing this to appease your ridiculous desire to get the dancer and her mother out of Russia. If you and this Skipper person want to make that harder for me, I'll simply drop the whole thing. I don't care."

"I could talk with her and ask for her help. She would do this thing for me."

White grunted. "Hang on a minute. I'm getting another call."

He clicked over. "Agent White."

"Okay, you check out. You're really with Justice, and your name really is Ray White. What do you want?"

Ray shook off the shock and leaned back in his chair. "First things first. You should know I'm sort of a friend of a friend, you might say."

Skipper said, "We're way past first things, White. I already told you I'm busy. Now, what do you want?"

Ray let out a long breath. "I want you to find out why someone is dead."

Skipper groaned. "People die for only one reason, Agent White. Lack of oxygen to their brain, regardless of what a coroner writes on their death certificate. Goodbye."

"No, wait. Don't hang up. I need to know how and why one specific Russian was murdered."

"A Russian?"

"Yes, a Russian."

Skipper was suddenly interested. "What's this Russian's name, and when were they killed?"

"That's the thing," White said. "I don't know the full name."

"Goodbye, Agent White. You're wasting my valuable time."

"No, no . . . wait. Here's everything I know. If you don't want to help after I finish, you can hang up."

"I don't think you understand, Agent White. I can hang up anytime I want."

"Yes, that's true, but just listen for two minutes. After that, I promise to never call again."

Skipper looked at her watch. "The clock is ticking, and you now have one hundred ten seconds."

"Okay, I need to know how and when the brother of Viktor Volkov was killed. He lived in or near Moscow, I believe, and he had a daughter named Anya Volkovna. She's a dancer in the Bolshoi second company."

Silence consumed the line until White believed she'd hung up. "Skipper?"

The silence continued, and White reached for the disconnect button to click back over to his problem children in New York.

An instant before he pressed the button, Skipper said, "Is Anya alive?"

White felt a bead of sweat form on his forehead. "Of course she's alive. She's only fifteen years old."

"Not that Anya, Agent White. *Our* Anya."

White felt at least half a dozen of his ulcers turn to raging pits of fire in his stomach. Suddenly he was standing on the precipice of a mighty chasm between doing what was right and doing his job. "I don't know what you're talking about."

He made the wrong choice.

Click.

21

EKSKURSIYA (FIELD TRIP)

Ray White immediately redialed Skipper's number and listened for an answer.

"We're sorry, but the number you have called has been disconnected or is no longer in service. If you feel you have reached this recording in error, please hang up and try your call again."

White slammed the phone back into its cradle, sending the handset and base careening off his desk.

Special Agent Gwynn Davis, who'd been holding on the second line, heard the commotion an instant before the line fell silent. Gwynn looked up at her partner. "I think Agent White just threw his phone across the room."

Anya smiled. "Skipper has this effect on some people."

Gwynn dialed White's office extension and heard only a long series of tones. She hung up and dialed his cell.

He snatched the phone from his pocket. "What!"

"Agent White, it's Davis. Is everything okay?"

"No, everything is not okay. Put the Russian on the phone, and turn off the damned speaker!"

Gwynn clicked off speaker and handed the phone to Anya.

She said, "Hello?"

"Your cocky little analyst cut me off. You and Davis better have your butts on the train to D.C. tonight."

"This is not possible."

White roared, "You don't tell me what is and isn't possible. You follow orders."

"Yes," Anya began, "and my orders are to infiltrate Viktor Volkov's operation. This is exactly what I am doing. I must be in my office matching diamonds tomorrow morning."

"Fine," White said. "You can ride the train back to New York tomorrow morning, or you can twitch your little nose and teleport back for all I care, but you and Davis will be in my office before the sun goes down. Otherwise, you can get accustomed to a six-by-nine prison cell. It's up to you."

Anya protested, but White had already hung up. She tossed the phone back to Gwynn. "It appears we are going back to Washington."

Gwynn reeled in disbelief. "What?"

"Agent White has ordered us back to Washington on the next train. He says it is up to me to get back in time for tomorrow's work."

* * *

Five hours later, Anya and Gwynn stepped from the train at Union Station and spotted Ray White leaning against a corner of aged brick. He acknowledged their arrival with only a single nod and then turned for the street. The two women gave chase, determined not to lose him in the crowd. When they finally caught up with him, he was waiting behind the wheel of his black government Suburban. Gwynn slid into the front while Anya made her way into the back seat.

Agent White eyed the two women. "No. Anya rides up front with me."

His tone left little room for misunderstanding, and the women didn't hesitate to exchange seats. He pulled from the curb without checking traffic and accelerated through sixty-five miles per hour.

White turned his attention to Anya. "We'll be in Silver Spring in twenty-five minutes, and you're going to tell me where to find Skipper."

Anya froze. "But I do not know where she lives or where she works. I have never been to Silver Spring, and I have no way to know if she is there."

White shrugged. "You'd better figure something out."

Anya turned to Gwynn, but she stared back in frightened uncertainty.

Anya spun in her seat and faced directly toward White. "Why are you doing this? What do you want from me?"

White quickly checked the mirror and stood on the brake pedal. To the blare of horns and screeching tires, he slid to a stop in the middle of North Capital Street Northwest. Cars flew by in both directions, but White never flinched.

He faced the Russian with steely-eyed resolve. "What I want from you is for you to prove you meant what you said to her." He jabbed an index finger directly at Gwynn. "I want you to do whatever the job requires, torpedoes be damned. I don't care who you kill or how many laws you break to get it done. I want to see you do it, just like you did it when you were SVR. Remember those days?"

Anya's anger rose, but she maintained the calm demeanor that made her so terrifying. "Yes, I remember when I was SVR officer. I was without limits. I worked alone, and I cut out the hearts of men like you. Is this what you want from me?"

"You're damned right, that's what I want from you! Quit asking permission, and start getting results. You told Davis you'd do this job even without the threat of prison hanging over your head. I think you're a liar, and you are the only person on Earth who can prove me wrong."

She leaned to within inches of his face and stared into his soul. "You do not understand this thing you are asking. You cannot stop the animal you are about to uncage."

He placed his hand in the center of her chest and shoved her back onto her side of the Suburban. "I don't believe that animal exists anymore."

As the steam inside the Russian continued to rise, a car pulled alongside, and two men hurled verbal volleys of profanity toward the Suburban. Anya narrowed her eyes, set her jaw, and grabbed the barrel of the shotgun locked in its bracket beside her left knee. The key to the locked bracket rested deep inside Ray White's pocket, but Anya had no need for a key. She sent a thundering elbow shot to the mechanism as she yanked the barrel to the side. The bracket gave way, and the weapon landed in Anya's waiting hand. She kicked open the door and stepped from the SUV, rage burning in her eyes.

The driver of the stopped car yanked the shifter into drive at the same instant Anya drove the butt of the shotgun through the car's window. Recoiling, she raised the weapon over her shoulder and sent the butt into the driver's face, spraying blood in every direction. She spun the weapon, racked the slide, and shoved the barrel into the man's neck just beneath his ear. The passenger panicked, threw open his door, and sprinted from the car. With trembling hands, the driver unfastened his seatbelt and followed his passenger across the front seat and into the street. Still in drive, the car rolled forward at a snail's pace. Anya opened the door then turned back to the government SUV. With two perfectly delivered rounds, she annihilated the passenger side tires of Ray's Suburban before leaping into the sedan and speeding northward.

At Kansas Avenue, she yanked the wheel hard over and slid the car onto the westbound lanes. Seconds later, she left the road and bounced the car into Fort Slocum Park, using a grove of tall trees for cover. In the next instant, her cell phone was pressed to her ear, and the phone she had dialed was ringing.

Skipper answered on the third ring. "Listen to me, and listen good. If this is White, you're playing games with the wrong—"

Anya shouted into the phone. "Skipper, it is me, Anya."

"Anya? What are you . . . I mean . . ."

"Listen to me, Skipper. Tell me where you are. I need your help."

"I'm at home in Silver Spring. Where are you?"

Anya scanned the environment around her. “I do not know, but I am close. I believe this is maybe Kansas Street or maybe Avenue.”

“In D.C.?”

“Yes, I think I am still in Washington, D.C.”

Skipper’s heart pounded as if it were coming out of her chest. “Anya, are you hurt? Are you in danger?”

“I am not hurt, but yes, I am in danger. I need your help. I cannot get out of this alone.”

Skipper gathered her wits. “What was the last street sign you saw?”

“I don’t know. I was riding north toward Silver Spring when I broke away and stole car.”

“Oh my God, Anya. What have you gotten into? Who’s chasing you?”

“A federal policeman called White.”

Skipper lowered her voice. “Listen closely, Anya. I’ve triangulated your position from your cell phone. You need to do exactly what I say. Open the hood of the car you stole. Find the hottest part of the engine, lay your cell phone on it, and leave the car running. If I can track your phone, so can White. Have you got all of that?”

“Yes, I understand.”

“Good. When you’ve done that, make your way due east across Kansas and Blair Road to the community gardens. You’ll know it when you get there. Dig in, and keep your head down. I’ll be there in ten minutes. I’ll be in a black Land Cruiser. Do you know what that is?”

“No, but is okay. I will come to your voice.”

Skipper shoved her phone into her pocket and ran for her car. Twelve minutes later, she left the pavement at the end of South Dakota Avenue Northeast and felt all four tires grip the soft, damp earth. Plowing through private plots, she powered ahead until she believed herself to be near the center of the gardens. With a throw of the shifter and a punch of the sunroof control, she leapt from the seat and climbed onto the roof of the Land

Cruiser. Drawing in a lungful of air, she prepared to yell for Anya, but one glance to the northwest made the call unnecessary.

She slid back through the sunroof and crushed the gas pedal, sending mud flying from all four tires. Anya ran as if pursued by lions. Twenty feet apart, Skipper spun the wheel and threw open the passenger door. Without breaking running stride, Anya dived through the open door and clung to the center console for her life. Skipper tapped the brake and then accelerated onto Sligo Mill. The transition forced Anya's door closed as she crawled between the seats and into the rear floorboard. Skipper continued off-road again and onto the gravel of the railroad track bed. Accelerating alongside the tracks, she pushed the Toyota's suspension to its limits and prayed the car would survive long enough to escape the enormous city surrounding them.

Running for the shore with no boat waiting was the worst possible decision and the last thing any rational pursuer would expect. Turning east through a neighborhood she didn't recognize, Skipper held the accelerator to the floor, and her prayers were answered. The car didn't fail them, and just under an hour later, they crossed a narrow finger of water into a small fishing village.

"Okay, you can come out. We're clear of the city, and no one would expect us to be here."

Anya climbed from the rear floorboard and into the front passenger seat, scanning the environment around her as she moved like a snake. "Where are we?"

"We're in a tiny little place called Deale, Maryland, on Chesapeake Bay, and it's time for you to tell me why a DOJ cop is chasing you through the streets of D.C. and why it has taken you so long to contact us."

"I will tell you everything. I promise this to you, but first I need you to find a little girl and her mother in Russia."

Skipper moaned. "Oh, boy. This is about Viktor Volkov's brother's murder, isn't it?"

"No," Anya said. "This is about the life and safety of a little girl who wants more than anything to come to America and never have to leave."

22

ZAOCHNOYE (ABSENTEE)

Skipper pulled the Land Cruiser into a dilapidated boatyard and nestled the vehicle between two rotting wooden fishing boats, making them all but invisible to the curious onlooker.

Skipper pulled off her sunglasses. "You knew I'd save your butt from the trap you've fallen into, but it's time to come clean. You've been missing too long to expect me and the rest of the team not to have some questions, so let's hear it. Where have you been?"

Anya's story could drag on for hours, but as usual, she condensed it into the abbreviated, yet still accurate, narrative. "I was captured by officers of your Justice Department after I killed those two men in Saint Augustine. My choices were go to prison for rest of life or work for American government to shut down Russian mafia. One of the requirements was that I could not contact anyone from my former life, especially any member of team."

Skipper dropped her chin and gave Anya a suspicious eye. "I'm not buying it. There are too many holes in that story. I know you were in Miami."

Anya nodded. "Yes, I was there. My friend, Gwynn—"

"Oh, so now you're making new friends, huh?"

"Yes, she was not friend at first, but she saved my life on yacht in Miami. She and I put ourselves inside—I cannot remember word for this—Russian mafia in Miami and killed a man named Leo."

"Infiltrated is the world you're looking for."

"Yes, this is word. We infiltrated, killed Leonid Petrovitch, and captured Antonio Alvarez, a man who calls himself new Pablo Escobar."

Skipper widened her eyes. "That was you?"

Anya slowly nodded. "Yes, me and my friend Special Agent Gwynn Davis."

A thousand questions churned in Skipper's mind. "But if you're working with the DOJ, why are they chasing you?"

Anya put on a mischievous smile. "This is part you will love. Person in charge is Supervisory Special Agent Ray White. He told me to break any law and kill anyone I wanted to get job done."

Skipper couldn't contain her laughter. "He had no idea, did he?"

"He did not, but this is why I am here. I stole shotgun from his Suburban, shot out two of his tires, hit driver of car in face with stock of shotgun, and stole car. You now know everything. Oh, except one thing. I have now beautiful dress made by Alexander McQueen."

Skipper shook off the randomness of the dress comment. "But if you killed Leo and captured Alvarez, why are you still working with the Feds?"

Leo and Alvarez were only one job. There are many more. I am now working in New York City to catch jewelry thief . . . sort of."

"You're trying to sort of catch a jewelry thief?"

"No, I said this wrong. I am sorry. There is man named Viktor Volkov. He is not really jewel thief, but he does steal diamonds."

"That's pretty much the textbook definition of a jewel thief, isn't it?"

"It is difficult to explain, but it doesn't matter now. I am working to catch him, but he has niece with same name as me, and she is dancer in second Bolshoi company in Moscow."

Skipper held up one finger. "Hang on. It's starting to come together for me. This Agent White guy. He called me and wanted my help finding Volkov's brother's murderer in Russia."

"Yes, he did this because I told him you were only person who could find missing pieces. And with these pieces, we can bring to America Anya the dancer and her mother."

"So, you're saying this Volkov guy in New York is connected, right?"

"Yes, he is Russian mafia, and he has partner named Sascha, but I do not know his last name."

Skipper silently processed everything Anya had told her before asking, "What do you want from me?"

Anya didn't hesitate. "I want you to tell Chase—and of course Marvin —I am okay, and I am sorry for making worries for them."

"They'll be relieved, but you could've done that by telephone. You didn't have to shoot up a Fed's SUV, steal a car, and have me perform a tactical exfiltration."

"Yes, I did have to do all of those things. I have to make Agent White know I am getting job done, just like he ordered. This is only way I will be free to come back and also bring Anya and her mother to America."

Skipper pressed her eyelids closed several times, trying to ward off the confusion-induced migraine. "That's not all you want, though, is it?"

Anya offered a genuine smile. "I want also your help to find murderer of Volkov's brother in Moscow."

"You know I can't do that."

Anya scowled. "Yes, you can. You are maybe only person who can."

Skipper laid her hand on Anya's. "Let me finish. I was going to say you know I can't do that without talking with Chase first. He's the boss . . . or so I sometimes let him believe."

"Yes, I understand this. So, you will help, yes?"

"I will help if Chase approves it."

The Russian's smoky blue eyes lit up, and she leaned across the console to embrace Skipper.

They shared a long hug before Skipper said, "I'm really glad you're okay. You had all of us worried, and Mongo—I mean, Marvin—is still out looking for you."

"My heart does not like to hurt him. He is good man."

"Yes, he is," Skipper said. "And he misses you more with every breath he takes."

"I will talk to him," Anya whispered. "It is only thing that is fair."

"What else?" Skipper asked.

"There is one more thing I need. I have to be at work tomorrow morning in New York. I have to catch train."

"Screw the train," Skipper said. "I'll take you. It's been a long time since I've been to the Big Apple, and I could use a beer and a good slice of authentic pizza pie."

Remembering the southbound train trip, Anya said, "I like this idea. It will be my treat."

"It's a deal," Skipper said. "Oh, I almost forgot. I brought you a gift. It's in the glove box."

Anya pressed the button, and the box opened, revealing a pair of Glock pistols, two passports, and a cell phone. She pulled one of the passports from the box and opened the cover. "This is no good for me. It has picture of you."

Skipper glanced over. "Yeah, that's not for you. Put that back. The phone is for you since I had you turn yours into a puddle of molten plastic on the engine of a stolen car."

Anya lifted the phone and programmed two dozen numbers from memory. "Thank you. Is nice working with team who is not government. They will give to me new phone, but it will take five days and will have inside tracking device."

As they accelerated on Interstate 95 north of Baltimore, Skipper turned to Anya. "It's really good to have you back."

Anya couldn't return the gaze. "I am sorry."

"Why are you sorry? You explained why you couldn't reach out. It wasn't your fault. It's just nice knowing you're okay."

"This is not why I am sorry. I am sorry because I am not back. I cannot be back with you and the others. I made promise to Gwynn."

Skipper frowned. "What kind of promise?"

"I promised to her I would work with government until we are finished fighting Russian mafia."

The analyst reached for the Russian's hand. "There's no reason you can't do both."

"There are many reasons I cannot do both. When I am inside . . . what is word again?"

"Infiltrate."

"Yes, infiltrate. When I infiltrate mafia with Gwynn, we are new people. You would say undercover. This means we must have large space between who we are pretending to be and people we love. It is too dangerous without this space."

"I understand," Skipper said, "but during the times you aren't undercover—you know, like between missions or whatever—we can hang out, right?"

"I do not know, but I want this hanging out with you and others."

"Speaking of the others, why haven't you called Mongo yet? I gave you a phone, and you've been playing with it for an hour."

"I do not know what to say to him."

"Just tell him you're okay. He's worried sick."

She dialed the number and let her finger hover over the key that would connect her with the man who worshipped the ground on which she walked.

Skipper eyed the phone and hovering finger, then quickly reached across the console and pushed the button. Anya watched the symbols on the screen indicating there was a phone ringing somewhere on Earth in the pocket of a gentle giant. She lifted the phone to her ear and heard the deep, kind voice of Marvin "Mongo" Malloy, former Airborne Ranger and current American covert operative.

"Hello."

She closed her eyes and pictured his enormous hand encircling the phone. "Marvin, it is me, Anya."

The giant froze in disbelief, too afraid to believe it was really her. "How do I know it's you?"

Anya swallowed the lump in her throat. "You once gave to me tiny purple flower for behind my ear on steps of Bonaventure Plantation."

His relief exploded through the phone. "Anya, where are you? Are you hurt? Are you safe? Where are you?"

"I am safe, Marvin. I am now with Skipper near Baltimore, and I am not hurt. I phoned to say I am sorry for hurting you."

"With Skipper? Why are you in Baltimore? Are you sure you're safe?"

"Yes, I am safe, but I cannot tell you why I am near Baltimore just now. I will tell you everything. I promise this to you."

"I'm coming to get you. I'll be at Baltimore-Washington International as soon as I can call Disco. It won't take long in the Citation."

"Marvin, no," she whispered. "You cannot do this. I cannot come back with you now. I am sorry. Please know that I am safe, and I will come . . ."

"Home," Mongo said. "You'll come home. Say it."

"I will come when I can, and I will explain everything, but I must now go. Please stop looking for me."

"Anya, I love you."

She pulled the phone from her ear and softly pressed the button, ending the call.

The two women rode in silence for another hour.

When Anya lifted her new phone again, Skipper laid her hand on top of the device. "No, Anya, don't call Chase. I'll brief him. Nothing good can come of you calling him right now."

"But there is something he must know. I cannot keep from him this secret any longer."

Skipper shook her head. "No, not now."

"But he is . . ."

Skipper turned stern. "Anya, listen to me. Whatever it is, it doesn't matter right now. He's in the middle of a mission, and he can't afford to lose his focus. Just don't."

Anya stared down at her phone for a long moment and then dialed the ten digits from memory. Skipper groaned in exasperation until Anya's call was answered.

"White."

"Agent White, she will do it. Skipper will find for us truth about Viktor Volkov's brother in Moscow, and I will be at work on time tomorrow morning. Goodbye."

23

SVYATOY BUBEN (THE SAINT OF DIAMONDS)

As promised, Anya stepped into the waiting car at precisely eight thirty the following morning. After two hours of sorting and matching diamonds, she looked up to Volkov standing in the doorway to her office.

"Good morning, Viktor. I have for you eight more pairs of matching stones."

Volkov ignored the progress report and crossed the room to within inches of Anya. "I have read stories of women working completely naked in drug processing operations, as well as counting rooms, where millions of dollars in cash flow through every day. Do you know why they do this?"

Anya spun in her seat and looked up. "Perhaps because boss is pig."

Volkov gave a half-smile. "Perhaps, but more likely, it is to keep the drugs and money inside the room instead of inside the pockets of the women."

Anya shrugged. "I believe boss is still pig."

The man picked at a fingernail as he intentionally avoided eye contact. "Your little sleight-of-hand work yesterday was impressive. There were only forty-nine stones in each of those bags when you arrived yesterday. I personally counted them twice."

Anya leaned close to inspect the fingernail that seemed to have Volkov's full attention. "Does this mean you are also pig and I must take off clothes? I am not afraid to show you my body, but I would prefer to do so in your bedroom and not inside office."

He dropped his hands, apparently no longer interested in the nail. "Show me."

Anya stood, slid off her shoes, and crossed her arms to pull off her sweatshirt, but Volkov caught her left wrist. The grab wasn't aggressive, and his grip was little more than light pressure, causing her to freeze in place.

He shook his head. "As much as I would love for you to continue removing your clothes, I meant, show me how you returned the diamonds to the bag."

She slid her feet back into the shoes she'd kicked off as she tried to decide how long to deny the accusation. "Maybe I let Sascha count forty-nine in first bag, then I moved two stones from first bag to pile from second bag, and I still have two stolen diamonds."

"That would've been a good plan," Volkov said. "But that would have left only forty-seven stones in the first bag, and we know that isn't the case. All three of us know one stone from each bag was in your possession for two days and not inside my vault."

Anya never changed expressions as Volkov continued.

"I've decided to believe you borrowed the stones for some reason and then returned them. I do not consider borrowing to be the same as stealing. Do you?"

"I do not."

He scoffed. "I can see this is going nowhere, but now you know I knew all along, and I let you lie to Sascha." He moved his finger beneath her chin, repositioning her face. "Look at me, Anya . . . if that is your name. I won't allow that again. Lying to him is the same as lying to me. He and I are partners . . . albeit not equal partners. I am, of course, the majority shareholder because I am the primary investor. I have many businesses around the world, and sometimes I allow people with a particularly rare skill or collection of skills to earn a small portion of these companies by committing their talents exclusively to my businesses. Do you understand?"

Anya nodded. "I think this is what Americans call sweat equity, yes?"

He took a step back. "So, you do understand. That's good. Now, on to the real reason I came in to interrupt your work . . ."

"So, accusing me of stealing your diamonds was not real reason?"

"I wasn't accusing you," he said. "I was simply making sure you knew that I knew . . . you know?"

She sighed. "English is ridiculous language."

"Yes, it is. We can speak in the tongue of our fathers, if you prefer."

"No, I must master the language. I have trouble with articles, but I am getting better. My friend, Gwynn, yells at me when I forget to say *the*."

Volkov scanned the worktable. "How many more matches are in those bags?"

Anya turned back to the piles of diamonds worth well into the hundreds of thousands of dollars. "Perhaps one or two more, but I can't be certain yet."

He impatiently drummed his fingers on the table. "When you are certain you've found them all, come find me. I will be in the vault or in my office, which is directly opposite your office. I have something special for you to work on."

Without another word, Anya moved her light back into place and returned to her task of matching stones.

Another half hour of peering through her magnifying loupe yielded three more matches. With the unmatched stones back in their velvet bags, she stretched, turned off her light, and rubbed her eyes.

The electric kettle had the distilled water hovering just below two hundred degrees when she spooned in the honey and dipped the teabag. As she turned to go in search of Volkov, she paused, turned back to the kettle, and poured another mug.

Viktor Volkov's office was exactly where he'd said, but it most certainly was not a mirror image of Anya's workspace. His desk looked like the deck of an aircraft carrier, and glass cases with some of the world's rarest stones lined the walls.

He motioned for her to have a seat as he finished a phone call in German, then he laid the handset back into its cradle. "How many more did you find?"

She placed the second mug of tea on his desk. "Three, but there are other near matches that may be close enough for earrings that will never be seen close together."

Volkov ignored the mug and turned away, apparently studying a Russian religious icon hanging where a window would've been if his office were atop one of Manhattan's ubiquitous skyscrapers instead of nestled in the corner of a vacant warehouse on the Upper East Side. He stood and ran his finger along the edge of the clear glass case housing the metal frame of the icon. "Have you ever heard of Andrei Rublev?"

Anya scoured her memory. "I have not."

"I'm not surprised. His name is known only to historians of Russian art and the most pious of Russian Orthodox scholars. Rublev was born in thirteen sixty. The exact date of his death is unknown, but most scholars believe he died between fourteen twenty-seven and fourteen thirty. He is the most important painter of Russian icons who ever lived. Every other icon ever painted would be compared to his work, and all would pale in comparison. Do you know why I'm telling you this story?"

She took a drink to hopefully buy enough time to think of a reasonable answer. After a long swallow, she said, "I do not."

Volkov held the pads of his fingers against his lips, kissed them, and then pressed them to the icon's airtight enclosure. "Because no matter how many thousands of icon painters came after Rublev, none could match the perfection of his work. He was finally glorified in nineteen eighty-eight. Do you know what this means?"

"No, I am sorry. I do not."

Volkov spent a long moment of silence staring at the priceless religious artifact. "It means the Moscow Patriarchate officially recognized him as a saint." He turned from the painting and settled back into his luxurious chair. "Thank you for the tea." Volkov touched the mug to his lips and let the smell of the aromatic tea fill his nostrils. Without tasting the steaming liquid, he said, "There is no such thing."

A pained expression overtook Anya's face. "There is no such thing as what, a saint?"

Finally, he let the warm liquid flow across his tongue and down his throat. "No, my angel, saints are quite real, and anyone who believes otherwise is a fool. What doesn't exist is the concept of 'close enough.' You see, thousands, perhaps even millions, of icons have been painted since the fourteenth century, but none have been close enough to the work of Rublev to gain their creator's glorification."

Anya leaned back in her chair, studying Volkov's cryptic words. "Is the same true of diamonds?"

Volkov raised his mug and smiled broadly. "You were paying attention. Forget about 'close enough.' Either stones match, or they do not."

He slid a key into a metallic mechanism behind his desk and produced three diamonds, each significantly larger than any Anya had matched in the previous two days. He clamped each of the stones into locking tweezers and slid them across the desk. Without being told to do so, Anya lifted each precious stone to her eye and examined them closely. When she'd nearly committed each one to memory, she slid the loupe into her other hand and examined the three stones with her left eye.

Volkov watched, intrigued. "Why did you change eyes?"

Anya stood, pocketed the loupe, and replaced the clamped diamond to the desk. "Stand and dance with me."

"What do you mean, dance with you?"

She stepped away from the desk and held up her arms in the perfect ballroom dancer's frame. "Come, come. Dance with me."

Hesitantly, Volkov stood, stepped into her frame, and felt her right hand fold over his left. She softly hummed the Viennese Waltz and made the opening step. "You are wonderful dance partner, Viktor."

"As are you, but I fail to see—"

"Shh. Just dance. And now, close right eye."

He did as she instructed, and as soon as she was confident his eye was truly closed, she moved her left hand to his cheek and laid the blade of the knife she'd been palming against the skin of his face. "Now, open both eyes, but do not stop dancing."

He reopened his eye and caught the glisten from the tip of the razor-sharp blade. In an instant, he recoiled and retreated several steps. "What is wrong with you?"

She smiled and sheathed the small blade. "Nothing is wrong with me, but when we choose to see the world with only one eye, we often overlook many of its dangers."

The look on his face made it clear he never expected his 'angel' to bear a sword of any length. "Why do you have a knife?"

"Because I am beautiful girl in dangerous city . . . Or perhaps I am dangerous girl in beautiful city."

Volkov returned to his seat, never taking his eyes from Anya. He motioned toward the stones on the desk. "Have you memorized these diamonds?"

"I have."

"Good. Come with me, but keep that knife out of your hands."

She followed him from the office and into the vault, where he pulled a ring of keys from his pocket. He opened a small door in the back wall of the vault and withdrew a velvet pouch from inside. Anya took the pouch from his hand and poured its contents onto the table. As she watched the light refract from every facet of the diamonds as they fell from the pouch, one by one, she counted eighteen stones.

Volkov motioned toward the scattered diamonds. "These few stones are valued at just under two million dollars on the retail market. Find the three matches to the ones you examined before threatening to cut my head off."

She glanced between the diamonds and the jeweler. "Cutting off someone's head with small blade is much harder than you think."

In less than five minutes, she set three stones to the side and bagged the remaining fifteen.

"Not possible," Viktor said. "No one can remember three stones and identify their matches so quickly."

"Perhaps no one other than me, but I have done it."

He lifted the diamonds from the table and headed for his office with Anya close in tow. "If you've done it, you may have any one of the six stones you wish."

He reclaimed his chair and pulled each stone to his eye in exaggerated motions. Pair by pair, he laid the diamonds aside until six nearly flawless gems rested beside their twins. Volkov motioned toward the desk. "Choose."

Anya set her face in the cold, stern look as only Russian women can do. "All of these are beautiful, but I choose, instead, to continue working for a bit of the sweat equity you mentioned earlier."

24

SOSHEDSHIY S REL'SOV (OFF THE RAILS)

Anya was only slightly surprised to find the door to her apartment unlocked and standing open a few inches. She stepped through the door with blade in hand and made her way through the darkened foyer without a sound. As she stepped from the kitchen into the living room, a deep, confident voice cut through the silence. "You owe me two tires and a new shotgun mount."

She switched on the lights, and Special Agent Ray White shielded his eyes against the sudden flood of fluorescence. "Do you want to tell me why you shot up my Suburban?"

"Because you ordered me to get the job done by any means. But you will be pleased to know I have not killed anyone yet."

"Sit down. We need to set some new ground rules."

Anya remained on her feet. "Where is Gwynn?"

"That's up to you, I'm afraid. Now, sit down."

She slid her knife back into its sheath and settled onto the sofa.

White stared her down. "It would appear we've developed a bit of a communication problem. I can do it in Russian if you're having trouble with the language barrier."

"I am not having any trouble at all. You told me to get the job done, and you didn't care how many laws I broke or who I killed. These are your words . . . in English."

White rubbed his forehead. "Not everything I say is meant to be taken to the extreme."

"I did not take it to extreme. I told you I have not killed anyone yet, but I did press my knife to Volkov's face today."

"I don't even want to hear that story. What I do want to hear is how you convinced Skipper to come onboard."

"I simply asked for her help, and she came for me. This is friendship."

White continued rubbing his head. "Speaking of friends, Agent Davis is not so patiently waiting to hear your decision."

"What decision?"

"It's become glaringly obvious to me that you prefer to work alone. When you don't have your sidekick hanging on, you make moves no one could anticipate, and you get things done. When Gwynn is weighing you down, things don't seem to happen as quickly. Gwynn has a skill you lack, though. It's called subtlety, and you could learn a great deal from her in that area."

Anya sat expressionless as he continued.

"So, I'm leaving it up to you. The reins are off. You can run all you want. You can butt-stroke drivers all day on the D.C. Beltway and steal all the cars you need. I don't care, as long as when this thing is over, Viktor Volkov and Sascha Goncharov are in prison . . . or dead."

"You did not tell me killing both of them would be satisfactory ending for this mission. I can do that tonight."

White held up a hand. "Calm down, warrior princess. We don't want them dead. That's a last resort when all else has failed. So far, we have no evidence either of them is dangerous to anyone except the diamond brokers and their bank accounts."

White sucked at his teeth. "I don't know what to do with you. On the one hand, I want Davis to learn from you, and I want her to keep an eye on you so you don't go off the rails. But on the other hand, I want to turn you loose on these bastards and let you do what you do best."

"Killing people with knives is what I do best."

"I know, but that's not all you're good at. So, let's hear it. What do you want?"

Anya didn't have to think. "I want to do whatever I must to bring Anya Volkovna and her mother to United States."

"I already told you what that requires. I'll get that done as long as you tie Volkov to his brother's murder and you put him and Sascha behind bars. The question is, are you going to do that with or without Agent Davis?"

"I want Gwynn to continue with me."

White rose from his seat and pointed at the Russian. "Then keep your butt on the reservation, and don't get arrested. If you do, I'm not bailing you out."

She gave him a simple nod of understanding and apparent compliance.

He looked down the hall. "Get in here, Davis. She wants you to stay."

Gwynn emerged from her bedroom looking like a scolded child.

White put a finger in her face. "She's your responsibility. You got that?"

"Yes, sir."

"You better, and for God's sake, find a way to control her."

He stomped from the living room into the kitchen and rifled through cabinets until Davis asked, "What are you looking for?"

"Something to drink. Don't you have any alcohol in this apartment?"

Barely loud enough to hear, Anya said, "I need a legend."

"What?" White said.

"I need a backstory. I believe Volkov will soon investigate my past. He does not know my last name yet, but some things happened today that make me believe he is going to open a door and let me put in one of my feet. Maybe the one with only four toes."

"Your legend is already in place in your real last name—if Burinkova really is your last name. You've been a working actress for three years. Your credit score is seven twenty-five, and you're an organ donor."

"My real last name is Fulton. I have passport and driving license."

White held up both palms. "Sure, we can make that change if you want Volkov and the whole Russian mafia to go knocking on your door in Athens, Georgia, and then on the door of that two-hundred-year-old plantation house on the coast."

"In that case," Anya said, "my last name is definitely Burinkova."

"I thought you'd see it our way. Now, about that drink?"

Anya pulled open an oversized drawer beside the stove and waved the back of her hand toward its contents of vodka, whiskey, and a bottle of merlot.

White pulled the Jack Daniel's from the drawer, poured three fingers over two cubes of ice, and swirled the glass. "Since everyone seems to be on the same sheet of music now, let's hear what your analyst had to say. Oh, and that reminds me. You owe three thousand dollars to the homeowners' association for the gardens you destroyed, and there's a guy with a badly broken nose who could use a new car."

Gwynn poured two glasses of red wine and handed one to Anya.

She accepted the glass and raised it to touch Gwynn's. "Here's to being together again."

White huffed and didn't join the toast.

Anya flicked the rim of his glass with her fingernail. "All of the damage you described happened in the line of duty while I was following *your* orders, so United States Justice Department will pay for tires and other things."

He wiped off the rim of his glass as if removing evidence. "You've been an American for fifteen minutes, and you're already a bureaucrat. Welcome to the circus."

Anya pulled the tiny plastic flag from her pocket and waved it as if on parade.

White snatched it from her hand. "So, tell me about this super analyst of yours. When will she have some background for us?"

Anya looked away. "Actually, I may have overstated her agreement to help us."

White pointed the stem of the flag at the Russian. "Overstated? What is that supposed to mean? You said she was on board."

"She is, but first she must confirm with Chase that it is okay for her to work with me."

"Chase? She's going to brief Chase Fulton in on this operation?"

Anya nodded. "Yes, this is how it works. Chase is commander of team, and Skipper—" Anya's phone vibrated, and she turned to the screen. "Speaking to devil. It is Skipper."

White groaned. "It's speak of the devil, you no-English-speaking freak. Answer the phone before I shoot you in the head."

"Hello, Skipper. You have good news, no? . . . This is good. . . . I will put phone on speaker so Agent White and my friend, Gwynn, can hear." She motioned toward the small table nestled in the corner of the room, and the three took seats. "Okay, Skipper, everyone is here."

"Yeah, well, like I was saying, Chase okayed the mission, but he's not exactly happy how it came about."

Anya reached for the phone and laid three fingers against the plastic case. "You said to him I am okay, yes?"

"Yeah, Anya. He knows you're okay. Are you guys ready for what I have?"

Everyone nodded.

Skipper said, "If you're nodding, you do know I can't hear you, right?"

White growled. "We're ready. Let's hear it, for God's sake."

"Chill. I'm doing this pro bono. That means you don't get to yell at me. Put me on the payroll, and you can yell all you want."

White eyed Anya. "Is that whole team like this?"

"No, the boys on team are terrible. Skipper is only good one."

The sound of Skipper banging on the phone rang through the air. "Hello! I'm trying to give a briefing here." The raucousness died down as Skipper began. "Okay, so here's the down and dirty. Before your guy Viktor Volkov went to prison and then came to the States, he was what we would call a cat burglar. His father, Dmitri Volkov, was a Communist Party official of some moderate rank. I didn't take the time to dig up anything on him because he doesn't really matter in all of this. The point is, Viktor and his brother—his name is, or was, Maxim Dmitrievich Volkov, by the way—were only eleven months apart. Maxim was the older one."

Gwynn scribbled furiously on a yellow legal pad as the briefing continued.

"Apparently, Maxim was the perfect little red commie—awesome grades in every class, athletic, hammer-and-sickle-flag-waving Russki. The problem was, even though they weren't twins, by the time the boys were teenagers, they were nearly impossible to tell apart. Same eyes, same size, you know the deal. Anyway, so his little brother, Viktor, despite being the spitting image of his perfect older brother, barely did well enough in school to make it to the tenth grade, and he dropped out some time during that year."

She paused to pour half an energy drink down her throat. "Ah, that's good. Sorry, I needed a drink. So, back to our fairy tale. Needless to say, their commie-party daddy was invited to all the little let's-hold-hands-and-hate-freedom parties or whatever they're called. Anyway, Maxim was always standing silently and obediently beside his party-official daddy like a good little Marxist, but our boy Viktor, who seems to have been a capitalist from the womb, wasn't big on the party scene. Instead, he was big on breaking into the houses of his daddy's commie buddies while they were drinking vodka and playing Cold War games or whatever. By the time Viktor was eighteen, he was already worth half a million, U.S. He stole everything from silverware to satellites. Okay, maybe not satellites, but you get the picture. It turns out little Viktor's favorite thing to steal was jewelry. In fact, he didn't just steal it, he learned to replicate it. Get this . . ." She paused for another drink. "Okay, I'm back. So, Viktor stole, bought, or borrowed one of those little spy cameras you see in all the old Cold War movies. You know the kind you can hide in the palm of your hand."

White rolled his eyes. "Yeah, yeah, we know. Get to it."

"I told you to chill, dude. I'm happy to hang up and you guys do this without me. It's not like I need the work. I've got plenty to do."

Anya gave White a shot to the shin beneath the table, and Skipper continued.

"Before I was so rudely interrupted, I was saying Viktor got a camera, but that's not all he got. He also became an apprentice in Moscow under a master jeweler whose name I can't pronounce, and it doesn't matter. Little Viktor, it seems, had quite the talent for creating look-alike replicas of real jewelry using fake stones and colored glass—that kind of stuff. He got so good at it, in fact, he would break into houses, lay out all the jewelry he wanted, take pictures, and then put the jewelry back."

White spoke up. "If all he did was take pictures, how did he end up in prison?"

"Patience, government dude, I'm getting to that part. So, Viktor would develop the pictures, make replicas of the pieces, and then wait for the next get-together of commie party yuckity-yucks. Then, he would break into the houses, swap out the real jewelry for the fakes he made, and vanish into the night. What do you think about that?"

"It's good stuff," White said. "But what does any of it have to do with Maxim's murder?"

"I'm getting to that part. Keep your pants on . . . unless you're more comfortable with them off . . . whatever. Here's the part where Mr. Good-Commie-Two-Shoes comes in. Maxim, as it turns out, wasn't as squeaky clean as everyone thought. Even though he was already married, he had a thing for the ladies . . . and I mean *all* the ladies. I'm talking eighteen to eighty, blind, crippled, or crazy. He loved 'em all. Now, don't forget Maxim and Viktor are practically body doubles for each other, but one of them is a jewel thief, and the other is a horndog, bedding everyone from Cindy Lou Whovna to Katherine the Great and everyone in between."

"Wait, wait, wait!" Gwynn yelled out. "I'm out of paper. Hang on just a second." She ran from the table and returned seconds later with two more writing pads. "Okay, keep going."

Skipper said, "Take it easy, chica. I'll send you a transcript when we're done."

"Yeah, but your transcript won't have my personal notes."

"Sure it will," Skipper said. "Didn't Anya tell you I'm not only the world's best analyst, but that I'm also a mind reader? By the way, I'm picking up some heavy lovey-dovey vibes from you about some girl named Sascha. What's that about?"

"Sascha's not a girl, he's a guy."

Skipper laughed. "Okay, that's cool. Like a boy named Sue or whatever."

Gwynn turned to Anya and mouthed, "How does she know?"

Anya smiled and shrugged as Skipper reclaimed the floor.

"Now that we're done with the background, and whatever Gwynn's thing for Sascha is, it's time for the good part. At some point, our little Russki slut-boy has a fling with a czarina or whatever. She was the wife of this KGB colonel who was on his way to a general's star in the Kremlin. So, little-miss-wife-of-colonel-come-general turns up pregnant, which is fine, except for one small detail. Her rock-star-one-star husband was aboard a ship in the Baltic Sea when said ship took a dive to the bottom. Before he was rescued, he spent enough time in the cold water to render his little trouser soldier unfit for duty, so needless to say, our friend, the colonel, had some questions about his lovely bride's swelling belly."

Gwynn froze with her pen hovering above her pad. "Did she just say 'trouser soldier'?"

Anya chuckled. "Yes, she did, and she is just getting warmed up."

Skipper said, "I'm on a roll here, so try not to interrupt. When Colonel Boris, or whatever his name is, figured out what was going on, he went on a manhunt. Now, the details are a little shaky from here, but it went something like this. He discovered Viktor trying to fence a necklace that had been in the colonel's family since Ivan the Terrible was in charge. Needless to say, the necklace was easily recognizable. The good colonel pulled his Makarov—that's a Russian pistol for the slow learners in the back."

"Wait a minute," White said. "We're talking about Maxim's murder here, but it was Viktor who was trying to sell the necklace."

Skipper sighed. "I told you not to interrupt. I'm going to land the plane. Just let me fly the approach first."

White threw up both hands in silent surrender, and Skipper continued rolling.

"Viktor, being a cat burglar, was fast. He apparently hit the back door like a jaguar. Is a jaguar the fastest cat? It doesn't matter. Suffice it to say, he was fast. The pissed-off colonel gave chase but couldn't quite keep up. Viktor made several ducks, dives, and dodges on his exfil route, but what the colonel didn't know was that Maxim had driven his brother, Viktor, to the shop, and he was waiting in the car around the corner, smoking a cigarette and singing whatever Russian horndogs sing. When the colonel came around the corner and saw Maxim behind the wheel of the car—remember, Maxim and Viktor might as well be twins from fifty feet away—Colonel Frozen-Pole emptied his Makarov into the wrong Volkov brother. Or maybe it was the right brother. I guess it depends on which one he wanted to kill—the jewel thief or the one responsible for the czarina's baby bump."

White scratched his chin and ran a hand through his hair. "How did you get all of this information in twenty-four hours?"

"It didn't take twenty-four hours. I only started on it just after lunch today, but I'm still not finished. When the colonel figured out which brother he'd killed, he had the other one, Viktor, sent to the Gulag. Okay, it wasn't really the Gulag, but it was prison. I just like the word Gulag and try to use it whenever possible. Somehow, Viktor ended up getting out of prison and finding his way to America."

"Wait a minute, though," Gwynn said. "What about baby Anya, the ballerina?"

"Oh, yeah, I almost forgot that part. It turns out Maxim wasn't only the baby daddy to the colonel's wife, but his own wife, Irina, was pregnant, as well. So, as Paul Harvey would say, now you know the rest of the story. Gotta run. Bye."

The three were left, jaws agape, staring at a dead phone.

White said, "How did she . . . ?"

Anya pocketed the silent phone. "It is what she does. I told you she would help us."

25

MAGICHESKAYA SHKOLA (MAGIC SCHOOL)

Like a good employee, Anya strolled into the diamond mine just before 9:00 a.m. to find Viktor Volkov's office door standing open. He rose when he saw her make her entrance and motioned for her to come into his inner sanctum.

"Good morning, Viktor. You are in good mood today."

"Come in, my angel. Have you had your tea?"

"Yes, but I would like another."

He poured them steaming mugs from the bar behind his desk and slid one across to his angel.

He held the mug to his lips and took a small taste. "I have to apologize to you."

Anya did the same. "Why would you apologize to me? You have done nothing wrong."

"Yes, I have," he said. "I have a bit of a paranoid personality. It comes with the business. I had some people do a little digging into your background without telling you."

Anya shot a wary glance into her mug, fearing it may be the final cup of tea in her short life. "And?"

He leaned back in his chair. "I learned some interesting things about you . . . some things you didn't mention."

She curled her toes inside her shoes, trying to focus the stress into her feet instead of letting it show her face. "What have I not told you?"

"Your real name, for one thing."

Anya swallowed hard. "Of course my real name is—"

"Tatiana, I know," he said. "And you're actually an American citizen already."

She breathed a sigh of relief but wished White had told her about changing her first name from Anastasia to Tatiana. "Yes, I am American citizen. See?" She pulled her plastic flag from her pocket and spun it between her fingers."

"Cute. You're a regular Betsy Ross," he said.

She turned her brain inside out, but she couldn't remember that name, so she took a gamble. "That is me, Betty Ross."

Volkov laughed. "Well, Tatiana, how would you feel about getting out of the office today?"

"I don't know. I would have to ask my boss, and he is terrible man."

Volkov's laughter continued. "Forget about him. Have you ever been to Nova Scotia?"

Still unsure if her background check was as clean as Agent White promised, her hesitance to answer left the beginnings of a frown falling over Volkov's face.

Allowing her cover as an actress to take over, she said, "I have been to only the airport in Halifax, but this is all I know of Nova Scotia."

He slapped both palms onto his enormous desk. "Then today shall be an adventure, and maybe you'll even learn a few new tricks."

"We are going today to Nova Scotia?"

"Yes, the airplane is waiting as we speak."

"But I do not have my passport. I will need to first go to my apartment."

Volkov waved off her concern. "Nonsense. You're with me, and when you're with Viktor Volkov, nobody checks for passports."

* * *

The drive to Teterboro took about half an hour, and after making their way through two security gates, they pulled inside a hangar where a

Hawker jet waited with the stairs deployed and a red carpet rolled out on the hangar floor.

The driver held open the rear door, and Anya stepped from inside.

"There is restroom inside your hangar, yes?"

Volkov motioned toward the rear of the vast space. "Yes, of course. They are back there, but we also have a lavatory on the airplane."

Anya looked between the back wall of the hangar and the airplane. "I would be more comfortable here if you do not mind."

He checked his watch. "We're already behind schedule."

"I will be quick. I promise this."

Before he could insist, she walked away, feeling for her phone. Inside the relative safety of the stall, she furiously typed a text message for Gwynn.

Viktor is taking me to Nova Scotia from Teterboro, and he thinks my name is Tatiana. His airplane is Hawker jet N111VV.

She pressed send and quickly deleted the text. If she were a sheep being led to slaughter, she wanted the DOJ to know where to find her body . . . if Nova Scotia was their true destination.

Anya climbed the stairs into the cabin of the Hawker and was surprised to see Volkov wasn't the only occupant.

"Good morning, Anya. It's nice to see you again."

The woman she'd known as Veronique a few days earlier had lost her French accent, and instead of two-thousand-dollar shoes and the elegant wardrobe of an aristocrat, she wore jeans, hiking boots, and a flannel shirt.

"Is nice to see you again, also, but I do not think your name is still Veronique."

The woman smiled and patted the seat beside her. "Come join me. I'm Veronica, but I enjoy being Veronique from time to time. I hear I'm not the only actress in Viktor's stable."

Anya took the offered seat. "I am sure you are better actress than me, but I am determined to become American star."

Veronica forced a warm smile. "You and a billion other beautiful girls. Once we're at cruising altitude, I have a few things to show you."

Curious, but less concerned for her life, Anya buckled her seatbelt and raised a finger for the flight attendant.

"Yes, ma'am. What would you like?"

"May I have blanket? I detest cold."

The uniform-clad young lady reached into a locker and produced a pair of blankets. The first was a lightweight cover, and the second was a heavier fleece-lined throw.

Anya pulled the heavier one onto her lap. "Thank you."

"You are welcome, ma'am. Is there anything else?"

Anya spread the blanket across her legs, snuck her phone from her pocket, and slid it between her thighs. "No, thank you."

The woman closed and sealed the door just as the jet began to move forward. The tow tractor pulled the gleaming white airplane from the hangar and onto the ramp. Minutes later, the engines whistled to life, and one of the pilots closed the cockpit door, separating the cabin from the brains of the craft.

After climbing out of Teterboro to the northeast, the pilots lowered the nose and settled the luxurious magic carpet into cruise flight at thirty-seven thousand feet for the short flight over the coast of New England.

As their speed increased, Veronica unbuckled her belt and slid forward in her seat. She held a fist toward Anya as if offering an unseen surprise. Anya instinctually stuck out her palm, and Veronica dropped one black marble into her hand.

"What is this?" Anya asked, inspecting the smooth glass orb.

"This is a prop. Think of it as a set of training wheels, for now."

Anya shook her head. "I do not know this term, training wheels."

Veronica looked up, wide-eyed. "You never had training wheels on your bicycle as a little girl?"

"I never had bicycle."

Veronica's expression fell. "Oh, I see. Well, never mind about the training wheels. I'm going to teach you to make your marble disappear."

Anya held the ball between her fingertips. "So, this is school of magic tricks."

"Yeah, you could say that. Watch me closely." Veronica held her white marble between the thumb and index finger of her left hand. She passed her right hand over the marble, lifting it from between her fingers. With the index finger of her left hand, she magically tapped the knuckles of her right, and opened her fist to reveal the marble gone. She crossed her hands again and tapped her left hand with the index finger from her right and revealed her empty left hand."

Anya smiled. "This is wonderful trick. But why do I need to see this?"

"You don't just need to *see* it. You need to master it. It's called the French Drop, and this is how it works."

Veronica talked Anya through the sleight-of-hand mechanics of the simple trick. After a few dozen iterations, each a little better than the previous, Anya could convincingly make the marble vanish.

"Good," Veronica said. "Now, let me show you a variation." She placed the white marble, once again, between the thumb and forefinger of her left hand, passed the right over, apparently lifting the marble as she went. "Now, you tap the right hand."

Anya leaned forward and touched the back of Veronica's right hand. She opened her fist to reveal a single black marble instead of the white one she had begun the trick with.

Anya gasped. "This is better trick. Teach this to me."

Veronica did, and soon, Anya had mastered the more complex movements of exchanging the black marble for the white one.

Veronica collected the marbles and pocketed them before producing two diamond-shaped pieces of painted glass about one fourth the size of the marbles. "Now, try with these."

Anya fumbled through the clumsiness with the smaller objects until she had the mechanics of the movements but still lacked the smooth flow of Veronica's hands.

Volkov stood from his seat and took a knee beside the two women. "How is your student coming along?"

Veronica turned to him. "Very well. She'll be a master by the end of the day."

Volkov turned to Anya. "Keep practicing, and Veronica will teach the advanced class on the flight home this evening."

Anya asked, "Are you taking me all the way to Nova Scotia to learn magic tricks?"

Viktor considered her question. "Yes, that's precisely what we're doing."

The flight attendant made her way through the cabin. "We're starting our descent now. We'll be on the ground in fifteen minutes."

Volkov returned to his seat, and everyone buckled in. The landing gear came down, and the pilots made a landing so smooth it was almost impossible to know when the jet stopped flying and started rolling.

Anya leaned toward the window. "This is not Halifax."

Volkov said, "No, it's Yarmouth, about two hundred kilometers southwest of Halifax."

She slid her hands beneath the blanket, feeling for her phone. She prayed the phone had found a local connection and that her thumb strokes were close enough to send the desired message.

She typed Yarmouth Veronique Volkov, and pressed what she hoped was the send key. The sleight-of-hand she'd learned on the flight made her manipulation of the cell phone far less clumsy.

The jet rolled to a stop and was, once again, towed into a waiting hangar. The flight attendant opened the door and deployed the stairs.

Veronica led the way from the plane, followed by Anya and then Volkov. A white Range Rover waited just beyond the wing tip, and Viktor ushered the women toward the vehicle.

Anya wasn't surprised to see who was behind the wheel when she slid onto the rear seat. "Hello, Sascha."

He turned with anticipation in his eyes. "Hello, Ms. Anya. Where is your friend?"

"You mean Gwynn?"

He smiled and nodded.

"I am afraid she is working today, but I think she would like to see you again soon."

He extended his hand, offering a card. "Have her call me anytime. I'd love to see her again, as well."

Anya took the card, gave it a cursory glance, and slid it into her pocket.

When Volkov was ensconced in the front seat beside his partner, Sascha pulled from the hangar and through the airport gate. The two-lane road was worn but sound, and the Land Rover gave them a smooth, comfortable ride across the rugged pavement.

"Where are we going?" Anya asked.

"We're headed to a place called Melbourne Lake to Dr. Sascha's laboratory. I think you'll find it fascinating."

The residential area near the airport soon gave way to tall evergreens and low green scrub brush. The scenery reminded Anya of the road leading from the chaos of Moscow to Sparrow school, tucked into the forest north of the massive city. The thought of what she endured in the dark, cold woods sent chills down her spine, and the bitter taste of hatred for the men who'd made her do things no teenage girl should ever have to experience left her mouth dry. Suddenly, Viktor Volkov was one of those men. The desire to draw her blade, insert it above the clavicle on the right side of his neck, and carve out his trachea was almost too much to resist.

26

PEKARNYA (THE BAKERY)

The assassin breathed in measured cadence: in through her nose and slowly out through her mouth until the need to tear the life from within Viktor Volkov for sins he'd never committed waned.

The paved road became gravel, and soon, a majestic shallow lake appeared through the trees as the stands of timber opened onto a wetland plain spreading to the southwest. The countryside was breathtakingly beautiful, with the few drifting white clouds in the endless blue sky reflecting from the glasslike surface of the serene lake.

Sascha pulled the Land Rover from the gravel drive and onto a concrete approach to a locked gate. A few keystrokes Anya couldn't see sent the first gate rolling along its tubular track, and they pulled forward into a sally port between gates. When the first gate had fully closed, Sascha entered a different code into the waiting keypad. Anya tried to imagine which tones corresponded with which keys, but she couldn't work it out. Soon, the second gate slid away just like the first one had, and they drove through.

Anya surveyed the security and counted four Belgian Malinois patrolling dogs along the perimeter of the five-meter-tall fence with coiled concertina running the length of the top. As they approached the only building inside the compound, she counted six security cameras with the tell-tale bulbous dome of motion detectors beneath each one.

They pulled beneath an awning on the northwest side of the building and came to a stop.

Veronica emptied her pockets into a plastic tray on the seat next to her and whispered, "Take everything out of your pockets, especially your cell phone. We're not allowed to take anything inside."

She pulled her jeweler's loupe and locking tweezers from her pocket and deposited them into the tray. As she pulled her cell phone from its position, she thumbed the screen to life and noticed a one-word text from Skipper.

Tracking.

She deleted the conversation as covertly as possible and added the phone to the contents of the tray. Next came her knives, all four of them, which garnered a look of suspicion from Veronica.

Anya caught her staring and said, "I have many things to cut."

Veronica shrugged. "I like to pretend to be French, so who am I to judge?"

With their pockets bare, the two women stepped from the vehicle and waited for Sascha to enter yet a third code and provide a thumbprint to a scanner beside the keypad. The locks built into the heavy steel door clicked, releasing at least three bolts. The foursome stepped inside to yet another sally port and repeated the entry security process.

Finally inside, Sascha turned to Volkov. "You're sure about this?"

Viktor silently nodded his approval, and the scientist led the way into a small but extremely well-appointed laboratory.

Anya committed every inch to memory as they traversed the room. Eighteen boxes shaped like microwave ovens lined three of the four walls. Although they resembled microwaves, they were much heavier, and instead of keypads to select cooking time, a collection of electrical lines and plumbing ran from each of them. They were like nothing she'd ever seen.

"These are our ovens," Sascha began. "Inside each oven, there are six small compartments with plates securely clamped inside each one. On each of those plates is a micro-thin layer of carbon. In a process we have perfected beyond any other facility in the world, we bombard each plate with plasma formed by combining hydrogen and methane at immense pressure and temperature. Under these conditions, carbon is stripped from the plasma and deposited on the base layer on each plate. Over time, as the carbon collects, diamonds are formed in exactly the same way nature created them eons ago. We've simply discovered, harnessed, and exponentially sped up the process. These are real, natural, authentic diamonds. The only difference is Mother Nature took her time forming her precious stones deep beneath the Earth's crust over centuries and allowed volcanic activity to bring them near the surface in certain parts of the world like Africa, and even the former Soviet Union. We grow ours in these ovens in a matter of weeks instead of eons."

Anya memorized every word as the scientist spoke, and she suddenly understood the operation. It was merely a high-tech version of exactly what Volkov had done by creating replicas of the jewelry worn by Russia's elite and exchanging his reproductions for the real thing.

Sascha ran his hand across the ovens as he slowly walked along the front of each one, peering lovingly inside through the treated glass fronts that must have been two inches thick. When he came to the end of the bank of ovens, he opened a blue metal box and pulled an object from inside. The object was roughly the shape of a cube, but the edges were far from uniform. In fact, they were jagged and malformed. The cube was a dingy brown color with streaks of darker colors randomly coursing around the surface. He held out the object for Anya to inspect.

She lifted it from his grasp and examined it from every angle with both eyes. When she'd memorized every surface of the object, she handed it back to Sascha. "What is it?"

His eyes lit up. "I'm glad you asked. It's my baby. Well, one of my many babies." He held up the rough cube. "This, as hideous as it may look to the untrained eye, is a three-and-a-half-carat diamond of unimaginable quality. Come with me, and I'll show you."

Through a pair of glass-paneled doors, he led them to a work area that resembled the small back room of Levi's jewelry store, where he mounted the diamond into Anya's setting. A man of indeterminate advanced age sat hunched over a spinning wheel resembling a small record player with a heavy arm where the needle should be.

"This is Sheldon. He prefers to be called Shel, and he is, in my humble opinion, the greatest diamond cutter who has ever lived. Here you go, Shel. Show Ms. Anya why we never judge a book by its cover."

The old man didn't look up. He clamped the brown, jagged cube into another heavy arm and applied the lab-grown blob to the spinning wheel. Soon, the unsightly dark surface vanished, revealing the clear, beautiful stone beneath.

Anya watched in fascination as the master craftsman continued to shape and polish the stone. When he was finished, he washed the diamond, rubbed it between the folds of a white cloth, and deposited it into Anya's waiting palm.

She reached for the loupe that had become part of her wardrobe but found only an empty pocket. Shel smiled and offered his loupe.

Anya inspected the stone from every imaginable angle and found herself lost in its utter brilliance and perfection. Reluctantly, she surrendered the flawless gem back to Shel. "I am without words. Why does the whole world not know about this?"

Sascha took the diamond from the old man and handed it to Volkov. "The world will know soon enough. Other labs are creating stones less than a fourth of the size of this one, but they lack the technology to push the limits as far as us. We are, perhaps, a quarter century ahead of our nearest competitor. As technology advances, this facility will cease to be an oddity and will sink into Melbourne Lake. Shel will be well over a hundred years old or dead by the time the others catch up."

The old man groaned. "Oy vey, I pray for being dead in these twenty-five years."

Volkov pressed the stone back into Shel's wrinkled, stained hand and motioned toward Anya.

The old man looked up. "Yeah? You sure?"

Volkov nodded, and Shel extended the diamond toward Anya for a second time. He closed her hand around the stone. "Young lady, you will someday have a beautiful daughter. Give this to her on the day she becomes a woman, and remind her that her mother was once also a beautiful, priceless gem in a world of worthless rocks . . . like these guys." He motioned toward Sascha and Viktor as Anya stared down at the breathtaking beauty lying in the palm of her hand.

She spun to face Volkov. "Viktor, I cannot accept such a gift. It is too much."

Viktor placed one hand on Sascha's shoulder and one on Shel's. "My dear, it is not a gift from me. It a gift from its creators, and you cannot rob them of the joy of sharing their creation with you."

She leaned down and kissed each of the old man's cheeks, and he blushed at the attention. "You must stop," he said. "You'll give an old man a heart attack. But oh, what a way to go."

She hugged Sascha and kissed his cheeks as well, but his heart was in no danger of stopping.

Back aboard the Hawker, Anya could not take her eyes from the enormous diamond from the lab.

Veronica leaned forward. "Are you ready to learn more of the real stuff?" Anya nodded, still transfixed on the stone, and Veronica held out her hand. "Let me have the stone."

Anya recoiled. No. I will not let you make it disappear."

"Fine," she said. "Give me the black-and-white glass fakes you were practicing with."

She handed over the painted glass and watched intently as the sorceress clamped the white one into a pair of tweezers. Veronica pretended to inspect the worthless piece of white painted glass through her loupe until she faked a sneeze.

"Bless you," Anya said as Veronica presented her with the tweezers that now contained the black painted piece of glass.

"This is what we do, dear. We find stones of exceptional beauty, replicate them down to the finest detail, and then make the swap. The dealer is none the wiser, and we then have possession of Mother Nature's creation while the dealer tucks away one of Sascha and Shel's masterpieces of a quarter the value, but practically indistinguishable from the original."

Anya spent half an hour perfecting the motions of switching one stone for another while clamped in a pair of tweezers.

The flight attendant materialized at her side with a terrified look on her face. "Ladies, I'm so sorry, but the pilots say we are experiencing a loss of cabin pressure. I need for you to sit one person per row and fasten your seatbelts securely."

Veronica moved one row forward while Anya stayed in place. She glanced to see Viktor pulling his seatbelt tight across his lap. The flight attendant then produced oxygen masks from compartments beside each seat and assisted each of the three in properly fitting the masks to their faces.

When she'd finished with each passenger, the flight attendant took a seat of her own, fastened the belt, and pulled on the oxygen mask.

Anya focused her attention out the window and watched the frigid water of the North Atlantic grow ever closer as the pilots descended the jet from altitudes where oxygen was essential for survival. She felt the jet slow and watched the flaps deploy from the trailing edge of the wing. The whir of hydraulic pumps followed by a solid thud in the floor of the cabin told her the landing gear had been deployed. She peered out the small window in search of the runway where the pilots obviously intended to land, but recoiled when one of the pilots, a husky, thick-armed man of perhaps thirty years old, emerged through the cockpit door.

They will surely not try to land the airplane with only one pilot in the cockpit, Anya thought as the ocean drew ever nearer to the belly of the jet.

She watched in horror as the pilot released the long red handle securing the door. He let the door open outward as the cabin filled with ice-cold air blowing in at whatever the airspeed of the plane was. The scene was utter chaos as everything that wasn't tied down in the cabin became airborne on the swirling, frigid wind.

The jet trembled violently as it flew in a condition it was never designed to experience. Suddenly, the muscled pilot drove a powerful fist into Veronica's face, rendering her immediately unconscious. Before Anya could react, the man yanked the unconscious body from the seat and shoved her feetfirst out the door. Without watching her fall, he reached through the opening and forced the heavy door against the violence of the wind until it was seated back in place, filling the hole in the side of the luxurious jet. With a gentle shove of the mechanism, the door was sealed back in place, and the pilot returned to the cockpit.

The flight attendant rose from her seat and returned the oxygen masks to their bins. "The situation has been remedied, but you may want to keep your seatbelts securely fastened until we land."

Back in the hangar at Teterboro, Volkov took Anya's elbow in his grip and spun her around as she moved to slide into the waiting car. "I trust you've learned all you need to know to replace our previous partner with whom we've, unfortunately, had a falling out."

27

MEZHDU DVUMYA MIRAMI (BETWEEN TWO WORLDS)

Gwynn met Anya at the door of the apartment as she was going out and the Russian was coming in. The look on the assassin's face immediately changed Agent Davis's plan. "What happened?"

Anya's non-answer spun Gwynn around and sent her following her partner back inside the apartment.

"Where is Agent White?" Anya asked as she poured half a glass of vodka.

"He's back in D.C. Why?"

"I made horrible mistake."

Gwynn took the glass from her. "What did you do, Anya?"

"I tried to be something I am not. I tried to be a normal person like you or Agent White or anyone we see on streets, but this is not what I can ever be."

Gwynn let Anya reclaim her glass. "What are you talking about?"

Anya stared off into distances Gwynn would never be able to fathom, remembering, in rapid succession, every training iteration, every press of the trigger, and every slice of her blade. Suddenly, every soul she'd torn from every target she'd faced since the lethal skills melded with her body and mind and consciousness flooded back to haunt and bewilder her.

As if speaking to no one and everyone simultaneously, she softly began. "I am killer. *Ubiytsa*. Assassin. I can never be less or more than this animal hiding inside this body of human." She turned to Gwynn and swallowed half the vodka. "I am sorry. I have put you in grave danger because I believed a lie of my own creation."

Gwynn took her hand, but Anya jerked away. "I cannot."

"Anya, you're not making any sense. What happened today?"

"Today, I realized I painted picture of Viktor Volkov as loving uncle to innocent, young girl. This picture I created gave to him wall to hide behind."

She took another swallow of the distilled spirit of the home to which she could never return. "He threw Veronica from airplane over ocean today."

Gwynn leaned in. "Who's Veronica?"

"The woman, Veronique, but this is not her name. She was Veronica, and they killed her, and I could not stop them because I was pretending to be normal person."

Gwynn squinted and held up a hand. "You have to slow down and tell me what happened."

She drained the glass and traced the rim with her fingertip. "I know everything now. Sascha has laboratory in Yarmouth, Nova Scotia. In this laboratory he makes diamonds."

"Wait a minute. You can't *make* a diamond," Gwynn argued.

Anya produced the stone Shel had given her. "Yes, it can be done, but it is terribly difficult without Sascha's equipment. This is diamond made inside lab."

Gwynn stared in mesmerized disbelief at the size of the diamond in her hand. "He just gave you this, or did you steal it?"

"He gave to me and said to one day give to my daughter."

"So, they're growing diamonds in a lab that are impossible to tell apart from natural ones? Is that what you're saying?"

"Yes, and then they exchange these diamonds for natural stones inside shops. This is what you saw Veronique do. She taught me how to do this, as well."

"Then they threw her out of an airplane?"

"Yes, and this is what they plan to do with me when I am no longer valuable to them."

"Well, you're a little harder to throw around than most people."

"Yes, but this is exactly what I am trying to tell you. I wanted to be normal girl, like you, who likes to go shopping and wear diamond ring, but I cannot be this thing and also protect people like Veronica or Veronique. I have to be what I am inside. I have to be killer without conscience."

Gwynn's mind flooded with the realization that she was sitting mere inches away from the woman she most admired and who she most wanted to emulate, but surrendering her innocence to become the machine Anastasia Robertovna Burinkova was would leave her dangling between two worlds—never able to truly exist in either.

"We have to brief Agent White. We probably have enough for an arrest warrant."

Gwynn made the call, and Anya briefed Supervisory Special Agent Ray White on every detail of Volkov's operation, including Veronica's murder.

He listened for fifteen minutes without saying a word or asking any questions. When she finished, he asked, "Is there anything else?"

Anya looked to Gwynn as if asking for help. "I gave to you murder. Is this not enough?"

White's voice echoed through the speakerphone. "Explain it to her, Davis."

Gwynn said, "Murder is only a federal crime under seven extremely specific conditions: if the victim is a federal judge or federal law enforcement official; an immediate family member of an enforcement official; elected or appointed officials; if committed during a bank robbery; if it takes place on a ship at sea per the Commerce Clause; if it's intended to influence a court case; or if it takes place on federal property."

Anya frowned. "Is airplane over ocean not considered a ship at sea?"

Gwynn remained in law professor mode. "Not unless it is engaged in interstate commerce as defined by the Commerce Clause."

Anya squeezed her temples. "It does not have to be federal crime. We can give Volkov over to the state."

It was White's turn to take the podium. "Which state were you over when Volkov threw that woman out of the airplane?"

Anya said, "I told you Volkov did not do this. It was one of the pilots."

"What was the pilot's name, age, address, and physical description? Exactly where was the aircraft when the alleged crime occurred? What was the alleged victim's name, and where is her body? When did Volkov instruct the pilot to kill the woman whose body we do not have and whose real name we don't know?"

"I do not know any of these things, but I know he threw her out of the airplane. This should be enough to arrest and convict him."

White said, "I agree. We could probably get one of the New England states to arrest the pilot, but even if he swears Volkov ordered the murder, it's still not a federal crime, and we have no jurisdiction. Arrest, trial, and sentencing, if convicted, falls to the state, and when was the last time you heard of anyone being convicted of conspiracy to commit murder when there's no dead body and no one knows the real name of the alleged victim who may or may not exist?"

Anya huffed. "American laws are too soft. In Russia, someone would shoot Volkov in his sleep."

"Maybe so," White said, "but we're the good guys, and that means we have to play by the rules . . . mostly."

Anya asked, "Does this mean you will not arrest Volkov if he has pilot throw me from airplane?"

White ached to offer any answer other than the truth, but he said, "We need you back inside, and we need you to actually exchange some fake diamonds for the real thing. And we need Volkov to instruct you to do so. We have to play by the rules if we're going to get an arrest and conviction in federal court."

Gwynn spoke up for the first time in several minutes. "What about the tariffs on imported goods intended for sale? How are Volkov and Sascha getting the diamonds into the country without going through customs and declaring the value of the diamonds?"

"That's an excellent question, and the answer is likely a federal crime. Anya, I need you to figure out how they're getting those stones into the country."

Everyone was silent until the silence bordered on uncomfortable.

"How much more?" Anya said.

"How much more what?" White said.

"How much more do I have to give you before you bring Irina and Anya to America? If I give to you Volkov's head inside box, is this enough?"

"Don't cut off anyone's head, Anya. You just keep yourself focused on gathering enough legal evidence on Volkov to get him put away for a long time, and I'll worry about the dancer and her mother. Got it?"

Gwynn said, "Okay, Agent White. I think we've got it under control. Anya goes back in, and we keep gathering evidence."

Anya held up a finger. "I have one more question. Am I federal law enforcement officer according to your law?"

White said, "No, you're a cooperating participant in a federal investigation."

"So, when Volkov tries to kill me, I am same as Veronica from airplane, yes?"

White cleared his throat. "That's not something we need to worry about right now."

Anya picked up the phone. "Wait for thirty seconds, and I will be back, Agent White."

Before he could answer, she pressed the mute button, temporarily blocking him from hearing anything she and Gwynn said. "Does person have to know the victim is a federal officer when he kills them for this to be federal crime?"

Gwynn pored through her memory for the exact wording of the law. "No, I don't think so, because there was a drunk driving case a few years ago in which an FBI agent was killed, and the driver of the other vehicle was charged with a federal crime."

Anya tilted her head. "Did this person get death penalty for killing FBI policeman?"

"No, he pled down the charge as I remember, but I can't recall exactly how the case ended."

Anya pressed the mute button again, opening the line. "I will go back inside business of Volkov and Sascha, but I will have federal badge when I do. You are powerful man, and this is simple thing for you to do. He will try to have me killed as soon as he finds someone else who can do what I can do. You would call this his business model."

"That's not something that I can make happen overnight, and I don't think you're in any position to start making demands."

"I am not making demands. I am giving to you a federal crime Volkov will commit. I will give back to you badge and credentials when you release me from my imprisonment with DOJ. Also, I am being patient. You do not have to do this thing overnight. I will wait as long as it takes. Goodbye, Agent White."

He blurted out the start of an argument, but Anya hung up before he could finish. "He will do this for me, yes?"

Gwynn smiled. "Yeah, he'll do it, but I have to tell you something. You're the first person I've ever seen who can manipulate Agent White. I've never seen anybody push him around like you do."

"I am trained to do this," she said. "But even if I was not, I am important piece of investigation. Without me, this would be much more difficult. Agent White is intelligent man, but I am maybe a little smarter. I am learning exactly how far I can push him and still have what I want. I think this time I may have pushed one meter too far."

Gwynn laughed. "No, I don't think you pushed it too far. You'll have your badge and credentials, but I think you should give it a little time before you push for anything else."

"This, I think, is good advice."

Gwynn motioned toward the empty glass beside Anya's hand. "I thought you didn't drink vodka."

The Russian tilted the glass toward herself and peered inside. "I did not say I do not drink it. I said I do not like it. I had excellent reason for drinking it tonight."

"Yeah, I'd say you did. Watching a woman get thrown out of an airplane is enough to drive anyone to drinking."

Anya shook her head. "No, this is not why I had vodka tonight. I have seen many people killed in terrible ways. Veronica was unconscious, so it was, for her, peaceful death."

"Then what's the good reason for drinking vodka tonight?"

Anya took Gwynn's hand and led her to the window. "All of this, and also you, are reasons."

"I don't get it," she said. "What are you talking about?"

"With you inside beautiful city like this one, it is easy for me to forget what I am and begin believing I am American girl. This will never be. I needed vodka to make my brain remember I am Russian killer."

"But, Anya, you are an American now."

"No, this is only true because of passport. You know how I became what I am. You know how I was trained and how I was treated. I was nothing except machine for them. This is what I am told for first twenty years of my life. I am only machine for Mother Russia. I am still this machine. Only flag under which I live has changed."

28

PODDERZHKA I ZASHCHITA (SUPPORT AND DEFEND)

Gwynn's phone chirped and yanked her from perfect sleep. "Yeah, hello."

"Davis, it's Agent White. Get up, and get your little girlfriend down to the Treasury Department at the corner of Broadway and Reade Street. Do you know where that is?"

Gwynn wiped the sleep from her eyes and yawned. "Yes, that's Federal Plaza at Foley Square, right?"

"That's right. Get her down there, and make it quick. Badge the security guy, and tell him who you are. He'll know what to do."

"Okay, fine. But why the rush?"

"Because Anya's ride to work always arrives at eight thirty, and today is not the best day for her to be late."

"Okay, I'll let you know when it's done."

She threw her legs over the edge of the bed and knocked on Anya's door. "Hey, wake up. Agent White says I have to take you to the Treasury Building before your ride gets here."

"Come in."

Gwynn opened the door to find Anya sitting on the floor and doing stretching exercises. She blinked several times and checked her watch. "It's four o'clock in the morning, and you're doing stretches?"

"Yes, my sleeping is finished. Why are we going to Treasury Building? Are we getting paid?"

"I don't know," Gwynn said. "But put on something other than yoga pants, and let's go."

The cab ride put Gwynn back to sleep, but Anya watched the city flash by the windows like a silent movie reel.

"That'll be thirty-two fifty."

The shrill voice of the cabbie yanked Gwynn awake for the second time. She slid two twenties through the glass and stepped from the taxi.

Just as she'd been instructed, Gwynn showed her credential pack to the uniformed security guard beside the metal detector. "Supervisory Special Agent Ray White told me to—"

"Yeah, I got it," the guard said. "Follow me."

He stood from his stool and pointed toward his machine. "Hey, Wilson, watch this for me, will you? I'll be right back."

"Yeah, sure, whatever, but don't leave me stranded down here."

The guard led them to a bank of elevators and up to the seventh floor. He pushed his way through a heavy oak door and into a conference room where three people sat near the end of an enormous table.

No one rose, but Gwynn produced her cred-pack. "I'm Special Agent Gwynn Davis, and . . ."

A white-haired man in a cheap suit and loosened necktie waved her off. "We don't care about you, Agent Davis. We're here for her. That is, if her name is Ana Fulton."

Anya and Gwynn exchanged looks. "Yes, I am Ana Fulton."

Gwynn was surprised how much of the accent was missing.

"Ms. Fulton, I'm Judge Carpenter. Come down here to this end of the room, raise your right hand, and repeat after me."

She moved to within a few feet of the judge, raised her right hand, and waited for him to speak.

He gave her the once-over. "Repeat after me. I, Ana Fulton, do solemnly swear that I will support and defend the Constitution of the United States against all enemies, foreign and domestic; that I will bear true faith and allegiance to the same; that I take this obligation freely, without any mental reservation or purpose of evasion; and that I will well and faithfully discharge the duties of the office on which I am about to enter. So help me, God."

She repeated every word of the Federal Government oath with only the slightest hint of an accent.

The woman to the judge's left stood and presented Anya with a black leather credential pack with the seal of the Treasury Department embossed on the outside. She opened the leather wallet to reveal a gold shield bearing the words "Department of the Treasury Special Agent" with the badge number stamped into the bottom. Adjacent the badge sat an official identification card with her photograph exactly where it should be.

The judge said, "I don't know kind of leash you are on, Ms. Fulton, but it just got tighter and a lot shorter. Whoever and whatever you are, that shield changes everything. Just ask Special Agent Davis, here."

Anya pocketed the credentials. "Thank you, sir."

"It's your honor," the judge said.

Anya turned back. "I'm sorry, what?"

"Ms. Fulton, you are to address me as your honor, not as sir."

She drew her cred-pack from her hip pocket and flipped it open in front of the judge. "And you will address me as Special Agent, not Miss."

Back at the apartment, Gwynn confiscated Anya's badge. "I'm putting this in my safe. If Volkov catches you with it, the whole world will come crashing down around you."

"Agent White was wrong. Apparently, he can get this done overnight."

"Yeah, he may have been wrong about that, but I was right when I told you that you shouldn't push him again anytime soon. By the way, what happened to your accent in there this morning?"

Anya shrugged. "When I concentrate on every word, I can hide accent sometimes. I think it was good to do so in front of his honor, the judge."

"You really are an actress, aren't you?"

* * *

Anya's car arrived exactly on time, but instead of heading for Volkov's office, the driver stopped at the corner of Forty-Seventh Street and Sixth Avenue.

"What are we doing here?"

Instead of turning around, the driver looked up into the rearview mirror, making eye contact with her. "Mr. Volkov said drop you here and pick you up again right here in a couple of hours."

"What am I supposed to do?" she asked.

"How should I know? I'm just a driver. There's an envelope back there. Maybe you should open it."

Anya tore open the plain white envelope to reveal a single square of paper. She read the short note:

Find, examine, and memorize four stones from four different dealers. 2.5 +/- .05 carat, round cut, D-E color, F-IF clarity.

She stepped from the car and leaned down to the driver's window.

He cracked the window an inch.

"I would like cigarette. You have one, yes?"

"Yeah, sure," he said as he rolled the window fully down and held up the pack.

She shook one from the pack and slid it between her lips. "You have also lighter, yes?"

"Geez, lady. You want me to smoke it for you, too?"

She took the lighter, lit the cigarette, and without letting the flame go out, she touched the corner of the note. The thin paper caught quickly, and she let it fall to the pavement. The driver motioned for his lighter. She slid it into his hand, pulled the cigarette from her lips, and crushed it out deep inside his left ear. The man howled like a dying animal, so Anya shoved his own hand into his mouth. "Stop yelling, and be nice to me. I am Viktor Volkov's angel."

He shoved her away from the car. "Yeah, maybe this week, bitch, but you'll be gone in no time, just like the others."

Careful to avoid Levi's shop, Anya strolled down Forty-Seventh Street, ignoring the hawkers as she went. Still fascinated by the Jewish men in their hats and dangling curls, she watched as they scampered about the street, ducking in and out of shops as they went about their day, seemingly oblivious to everyone else on the street.

The first shop she entered was crowded with shoppers, mostly young couples in the market for an engagement ring but unwilling or unable to pay shopping mall prices back in Arkansas or a thousand other places that weren't New York City's Diamond District.

The diamonds she wanted to see would be in quite a different atmosphere. She found that atmosphere three doors down. There were no Midwestern lovebirds milling about, only serious players in the high-end diamond game . . . "How you doing?" . . . "What can I show you?"

Anya smiled and stepped toward the forty-something, balding man who believed the three-days' growth on his chin made him irresistible.

"Hello, I am Tatiana. And you are?"

"I'm Armond. Nice to meet you, Tatiana. What's on your mind today?"

"I like big diamonds, and my husband, who is never home, likes to buy for me things I like so I will not leave him for younger man like you. Do you have anything big enough to make me smile, Armond?"

"Just how big are we talking, Tatiana? Three carats, maybe?"

She stared through the glass of the cases holding millions of dollars in beautiful diamonds. "I think maybe this is too big. Maybe two and a half carats is better, and I like round diamonds."

Armond unfolded a felt-covered pad and pulled a tray of stones from the glass case. He selected a stone, clamped it into his tweezers, and pressed the loupe to his cheek. "This one is beautiful. It's two-point-five five carats, D, IF. Here, have a look."

Anya took the loupe and tweezers and examined the stone from every angle, committing every facet to memory. "It is breathtaking, Armond, but I think price would also take away my breath, no?"

The man looked around as if being overheard would be a mortal sin. "It's marked at just under seventy-five, but if you love it, I think I can get if for you for . . ." He paused and rattled the buttons of an old calculator, then he spun the machine toward her, revealing the price of sixty-six thousand eight hundred dollars. "What do you think?"

"I think I should make sure I am getting best deal. My husband works hard for his money. If I spend it frivolously, he will maybe not let me keep spending so much."

"Hold on for just a minute," Armond said. "Let me see what I can do. I'll be right back." He took the stone, replaced it in the tray, and returned the tray inside the case.

When he returned, the beautiful Russian with her husband's credit card had vanished.

Slightly modified versions of Armond greeted her at five more shops over the remaining ninety minutes, and she left each of the shops empty-handed but with six spectacular diamonds firmly ensconced in her mind. They ranged in price from sixty-five thousand to nearly one hundred, and Anya knew every detail of each of the six stones.

When the driver pulled to the curb at Sixth Avenue, Anya was surprised to see a man behind the wheel she didn't recognize. He leapt from the car and held the rear door for her. "You must be Ms. Burinkova."

The demeanor of the new driver gave her a chuckle. "What happened to other driver?"

"He had an earache, and Mr. Volkov isn't tolerant of people who look for an excuse to get out of work."

She smiled and slid onto the opulent rear seat. They pulled through the automatic door in the nondescript warehouse and stopped at the door to the offices.

Anya stepped from the car, and the driver held the door attentively. "Thank you. I'll be sure to tell Mr. Volkov how kind you are."

Without a word, the man bowed slightly and closed the door.

The office door emitted an audible click as she approached, and she pulled it open and strolled through.

"Ah, my angel has returned. Come inside and tell me about your shopping trip."

Anya was amazed by the man's ability to sit idly by and order the death of an employee one day while appearing to be the kindest, most sincere man alive on the next.

He poured tea, and they sat together on the sofa in his office. "You found four diamonds like I asked, correct?"

She shook her head. "No."

His demeanor fell. "What do you mean, no? You read my instructions, didn't you?"

"Yes, I read them. What happened to first driver?"

"What difference does that make?" he growled. "Why didn't you follow my instructions?"

"The driver," Anya said. "What happened to him?"

Volkov narrowed his gaze. "He complained that you were demanding and claimed you put out a cigarette in his ear. Did you do that?"

"I was not demanding. I have grown accustomed to being pampered by your staff, and I enjoy this. He did not open door for me, and he spoke harshly to me. I asked him to be kind, but he refused, so, yes, I put burning cigarette inside his ear instead of inside eye."

Volkov tried to mask the amused smile. "Indeed, but the question remains. Why did you not find four diamonds as I instructed?"

She took a long sip of her tea. "I found six instead of only four. If we are doing what I hope, it will be much easier to pair four diamonds if I have six to begin."

He took her face in his hands and kissed each cheek twice. "Where have you been all my life, and how is it possible for your mind to hold so much information?"

"I have been waiting for you to come for me, and now, you are here. I must tell you of the stones." She widened her eyes and played the role of her life. With exaggerated excitement, she poured out every detail of the six stones, growing more animated with every word. By the time she'd finished, her face was flush, and her breath was coming in short bursts.

Volkov beamed. "You are perfect for this job. I remember when I first studied gems. I was just as excited as you every time I held a brilliant, rare stone I'd never seen before."

"It is all so exciting," she said. "I can find matching diamonds from inside vault for the ones I found this morning, yes?"

He patted her thigh. "I love your excitement, but the stones you'll be matching haven't arrived yet."

Sensing the opening she—and Agent White—needed, she took Volkov's hand. "When will they come? Sascha is bringing these diamonds, yes? My friend, Gwynn, talks of him always. She would love to see him again. Is this possible?"

He paused, seeming to consider her question. "Gwynn . . . She is the contract attorney in Connecticut, correct?"

Anya caught the attempt to tear at their cover story. "No, New Jersey, but I know you are too busy to remember details of other women. You've not forgotten me, have you?"

He traced the back of his hand lightly against her cheek. "I could never forget every detail of my angel."

She feigned embarrassment and looked away. "Perhaps you could tell Sascha my friend would like to see him again when he brings diamonds."

"Actually, he doesn't come into the city very often. You know how those scientific types are. He loves to be near his work."

"That is too bad for Gwynn, but I still have you."

She pulled at his leg, encouraging him to come closer, but he lifted her hand from his thigh. "I told you that I never mix business with pleasure. Nothing good can come of it, so, as much as I enjoy your attention, we must keep that outside of the office. Inside these walls, I am a businessman and nothing more."

Changing tack, she folded her hands into her lap. "I understand this, and I am sorry for being so excited about the diamonds, but they make me feel like animal inside. Nothing has ever had this effect on me before. I love you for bringing such beautiful things into my life."

"You are welcome, my angel, and I am happy you are happy."

Daring to push the conversation even further, she asked, "Speaking of beautiful things that make us happy . . . When can we see Anya dance again?"

29

SLUSHAY KAMEN' (LISTEN TO THE STONE)

Volkov's gaze fell to the floor of his office at the sound of Anya's question. "I don't know. I have left several messages, but she won't return my call. She's still angry with me."

Anya turned in her seat to face him more directly. "I am certain she isn't angry with you. She is only a child, and she has so much responsibility with the ballet company. How long will she be in New York? I would love to see her dance again."

"I'm afraid that will be challenging. They are scheduled in Chicago, Atlanta, and Miami on this tour, but I don't know the dates. We will be very busy after we pick up the diamonds . . ."

Anya stopped listening after his diamond comment. "Perhaps we can see her dance again next time she comes to New York. But I understand, the diamonds are important. When will we pick them up?"

Seeming to surrender to her questioning, Volkov said, "When Shel finishes cutting and polishing them."

Anya leapt at the door Volkov had left ajar. "I have great idea!"

Volkov recoiled. "There's no need to yell, my dear. I'm right here."

"I am sorry, but I have brilliant idea. If I can see stones while Shel is cutting them, I can describe to him how they should look to match the ones in shops."

Viktor held up a finger. "Don't go anywhere."

He stood from the sofa and nestled into his chair behind the enormous desk. With the phone in hand, he dialed the long number. "Sascha, stop Shel. Do not let him cut anything else until tomorrow when we arrive."

"We? Who is we, and why would I stop Shel?"

"Anya and I will be in Yarmouth tomorrow morning, and she will work with Shel to cut the stones perfectly."

Sascha sighed. "I don't know if this is a good idea. Bringing her here once was dangerous enough. She still has a lot to prove."

"I understand your concern, and with anyone else, it would be valid, but you haven't seen her come alive when she works."

Sascha groaned. "She is an actress, Viktor. Lying to her audience and making them believe it is authentic. This is what she does. Yes, she has a magnificent memory, but there is so much more to what we do. Viktor, this is our life. Our everything. We have to be careful."

"Listen to me, Sascha. I've done this since I was ten years old. I know what I'm doing."

Sascha surrendered. "I know you do, my friend, but we have so much to lose. I am afraid—"

"Yes, you are afraid, and no one can do his best work when he is afraid, so find a way, Sascha. Find a way to have faith in me. I need you, and you need me. We're in this together, but never forget your position."

"Yes, Viktor, I am the minority shareholder, and you never let that fact drift far from my mind. Of course I'll do what you ask, but in return, I want you to be careful for both of us."

Volkov gave a satisfied nod. "Good. I'm happy you haven't forgotten. Anya and I will be there tomorrow, and Shel does not cut another stone until we get there. This is agreed, right?"

"Agreed," Sascha whispered. "No more cutting until you arrive. I will see you tomorrow, my friend . . . and majority partner."

Without ceremony, Volkov returned the handset to the cradle and slapped his hand on the desk. "Sascha is excited that we are coming, and he loves your idea. We will leave from Teterboro tomorrow morning at nine. I will pick you up at eight thirty."

"I'm so excited," Anya said. 'How long will we be there?"

"Perhaps two days, no more."

"I cannot wait, and Gwynn can come to make Sascha feel better? I could hear only your side of conversation, but perhaps a beautiful woman would make him feel better. He puts himself under so much stress."

"You're exactly right. He does put himself under too much stress. He likes to blame me for that, but he does it to himself. Yes, Gwynn can come. She will be a fine stress reliever for him."

* * *

"What? Are you serious? No, I'm not getting on a plane with a history of women being thrown in the ocean. You've lost your mind."

Anya laughed. "You are not afraid, are you? Remember, we took an oath, and it is our job to stop these people."

"Yeah, I took an oath. I don't know what that was you took this morning, but we are not the same. You can fight off a musclebound pilot and probably throw him out the door, but I can't do that."

"Yes, I can do this, and I can also land airplane when he is gone, but there is something else I can do. I can protect you because you are my friend."

"Oh, boy," Gwynn said. "Here we go again with the friend stuff. I don't know. Regardless of what I say, it's not up to me. We have to call Agent White."

He answered almost before the phone rang. "White."

"Agent White, it's Davis and Anya. There's a twist, and you need to know about it."

"Don't keep me waiting. Spit it out."

Gwynn motioned toward the phone as it lay on the table on speaker.

Anya wasted no time. "I am flying back to Nova Scotia with Volkov tomorrow to work with Shel, the diamond cutter, and Gwynn is coming with me to gather evidence. Oh, and thank you for my badge."

"I think you may have forgotten how this works. You don't call me and dictate what's going to happen. In this case, though, you guessed right. You're both going, and you're coming back with enough to put these guys away for a long time."

Gwynn said, "I want to go on the record here as saying if I get thrown off that airplane, I'm coming back, and I'm going to haunt both of you for the rest of your lives."

Anya let out a laugh. "I do not know about you, Agent White, but I am already haunted by so many demons I will hardly notice one more."

White said, "Trust me, Davis. You don't want to live in my head. It's dark and scary in there."

* * *

Viktor Volkov was waiting on the curb when Gwynn and Anya emerged from their building, each with an overnight bag in hand. The driver kept his seat while Volkov ushered the women into the back. Traffic was light, and they pulled into the private hangar less than forty-five minutes after leaving Times Square.

They slid from the car, and the bulky pilot who'd done the dirty work on the previous flight reached for their overnight bags. "It's nice to see you again, Ms. Anya. Let me take your bags. We wouldn't want anything to happen to them along the way, would we?"

They climbed the stairs into the luxurious jet.

"This is impressive," Gwynn said as she nestled into the leather seat.

Anya sat beside her and fastened her seatbelt. The flight attendant immediately handed Anya a blanket, and she looked up. "Thank you for remembering."

The woman lost her smile. "I never forget anything, and I hear the same is true for you."

Anya kept her smile. "I am simple actress, nothing more."

The flight attendant said, "Aren't we all?"

Volkov climbed the stairs and leaned into the cockpit momentarily. Neither woman could hear what he was saying, but unlike Gwynn, Anya didn't suspect anything sinister.

Just as they'd done on the previous flight, someone towed the Hawker jet from the hangar, and the engines came alive. The wait for departure was a little less efficient than the exit from the hangar. A long line of airliners and business jets strung its way from the departure runway down the taxiway. After nearly half an hour on the taxiway, N111VV was finally cleared for takeoff, and the jet blasted into the sky like a homesick angel.

As the jet and its passengers winged their way to the northeast, Anya mentally replayed the sleight-of-hand techniques Veronica had taught her. She couldn't avoid replaying Veronica's untimely departure from the flight, but she tried to banish that thought from her head. There were too many other things needing her attention, and she didn't need distractions like a dead woman who enjoyed pretending to be French.

Gwynn leaned over. "Uh, Earth to Anya. Where are you?"

She shook off the mental film roll playing in her head. "I am sorry. I was thinking about my last flight."

Gwynn checked across her shoulder. "Well, how about staying in the moment . . . with me? I'd like to make the *full* round trip."

"Do not worry. I won't let the big, scary man hurt you."

Gwynn scowled. "Don't make me shoot you in the eye."

It was Anya's turn to check for prying ears before she leaned near her partner. "You will not shoot me in my eye because I am now federal police officer like you, and it is federal crime to kill me, remember?"

"I'll claim self-defense, and everyone will believe me."

The landing was less elegant than before, but the pilots got the jet safely back on Earth and parked on the ramp at Yarmouth.

Unlike the first flight, the flight attendant gathered everyone's passports and handed them to one of the pilots. He held up the little blue booklets. "I'll check us in, and you'll be able to get off in a few minutes. It won't take long."

Anya turned to Volkov. "We did not have to do this last time."

He subconsciously shot a look at Gwynn and back to Anya. "Sometimes, this is necessary. It will not take long. It never does."

The pilot returned with a customs agent who followed him onboard the Hawker.

The agent gave a cursory glance around the interior. "Does everyone speak English?"

Heads nodded, so he continued. "Welcome to Yarmouth, Nova Scotia. Enjoy your stay. You're free to deplane whenever you'd like." With that, he hopped down the stairs and disappeared inside the terminal.

The pilot stepped from the cockpit again and handed Volkov his passport. He held up the other two. "I'll hang onto these until we leave the country. We wouldn't want you losing them all the way up here."

Neither passport was authentic, so Gwynn and Anya offered no argument. Everyone deplaned without issue, but Volkov spent another long moment conversing with the pilots.

Gwynn's eyes lit up when Sascha stepped from the Land Rover.

He ambled over, ignoring Anya. "Well, hello, Gwynn. What a treat this is. I was hoping to see you again."

She shot a look at Anya, then turned back to Sascha. "This place is beautiful. Do you live up here?"

He looked around. "This is an airport. You've not seen beautiful yet. Just wait until we get to the lake. It's breathtaking."

Volkov and Anya climbed into the back while Gwynn slid onto the passenger's seat beside the scientist. She was as enamored by the scenery as Anya had been on her first trip from the airport to the lab. Sascha manipulated the security keypads just as he'd done before, and they drove through the sally port and into the enclosure. Once inside the lab, Volkov led Anya directly to Shel's workshop, where they found the old man napping in an upright position in his chair.

Volkov cleared his throat several times with increasing volume each time.

Finally, the diamond cutter opened one eye and then the other. "It isn't polite to interrupt an observant Jew during his prayers."

"The only thing you were praying to was the inside of your eyelids. It's time to go to work, you old relic."

"I'll have you know that without this old relic, you'd still be"—he paused and gave Anya a glance—"doing whatever you did before I made you rich."

Volkov pointed to a second rolling chair behind Shel. "See if you can keep him awake long enough to cut my diamonds."

She took the seat and pulled a pen and paper from the desk. "I will draw for you first stone."

When she finished, Shel held the paper at arm's length and studied the sketch. "This is a beautiful work of art. I hope I can turn this ugly old lump of carbon into something close. Young men who think they are master diamond cutters rely on electronic mapping software to plan the marking and cutting for them. A true master needs only his eye, his imagination, and his willingness to listen to the stone. They whisper to me, even in my sleep."

He went to work shaping the rough diamond and inspecting every surface after only seconds on the wheel. Two hours later, he wiped his hands and the stone with a delicate cloth and laid the diamond in Anya's palm.

She clamped the stone and studied its every surface through her loupe. "It is perfect, Shel. You are truly a master of your craft."

He blushed and rose from his chair. "An old man has to visit the water closet more often than a young man. By the time you have another sketch, I will be back and refreshed."

They repeated the process five more times with precisely the same result every time. Shel studied Anya's drawings and listened to the stones as they claimed their shapes under the master's hand.

When they finished, Shel looked as if he'd aged a decade. "I have reached my limit for the day, my dear. If you have more diamonds in your beautiful head, they will have to wait until morning."

She stood and helped him from his chair. A kiss on each of his cheeks seemed to revitalize him as the worn expression drained from his eyes.

"You know," he said, "I once knew a woman as beautiful as you. She broke my heart a thousand times before she became an old woman. And then, she broke it a thousand more. I've been married to her for twice as long as you've been alive. Goodnight, my dear. Whatever you're doing, please be careful. There are wolves afoot."

30

ETO GAZ (IT'S A GAS)

Gwynn stretched and forced her eyes open. "Where have you been?"

Anya whispered, "I am sorry to wake you. I have been working."

"Working? On what?"

"Go back to sleep. I will tell you in the morning."

Gwynn pawed at the nightstand and lifted her cell phone. "It's already morning. Tell me what's going on."

Anya sat on the edge of the adjacent bed and pulled off her shoes. "First, you must tell me what you learned."

Gwynn sat up and gathered the sheet around her. "I guess you already know what's going on in this place, but Sascha is creating diamonds. It's the most incredible thing I've ever seen. I can't even bake a cake, and this guy's baking diamonds."

"Yes, it is amazing. I cannot understand the science."

"Nobody can understand the science. Otherwise, the whole world would be cooking diamonds instead of crystal meth. It's clearly Sascha's baby. I think he may be the actual father of the process. If not, he's at least its fairy godmother. He says nobody can do it in the sizes he can. He may have just been bragging, but if he's telling the truth, this place is a gold mine. Well, I guess it's actually a diamond mine."

Anya shivered. "It is cold in here. I must get beneath covers." She undressed and slid into the bed, then adjusted to see her partner beyond the nightstand separating the two beds. "I have been with Shel. He is their diamond cutter."

"Is he as cute as Sascha?"

"Perhaps he was sixty years ago."

"Oh, I see. So, what did you learn from this Shel guy?"

Anya surrendered to the coming yawn. "He is not only diamond cutter. He is master of this craft. He made perfect recreations of the six diamonds I memorized from yesterday morning."

"How do you do that?"

"How do I do what?"

"Remember every detail of a diamond you've only seen once."

Anya turned from enthusiastic undercover cop to a tortured little girl in an instant. "It is skill I was forced to learn as child. You know everything about my training at Sparrow School, as you call it."

"Yes, that's where they taught you to get anything you wanted from a man by using, we'll say, your charms."

"Our bodies. Not our charms."

"Yes, but I was trying to be polite."

"It is three o'clock in morning. Time for polite ended hours ago. Anyway, when a man begins to talk after tasting our charms, it is not possible to press record button or take notes. We must remember every detail and recite exactly what we are told to analysts. Sometimes, also, we are required to make mental photograph of documents and recreate these papers later. I excelled in this part of training. Perhaps it is because I was so happy to no longer be inside whore school. Using my brain is better than other."

Gwynn sat up straight, her interest piqued. "So, you can remember every detail of everything you see?"

"Not everything, but if I choose to remember every detail of one thing, I can focus on this thing, and it will stay inside my mind for a very long time."

"Can you teach me to do that?"

Anya smiled. "You must first go to Sparrow School. Obviously, you are not very good at this because you are in hotel room with me and not in Sascha's bed."

Gwynn threw a pillow at Anya's head. "Cut it out. I think he may be gay, or maybe he prefers blondes. He kept telling me how he doesn't mix work with play."

Anya sat up and returned the pillow with much better accuracy than Gwynn's effort. "This is exactly same thing Viktor tells me."

Gwynn shrugged. "Who knows? Maybe they're more than just business partners."

Anya turned off the lamp. "I need to get some sleep. We will fly home later today with new diamonds."

She breathed in slow, rhythmic breaths in no time while Gwynn lay awake, piecing together the puzzle of Volkov's operation.

* * *

The sun filtered through the east-facing window of the small hotel room and drew Anya from her sleep.

Gwynn came from the bathroom with her hair in a towel. "Good morning."

Anya rubbed at her eyes. "What time is it?"

"A quarter to nine, sleepyhead. I talked with the boys already. They're picking us up on their way to the airport. They'll be here around nine thirty."

"That means I can sleep for another half hour. Try to be quiet."

Gwynn turned on the lights and the TV. The French-speaking anchor was reading the morning news.

Two minutes later, Anya threw back the cover and stomped to the bathroom. She returned with a toothbrush clamped in her grip. "Do you see this?"

Gwynn looked at the brush. "What are you going to do, brush my teeth for me?"

"No, I'm going to stab you with it as soon as I can find a way to sharpen it."

Gwynn slapped away the weapon and stepped close to Anya. She whispered, "I was thinking this morning while you were sleeping. If they're paranoid enough to keep our passports and refuse our charms, they're probably paranoid enough to bug this room. The TV will help mask our voices."

"Okay, maybe I will not stab you. Did we say anything incriminating when I came in early this morning?"

"How should I know? I was barely awake, and you're the one with the eidetic memory."

"Is not eidetic. Is selective photographic."

"Whatever. Just get ready to go. There's a restaurant in the hotel. We can grab some breakfast before they pick us up."

* * *

Breakfast was coffee, Danishes, and fruit.

"You don't think they suspect us of being feds, do you?"

Anya thought about the question. "I do not think so. We would not be here if this is what they believe. I think they are cautious, especially Sascha."

Gwynn wiped her mouth with a paper napkin. "Speak of the devil . . . They're here."

They left the restaurant and climbed into the Land Rover for the ride back to the airport.

"Good morning," Volkov said. "Did you get some rest after your long night at the lab?"

"Yes, but Gwynn was very rude this morning and turned on French television."

He said, "You can get some sleep on the plane."

Gwynn tried not to let her fear of Anya sleeping on the plane show on her face. There was no way she'd let her sleep, especially if they had a second "pressurization issue" over the ocean. She laid a hand across Sascha's shoulder. "Are you coming back to New York with us?"

"Yes, I have some things to do in the city. I'll be there for a few days."

Gwynn smiled. "Maybe we can spend a little time away from work while you're there."

He met her eyes in the mirror. "I'd like that. We all need an escape from work from time to time."

Compared to Sascha's lab, security at the Yarmouth Airport was nonexistent. Anya recorded every detail of the scene as Volkov handed a metallic change purse to the bulky pilot, who nodded and pocketed the bag that looked minuscule in his enormous hand.

A fuel truck arrived, and the driver approached the uniformed pilot, who slid a few bills of Canadian cash into his palm. In return, the driver pulled the hose from the jet fuel reel and handed it to the pilot. The oddity of the exchange struck Anya, so she slowed her pace to continue watching the scene unfold. By the time she reached the bottom of the stairs into the Hawker, the pilot was beneath the tail of the aircraft. He knelt, pulled the metal change purse from his pocket, and carefully laid it inside the fuel nozzle. He reached above his head, opened the access panel, and removed the fuel cap.

Making the connection of the nozzle to the filler valve, he tapped on the side of the plane and yelled, "Open up!"

Anya shot a glance up the stairs to see the second pilot pressing a series of switches on the fueling panel. He looked down the stairs and noticed her. "Tell him the valves are open."

Anya leaned down and made eye contact with the muscular pilot. "Valves are open."

He gave a nod and opened the valve on the hose, sending jet fuel—and the coin purse—rushing into the ventral tank of the Hawker.

She climbed the stairs and noticed Gwynn sitting beside Sascha instead of saving the seat for her. Anya chose an empty seat that looked like it would make a perfectly comfortable sleeping nest.

When Volkov boarded the plane, he, once again, leaned into the cockpit for a thirty-second conversation. This time, though, he pocketed a pair of American passports before making his way to his preferred seat.

Before they'd leveled in cruise flight, Anya was sleeping like a kitten, and Gwynn was interrogating the scientist under the guise of getting to know him.

Almost an hour into the flight, the plane bucked as if it were being tossed around inside a washing machine. Anya opened her eyes to see the thick-chested pilot emerge from the cockpit. Gwynn turned in her seat to make eye contact with her, and Anya gave her a little wink.

The pilot held up both hands. "There's no need to worry. We're experiencing a little turbulence, but air traffic control has just cleared us to descend a little early. We should be back in smooth air in no time, but if you wouldn't mind, we'd like you to put on your seatbelts nice and snug for the duration of the flight.

Less dramatic than loss of cabin pressure, but equally effective to explain an early descent and seatbelts, Anya thought as she poised to defend her friend and partner, should it become necessary. Her hand slid instinctually to the four-inch fighting knife concealed in her belt. It was still there and ready for use if muscle-boy fly-guy opened the door again.

Gwynn dug her fingernails into the arms of the luxurious seat as the turbulence worsened in their descent.

Sascha pulled her hand from the armrest and wrapped it in his own. "It's okay. It's just a little rough air. We'll be fine in a few minutes. These pilots are excellent."

Gwynn squeezed his hand. "I'm just a nervous flyer, that's all."

Anya made a show of tightening her belt, but when she was certain no one was watching, she freed the buckle, leaving it to look as if it were secure. Should Captain America come back out of the cockpit with the intention of tossing her partner into the ocean, every advantage would be crucial.

As the descent continued, the bumps lessened until the air was smooth, and Gwynn released her crushing grasp of Sascha's hand. Anya pressed the blade back into its sheath beneath her belt until she felt the click.

The wheels kissed the runway back at Teterboro, and the pilots taxied the Hawker to Volkov's hangar, where a customs officer waited to board the plane. The inspection that followed was a bit more thorough than the cursory glance at Yarmouth, but the officer dug no deeper than unzipping a pair of overnight bags and asking, "Does anyone have anything to declare?"

Volkov's private fuel truck pulled to the rear of the plane, and the driver connected a nozzle to the fill valve on the ventral tank. Seconds later, he closed the valve, stood, and returned to his truck, where the waiting pilot collected the metallic change purse in a plastic bag.

31

SOSTOYANIYE SERDTSA (HEART CONDITION)

The debriefing conducted by Special Agent White was unlike anything Anya had experienced. "We're on the verge of making the biggest non-drug-related bust of my career. We've got one more crucial step to make, and as long as Anya doesn't blow it, we've got these guys nailed to the wall."

Anya said, "I promise I will not steal anymore shotguns or break anyone's nose this time."

"Break all the noses you want, Treasury Agent Fulton. Just make sure you put the real diamonds in Volkov's hand before the sun goes down tomorrow."

"Is this the plan? You will make arrest when Volkov has diamonds?"

"You bet it is, Red Sonja. The second you deliver the real diamonds, we're crashing the gate, and everybody's going to jail, including you. I want you to put up a fight, too. Don't go quietly. The SWAT team may rough you up a little, but Volkov needs to believe you're on his team the whole time."

"In this case, am I allowed to hurt people?"

"You can get a little rough with them. They like a challenge, but don't pull a knife on them. They'll drill you full of holes if you draw a weapon."

* * *

Anya's attire wasn't blue jeans and a sweatshirt when she arrived at the office the next morning.

"You look spectacular, like the gorgeous Russian princess you are."

Volkov couldn't tear his eyes away from the skirt and sweater combination Gwynn had insisted Anya wear to make the diamond swaps.

"Spasibo, Viktor. I like when you are pleased."

"I can't imagine any man being displeased with you. Are you certain you understand the task today?"

She nodded with confidence. "Yes, I will exchange each of your stones for the six diamonds in the shops if they have not sold since I saw them two days ago."

"Not exactly."

Anya raised an eyebrow. "There is change of plan?"

"Yes. Wait here." He turned for the vault and returned a moment later with a stack of cash and the metal change purse. "Here are the diamonds. You'll want to sort them so you don't make a mistake during the exchange."

"I understand, but why do I need all this money?"

Viktor tapped his fingers on the banded bills. "This is contingency money in case someone gets suspicious. If you believe you have been caught, immediately purchase the diamond but negotiate the price. Five percent is reasonable, but first, ask for ten percent off."

"I will not get caught. This is for certain."

Viktor smiled. "Even the best get caught sooner or later, my angel. Take the money. We cannot afford to have you discovered. Diamonds in the city are a small community, and that community talks incessantly. This is a temporary game at best. Knowing when to get out is the key, but before that time comes, you and I will make a fortune together."

Anya slid the cash into her purse and separated the stones in the order of the shops she would visit. "Speaking of making a fortune together, we have not discussed my percentage."

Viktor lowered his chin. "You agreed to a set rate of five thousand dollars per week."

Anya handed her purse to him. "You are correct. This was our agreement, so I will go back inside office and continue matching stones. This is what we agreed."

Volkov waggled a finger. "I should've known. You're a shrewd one. What is your proposal?"

Anya reclaimed her purse and counted ninety thousand dollars in banded bills inside. "I will bring to you six diamonds at end of day, and I will keep money. If I have to make purchase, I will keep nothing."

"No one can exchange six diamonds in the same day without getting caught at least once. There's no chance of you keeping that money, but I'll agree to your terms just to teach you a lesson."

The more courteous driver held the door for her, and Viktor gave her a peck on the cheek for good luck. "I will see you in a few hours. Oh, and just in case you get any ideas about running off with my diamonds and my cash, don't forget how accidents can happen. Poor Veronique."

The longing to break his neck was almost impossible to resist, but instead, she bowed her head in submission and slid onto the rear seat of the Bentley.

The warehouse door opened, allowing them to pull onto the street before it quickly closed behind them.

"If you wouldn't mind," Anya said, "I must go to my apartment before you take me to Diamond District. I have small medical condition, and I did not take medicine this morning. I was so excited for today."

The driver looked up in the mirror and sighed. "Mr. Volkov made it clear that I was to drop you at Forty-Seventh and Sixth and nowhere else."

"Then we must go back inside so I can explain to him about my heart condition."

The driver checked his watch. "You're just going to run straight up, grab the meds, and right back down, right?"

"Yes, I promise I will only be a minute."

He wiped a bead of sweat from his forehead. "If he finds out, we're both dead, so don't hang me out to dry."

"I will not, I promise.

"Me neither, but you can't tell the boss. Oh, and how 'bout you leave your purse in the car? You know, just for a little insurance for me."

She gave him the smile she'd practiced endlessly in the woods outside Moscow when she learned to turn her body into the bait no man could resist.

Traffic was heavy, but they made the drive to Times Square in fifteen minutes. Anya didn't wait for him to open the door. She bolted from the back seat and up the stairs with her purse tucked beneath her arm.

The driver rolled down the window and yelled, "Hey! The purse!"

She ignored him and continued through the door and into the elevator. When she returned to the car, she slid onto the seat. "I am sorry. It is habit for me to always keep purse under my arm in city."

"It's okay," he said, "but only 'cause you're back. I just wanted a little insurance policy to make sure you weren't going to rabbit on me. It's all good now. Did you get your medicine?"

"Yes, I did. Thank you."

"Yeah, my sister's got a heart thing, too. Vitribu-something or another. I don't know. But she takes a pill every day."

"Same for me. Thank you again for making the stop."

She stepped from the car at Forty-Seventh and Sixth with everything she needed tucked beneath her arm. When she walked into the first shop, she did a double take when she saw Special Agent Johnathon Johnny-Mac McIntyre leaning against the counter and talking with one of the brokers. He immediately looked away from the leggy blonde wearing the skirt she thought would get the attention she deserved.

She spotted the gentleman who'd shown her the eighty-thousand-dollar diamond two days before and gave him a little wave.

He blushed and held up a hand. "I see you've come back. Your stone is still available, but a couple came in here last night and fell in love with it. It may not be here much longer if you don't grab it today."

Anya pulled a chair to the glass case. "Let me take one more look at it, please."

Instead of pulling the entire tray, the man plucked the stone with his tweezers and offered it to her. She reached up, took the tweezers from his hand, and stared at the broker.

"Ah, forgive me," he said. "I almost forgot. Here's a loupe." He handed her the magnifier and waited patiently for her to examine the stone.

As she studied the facets, Johnny-Mac dropped the loupe he'd been using. As it bounced across the top of the glass case, he made a show of dropping the tweezers and diamond. This gave Anya the diversion she needed to make her first exchange. The trade happened too fast for even the security cameras to catch, and she handed the lab-created stone back to the broker as she pocketed the authentic, natural diamond.

"How much did you say it cost? I am sorry, but I cannot remember."

He gave the stone a look through his loupe. "It is a beautiful diamond. I'm sure you know quality when you see it. Since there is other interest in the stone, it's risky for me to discount it for you."

She laid a hand across his wrist. "But I saw it first."

"Yes, you did, so because of that, it's sixty-five for you. But only today. If you walk away, I have to rescind the offer."

She smiled. "It's a fifty-five-thousand-dollar diamond, and I have cash."

He recoiled. "I'm sorry, but sixty-five is the best I can do."

She shrugged, stood, and walked from the shop. The pen camera protruding from Johnny-Mac's pocket captured a barely perceptible wink and nod from the Russian.

Five more shops yielded nearly identical results with Johnny-Mac present for the first, third, and sixth. Other agents masquerading as customers in the three remaining shops captured the video evidence the Justice Department needed, and Anya never came close to being caught by any of the brokers. Her hands moved like lightning as she exchanged stone after stone with Sascha's near-perfect replicas.

This time, the driver was waiting at Fifth Avenue and Forty-Seventh with the rear door held open. "I hope you had a pleasant day of shopping."

"I did," she said as she situated herself on the rear seat. "It was perfectly delightful. I am sorry you had to wait for me all day."

"I don't mind waiting," he said. "Mr. Volkov pays me well."

"I am sure he does."

Approaching the warehouse, Anya noticed a telephone service van parked thirty yards down the street from the entrance. Beyond the van, a pair of traffic cones stood to eliminate any unwanted visitors from turning onto the street. As the driver made the turn into the warehouse, Anya saw the eyes and salt-and-pepper hair of Supervisory Special Agent Ray White in the cracked mirror of the van.

As the door closed behind the car when they pulled into the warehouse, Anya turned just in time to see a fiber-optic camera lens being slid beneath the rubber seal of the heavy door.

32

SNOVA PROPAL (MISSING AGAIN)

Supervisory Special Agent Ray White keyed the microphone on his two-way radio. "The clock is running. I need everybody on their toes. When we hit it, we hit hard, and everybody comes out alive. Call your positions."

"Entry Team is go."

"Commo is go."

"EMS is go."

"Legal is go."

"Perimeter is no go."

White keyed up again. "Stand by. Perimeter, say condition."

"Perimeter is no go. There's a garbage truck broken down in the alley on the southeast corner. We can't get in position."

"Roger, stand by, Perimeter. Legal, Command-One."

"Go for Legal."

White said, "Can I move that garbage truck by force?"

The attorney from the Southern District of New York said, "Stand by, Command. We're checking."

"We don't have time to stand by, Legal. I need that truck moved, now."

The attorney keyed her mic again. "I said stand by, Command-One. I'll get back to you."

White threw the radio onto the seat and cursed the necktie army. He threw open the door of the van and leapt from the seat. Two hundred strides later, he was standing in front of a heavy tow truck in the process of repossessing some poor sap's Mustang. "Hey, buddy!"

The tow truck driver looked up. "Look, man, I'm just doing my job. This ain't personal, but you gotta make your payments, man."

White stopped a few strides in front of the burly driver and held up his badge.

The driver threw up both hands. "Look, man, I don't know what that crazy broad told you, but I didn't do nothin' to her."

White shoved the four hundred bucks back into his pocket, suddenly realizing he had a much better negotiating tool. "Oh, yeah. That's what she said you'd say when we picked you up, but look . . . I can probably look the other way on that thing. Who needs that kinda headache anyway, right?"

"Yeah, that's right, man. But I know cops don't do nothing for free. What do you want from me?"

White hid the smile, but inside he was doing the happy puppy dance. "There's a broken-down garbage truck in the alley back there, and I need it moved."

"Is it one of them big ones, or the little community trucks?"

"What difference does it make? I only need you to move it ten feet. That is, unless your little truck can't handle it, in which case, I guess you've got the right to remain silent."

The tow truck driver threw his gloves into the toolbox and laid his meaty arm across a series of levers, sending the Mustang banging back to the ground. "Just ten feet, you say?"

"That's right. Just pull it out of the alley enough to get a few guys in there."

The driver wiped his brow. "If I do this thing, you're gonna look the other way on that other thing, right? And I got your word on that?"

"You got it. I swear I won't be looking for you, and I'll make sure nobody in my precinct is coming after you. But you gotta leave that girl alone, you hear me?"

He yanked open the door and slid behind the wheel. "Trust me, man. I don't want nothin' else to do with that crazy chick."

Five minutes later, the agent in command of the perimeter team keyed his mic. "Nice going, Command. Perimeter is a go."

White picked up his radio. "Roger, Perimeter."

Almost before he'd stopped talking, the radio squawked to life. "Command-One, this is Legal. Stand down. Sanitation says they'll have the truck removed within an hour."

White couldn't hold back the smile any longer. "Roger, Legal. You're breaking up a little. Go to channel two, and stand by."

"Roger. Legal will be standing by on channel two."

"Hey, SWAT. Are you guys ready to have a little fun?"

"Affirmative, sir."

White checked his watch. "Commo, say interior condition."

"Interior is condition two. Your girl is inside the interior, and the driver is sitting on the hood of the car, smoking a cigarette. No obstructions, no security, no problems. Hit 'em at will."

"Roger, Commo. Did you hear that, Entry?"

The Entry Team commander motioned for helmets on and face shields down, then keyed his mic. "Rock and roll."

White took a long breath and keyed up. "Okay, Entry, knock on the door nice and polite, and SWAT, you go ahead and do the same."

"Entry, rolling!"

"SWAT, rolling!"

White pulled the old-fashioned stopwatch from his pocket and pressed the single button on the crown.

The mirror of White's van provided a six-inch square view of the action, but he wanted a wide-screen high-definition view. A spin of the wheel and a size eleven boot on the accelerator spun the van and changed his perspective.

The solid black armored entry vehicle with the triangular cow catcher on the front accelerated down the street with black diesel smoke boiling from the stacks. The SWAT van with eight heavily armed commandos hanging off the sides followed less than one car length behind the Entry Team.

The Commo officer yanked the fiber-optic camera lens from beneath at the same instant the entry vehicle collided with the steel roll-up door. Sparks, flying debris, and radio calls filled the air.

"Entry Team is in!"

"SWAT's in!"

White hammered the accelerator to the floor, sending white smoke pouring from the rear tires of his van. He fell in behind the SWAT vehicle and braked hard as soon as the full length of the van was inside the warehouse. Sliding the van into place, he blocked the exit door and leapt from the vehicle with his pistol drawn and ballistic vest in place.

The point man from SWAT set a pair of charges on the doors of the office and yelled, "Fire in the hole!"

Almost before he'd taken cover behind the van, the doors exploded from their hinges, filling the entryway with dust and debris.

One of the entry team officers pinned Volkov's driver to the floor of the warehouse and secured his wrists with flex-cuffs. "Don't move, and you won't get hurt. Got it?"

The driver nodded in a silent, knowing reply.

White pressed his left hand against the back of the last SWAT officer and made entry into the office space right on their heels.

The lead SWAT officer yelled, "Get down! Get down! Get down!"

As the chaos calmed and the dust and smoke parted, one of the SWAT team members called out, "Right office, clear!"

"Lobby, clear!"

"Left office, clear!"

"Interior, clear! Stand by to blow the vault!"

"Blow it!" White commanded.

The breaching officer yelled, “Fire in the hole!”

With a thundering roar, the heavy vault door caved inward beneath the force of the shaped charge, and the concrete pillars supporting its weight collapsed.

“Vault, clear!”

White coughed and wiped his face on his sleeve. “Nice work, guys. Count ’em down.”

The officer from the warehouse yelled, “I’ve got one on the concrete. He’s cuffed and secure.”

Special Agent Gwynn Davis pulled off her helmet, wiped the sweat from her brow, and yelled, “Two cuffed and secure in the right office.”

No one else made any reports, and White felt his heart stop beating. “There should’ve been four!”

Gwynn yelled, “We’ve got Volkov and Sascha.”

From the warehouse, another yelled, “I’ve got the driver!”

“Where’s the woman?” White shouted. “Find the woman!”

He drove his thumb into his push-to-talk button. “Perimeter, Command-One, we may have a runner. Keep your eyes open.”

“Roger, Command-One. Looking for the runner.”

The SWAT team scoured the interior of the offices in two-man search teams while Agent White knelt beside the driver. “Where’s the woman?”

The officer still had a knee in the driver’s back, so White ordered, “Let him sit up.”

The officer helped the driver roll over and sit up with his back against the Bentley.

White grabbed the man’s shirt and stuck his face within inches of his. “I said, where’s the girl?”

The driver smiled, leaned his face even closer to White’s, and shot his eyes toward the demolished roll-up door. “I’ve got a better question . . . Where’s your van?”

EPILOGUE

Fox Theater, Atlanta, Georgia

Anastasia Robertovna Burinkova stood beside the stage surrounded by throngs of adoring audience members as the prima ballerina of the Bolshoi second company stood only inches away on pointe, posing for pictures with every would-be ballerina in the audience.

In her native Russian, Anya, the elder, said, "Sometimes I pretend I can't speak English."

Anya, the younger, looked up to see the face of the beautiful, former Russian SVR officer standing in the shadows, and she released from pointe, landing on her heels and running to her American namesake. "Miss Anya, I can't believe you came. Where is my uncle?"

"He couldn't come, but I am here. Do you have a change of clothes?"

The ballerina's eyes exploded in excitement. "I will meet you at door six in five minutes."

Two hours . . . and five minutes later, Anya and Anya pulled into the driveway of a simple ranch-style house near the University of Georgia in Athens.

"What is this place?" asked the dancer.

"This was my father's house, and now it is your house."

"My house? But how can this be?"

Anya slid her oversized purse containing ninety thousand dollars in cash across the seat. "It is your house because I say it is so, and this purse is for your mother."

The porch light illuminated the elevated concrete landing by the front door, and Irina Volkovna emerged from the house with tears streaming from her face as fifteen-year-old Anya ran into her mother's arms for the first time on American soil.

PRIMECHANIYE AVTORA (AUTHOR'S NOTE)

Several months ago, one of the readers of my Chase Fulton Novels series emailed to share a wonderfully touching story. He told me the story of his granddaughter named Anya, and how much she enjoyed hearing about a character who shares her somewhat unusual name. Over the course of dozens of emails with this gentleman, he and I formed a friendship for which I am deeply thankful. In a bit of an off-the-cuff comment, I mentioned that it would be fun to work his granddaughter into a scene in an upcoming story. At the time, I thought I might create a scene in which the young Anya would make a passing appearance and offer a bit of lightheartedness and possibly serve as a trigger for a memory sequence for Anya Burinkova, but, obviously, that's not what happened. As you read in the pages of this novel, Anya Volkovna, just like big Anya, has a way of taking over every scene in which she appears. She grew from a momentary character into the primary subplot of *The Russian's Greed*, and something tells me we're not finished with her. She managed to weave herself into the ending of this story, setting up her likely return in future novels. I hope you enjoyed meeting Ms. Volkovna "Little Anya" as much as I did.

This story, circumstances, characters, and premise are entirely the products of my imagination. To my knowledge, there is no evidence of any degree of corruption in the diamond trade on New York City's Diamond Row. I found no evidence of involvement of any faction of the Russian mafia in the diamond industry anywhere in the world. By all evidence and accounts, the diamond dealers of New York City conduct a reasonable, respectable, and honorable business, and none of my research for this novel produced any evidence to the contrary.

The scene involving opening the cabin door in the airborne Hawker jet is purely fictional, and it is likely the events described in that scene are completely impossible. I took enormous liberties in the creation of that scene.

Although the science of creating diamonds in a laboratory exists and is in practice today, I greatly exaggerated the capabilities of that science for dramatic effect in this novel. I have no evidence of anyone exchanging laboratory-created diamonds for natural diamonds in any setting anywhere in the world. Although almost impossible to discern with the human eye, there are laboratory tests capable of determining the difference between a lab-created diamond and a natural stone. The science fascinated me enough to construct a fictional story around the premise purely for entertainment value.

To my knowledge, there is no Bolshoi Ballet second company, and the Bolshoi does not designate a prima ballerina. Their designations are principals, leading soloists, first soloists, and soloists. My representations of life in Russia, as well as involvement with the Bolshoi Theater, are purely fictional.

Further, my depictions of field agents of the United States Department of Justice, their tactics, and procedures are purely fictional and have no basis in actual operations of the DOJ . . . unless, of course, they aren't fictional and I made some lucky guesses.

Ultimately, I made it all up and used the real names of some real places while doing so. My only intention in the creation of this work of fiction was to entertain the reader. I hope I pulled it off.

ABOUT THE AUTHOR

CAP DANIELS

Cap Daniels is a former sailing charter captain, scuba and sailing instructor, pilot, Air Force combat veteran, and civil servant of the U.S. Department of Defense. Raised far from the ocean in rural East Tennessee, his early infatuation with salt water was sparked by the fascinating, and sometimes true, sea stories told by his father, a retired Navy Chief Petty Officer. Those stories of adventure on the high seas sent Cap in search of adventure of his own, which eventually landed him on Florida's Gulf Coast where he spends as much time as possible on, in, and under the waters of the Emerald Coast.

With a headful of larger-than-life characters and their thrilling exploits, Cap pours his love of adventure and passion for the ocean onto the pages of his work.

Visit www.CapDaniels.com to join the mailing list to receive newsletter and release updates.

Connect with Cap Daniels

Facebook: www.Facebook.com/WriterCapDaniels
Instagram: https://www.instagram.com/authorcapdaniels/
BookBub: https://www.bookbub.com/profile/cap-daniels

Made in the USA
Monee, IL
15 April 2022

94756314R00142